What She's Having

LAURA MOHER

sourcebooks
casablanca

Published by Sourcebooks Casablanca, an imprint of Sourcebooks
P.O. Box 4410, Naperville, Illinois 60567-4410
(630) 961-3900
sourcebooks.com

Cataloging-in-Publication Data is on file with the Library of Congress.

Printed and bound in Canada.
MBP 10 9 8 7 6 5 4 3 2 1

In memory of Marie R.,
the "Mother Teresa" of my folks' hometown
and the inspiration for Angus's grandma
(and thus indirectly for July)

———————

Joe B.,
one of the loveliest men I've ever known and
part of the inspiration for July's Joe

CHAPTER 1

Joe

"YOU'RE A GOOD SON, JOE. I just...really wanted grandkids."

Okay. I guess we're done reading. I shove in the bookmark and set aside her battered copy of *Wuthering Heights*. Not that I mind—Heathcliff's an ass, which probably explains my mom's attraction to him—but I'm tired of this particular conversation.

Her voice isn't as thready or dreamy as when she's just cranked up the meds though.

"You okay, Ma?"

She lifts one hand an inch off the bed. Waves it dismissively. "Why didn't you ever settle down?"

"Restless, I guess." Not entirely true until recently. I've been in Fort Collins ten years, long enough to make a success of the restaurant and open a second in Loveland. Long enough for Dad to die and Mom to get sick.

She shakes her head, grimacing, her face grayer, her papery wrinkles deeper than last week. Deeper than yesterday. "No, no. In a relationship. There something you want to tell me?"

She means am I gay. We both know where she got *that* idea. Dad was fixated on it.

"Still not gay, Ma."

Her eyes open, pierce me. "Would you tell me if you were, Joey? Honestly. It's okay."

"Yeah, I would."

"Then why? Girls always liked you."

I shrug and look away. "Haven't found anybody I want that with."

"In a few years, you'll be forty and I won't be around. I don't want you to be alone, Joe." She scratches at the sheet with a fingernail like she does when she's worried, and I pick up her hand.

"Better alone than in a bad relationship, Ma." That may be a little too much truth, given her choices.

Her grip weakens. "Hasn't there ever been anybody though?"

I look into her watery eyes. "Not for twenty years, Ma. And I was wrong about her."

Her voice drops so low I can barely hear her. "You mean that girl in North Carolina."

I jerk my head in a nod. July. Girl as warm as her name.

Well, until she wasn't.

But suddenly I'm back at Galway Lake, her smile is shining down on me, the sun is making the water and the paler strands of her hair sparkle, and I'm hit in the gut again with a rush of want and lust and yearning so strong it almost knocks me out of my chair.

Twenty fucking years and it's still that strong.

Last time I looked her up online, it seemed she'd gotten her dream. Opened a restaurant on the old town square. Filled it with loyal townies and tourists who give rave reviews. No pictures on the website of July herself, but the place and the menu look great.

I promised to help her try out recipes for that menu back when we were kids and the restaurant was just a gleam in her eye. Guess she didn't need me.

I couldn't find her on social media except for the restaurant's Facebook page. Couldn't find a personal phone number for her, but her address is the same as the restaurant, and her last name hasn't changed.

Not that any of this matters. I'm not going to contact her. I'll never see her again. It's not like she'd remember me anyway.

Mom makes a tiny sound, and when I look, her face is streaming with tears.

"Ma, what's wrong? What hurts?" I twist around, praying to see the hospice worker, Frances, in the kitchen, but she's gone on her break. I'm half out of my chair, fumbling in my pocket for my phone, when Mom speaks again.

"'S'okay." She gestures to the tissues on the bedside table.

I pluck a bunch of them and dab at her face, her fragile state a terrifying reality in a way it wasn't a few minutes ago.

She takes the tissues and squeezes them into a ball, gripping them like she needs to hold on to something. "Honey." Her voice is a rasp. "Go in my closet. Top shelf. Back left. Shoebox."

"Sure, Ma. Be right back."

The sweet powdery scent of her perfume hits me when I pull open the closet door, and I get a glimpse into the not-too-distant future when I'll be doing this again to clean out her things. Something heavy and burning rises in my throat. I choke it down.

Her shoes are lined neatly on the floor beneath her hanging clothes. The box at the back of the top shelf is nearly hidden behind a pile of scarves—handy for covering bruises—and gloves.

I pull it down. The label shows a pair of tan dress shoes, size seven, but the box feels too heavy for that.

I take it to her fast in case it's my last-ever chance to help. Settle it gently between her hands.

She shakes her head. "For you." Her voice is heavy. Dread? Exhaustion? Both?

What terrible piece of our past is she dredging up now? Family photos? Dad's wallet? Locks of his hair? Fine, but I'm burning those motherfuckers as soon as she's not around to know.

I sink back into my chair and, at her nod, slide the box onto my knee and ease the lid off, bracing for anything.

Envelopes. Tightly packed, the once-white paper yellowing. Shit. I'd do almost anything for her, but if she expects me to read love letters to or from my dad, I'm gonna have to draw the line. That wouldn't disappoint her as much as not having grandkids, right?

Ma gestures at the box. "Go on. Look at them."

I sigh. Work my fingers into the mass of envelopes to close around the first one. Ease it out. "Ma, I don't—"

The envelope comes free and her dread becomes mine.

July Tate. 210 Mockingbird Circle. Galway, North Carolina.

The handwriting is mine.

The envelope is unopened. Unpostmarked.

I reach back into the box and pull out another envelope. And another and another. All the same plain white stationery I used when I was sixteen and found myself in Germany against my will.

I count them. One hundred never-sent, never-received, never-read letters in all.

Things I thought I knew—things I had resigned myself to,

beliefs I'd used to chart the course of more than half my life—crumble and smear around me like fresh ash, singeing me.

The eyes I raise to her are murderous, and Ma flinches. She's seen that face too many times, though never on me.

"I'm sorry, Joey," she whispers, and the tears start again.

I rise with the box, cramming the envelopes in every which way, and bolt out of the room. It's the only not-terrible thing I can do.

I throw it on my dresser like it's poisonous. Strip off my jeans and yank on running gear. As soon as Frances gets back from break, I'm out the door and headed for the Poudre Trail, Evanescence and my own blood pounding in my ears.

My letters—all those letters—never went out.

July never got my letters.

Miles and miles later, I slip back into my house, not bothering to shower before I go to the room that's been Ma's since her diagnosis.

Frances looks up with a tiny smile and gathers her knitting, retreating to the kitchen, leaving me her seat. This is our routine. Usually I read out loud for a while, whatever Ma wants. Tonight I settle into the chair and study her as she sleeps.

She's not that old—not seventy yet—but she's shrunk and paled and faded out before the life has even left her body. A horrible, wasting end to a wasted life. She wouldn't say so, but it's true. Outliving her monster of a husband but missing out on the joy of grandchildren...

Because she played some role in making it so.

I had tried to grasp all the implications as I ran. If I had known my letters hadn't been sent, I could have found some other way to contact July to let her know what happened. Where I went. Why I didn't have any choice. I could have left Germany as soon as

I turned eighteen. Could've been back in Galway these past eighteen years, maybe with the girl I've spent that time hating instead.

She might've waited for me for two years.

I wouldn't have felt my hope and my future cracking and peeling away a little more each day, leaving me an empty, bitter, faithless husk convinced that love doesn't really exist and that I'd been a fool to believe, even for one perfect summer, that it did.

And what about July? How must she have felt, having me stand her up the day after we...? Having me disappear and never contact her again?

My mom murmurs something, her head moving restlessly.

I pick up her hand. Stare down at the pale skin, the veins that have been poked too many times lately. Sigh, rub my thumb over her frail knuckles as her eyes open.

"Ma." My voice is gravel. "It's okay. Tell me."

July

"Oh, hey, July." Sonya pauses just inside the kitchen doorway, two servings of perfectly-plated-if-I-do-say-so-myself eggs Benedict in her hands. "Tom Reid was in. Said to tell you to come over tonight if you want to talk about the team." She winks and pushes on through the swinging door to the noisy dining room.

Donna snorts but doesn't raise her gaze from the soup she's seasoning.

"'Talk about the team.' That what the kids are calling it these days?" My friend Andi's poking around in the bags of quiche and fruit and cinnamon rolls we've fixed for her women's shelter board meeting this morning. Light's doing that annoying thing it always does around her, glinting off her shiny hair and her smile, and airbrushing her skin.

I shake my head and grin, not confirming or denying a damn thing.

Tina's frowning. "He can't even be bothered to ask you himself?"

"The man lacks subtlety, it's true." No point telling them to mind their own business. I slip omelets onto three plates and add fruit garnishes and croissants.

"That's not all he lacks," Tina mutters, sliding a hot tray of cinnamon rolls out of the oven.

"What y'all got against him? He's not a bad guy." I'm just curious. It doesn't really matter. Things'll never be serious between Tom and me.

Donna levels a look at me as she adds cumin and stirs the soup, her dark hands quick and sure. "He's gonna always want to be taken care of. Never do any caring in return."

Tina nods, fanning the hot rolls, then reaches for the glaze she's made. "That's it exactly. You deserve more, July."

At first glance they're an unlikely couple, Donna a lean, serious, quiet Black woman almost as tall as me, and Tina a bubbly, little, white, ginger busybody. But when you see the way they look at each other, the way they back each other up, it suddenly makes perfect sense. They balance each other in every way.

Last Halloween they came in wearing complementary T-shirts: *Melanin and Mela-none.* I amused myself all day imagining Tina talking Donna into that, probably after Donna talked Tina down from something wackier.

Tina's the finest baker in town, and Donna is the most creative cook I've ever seen. I'm lucky to have them working with me and luckier still to have them as friends.

"You have somebody better in mind? Galway's not exactly overflowing with prospects." Not that I'm looking. I line up the next few orders.

Sonya comes back for the omelets, and I set about making veggie hash and eggs over easy.

"That's 'cause you intimidate the weak ones and let the good ones marry other people." Tina brushes the rolls with her secret-recipe glaze. Even I don't know what all's in it, but some people drive thirty mountain miles for her cinnamon rolls.

"I think your heart's not in it." Donna's finished with the soup and is juicing oranges.

Tina wrinkles her nose. "Is sex with him even any good? I can't imagine that it would be."

I laugh. "I am not gonna talk about that."

But she's got a point. It's not very good. Tom is…someone who will never break my heart and will never have his broken by me. I don't put much energy into it, and neither does he. He's just somebody to spend a couple of hours with when I've got down-time I don't know what to do with.

Because sometimes, if I spend too many nights alone, I start to think about what's missing. And it's pathetic that twenty years after the fact, I'm still feeling it.

Especially over somebody who didn't deserve it.

It's just…he was just so *believable*.

"Seriously though, don't you want somebody of your own? Somebody permanent?" Tina's moved on to the sourdough, punching it down, forming it into mini baguettes for the lunch crowd.

"Babe." Donna's voice is soft as she touches Tina's shoulder.

Tina glances up at me. Must see something in my face, because she nods at Donna and falls silent.

"I used to. There was somebody in high school. I was young and thought… Well. It was really hard when he left." I wipe down my workspace. "Never felt like making that mistake again."

But at night sometimes, he comes to me in my dreams, his smile quicksilver, his eyes bright and changing like a mountain river slipping around rocks, his voice dipping low so only I can hear.

"Boy was a fool to leave you." Donna covers the fresh juice and stalks over to the walk-in with it. Comes back with the roasted chickens for her chicken salad. Her knife flashes quick and sharp as she cuts up the meat.

"Maybe we should find somebody to fix her up with." Andi again, piping up oh so helpfully from behind her bags.

I roll my eyes as I slice open fresh biscuits to layer with pancetta and cheeses and caramelized onion. "Oh, you're a fine one to talk, Ms. Always-been-single-always-gonna-be-single-don't-even-try-to-change-my-mind."

"It's no trouble—we can fix you both up!" Tina's mainly messing with us, but there is some matchmaker in her.

"No." Andi and I say it with equal conviction.

"Seriously, y'all are at a disadvantage, looking for good *men*. Maybe you should give up on them, like Donna and I did." She smiles across the worktable at her sweetie, whose face softens adorably.

Andi sets her jaw and shakes her head. "No partner for me. July's the one we're helping here."

I wave my spatula at them, even Donna, who didn't really say much but is clearly in league with the others. "You're fired. And you're fired. And you're fired." The swinging door opens. It's Sonya, so I fire her too.

Tina raises her brows and bobbles her head as she forms another mini baguette. "I mean, Oprah gave out cars…"

Andi leans against the doorframe and studies her nails. "I mean, *I* don't work here."

Sonya looks at Donna. "What are we up to?"

Donna does the math. "Six, just this morning."

Sonya whistles. "Wow! Usually she only fires us six or seven times in a whole week."

"Y'all are extra deserving of unemployment today."

Friends like these are a blessing. I do have just about everything in the world. I do.

The rest of the day passes with no one bringing up topics I need to leave buried. Mealtime rushes give way to prep and cleanup before the next rush. My brother brings our pregnant little sister in for lunch. Half the town wants to chat when I go out to tell them hi. A volunteer picks up the lunches I've made for the free-clinic staff. I talk and laugh and tease and fix meal after meal after meal, my hands working on their own while my mind is other places.

Like how glad I am that Tina didn't ask if I've ever tried to find out what Joe's doing now. So I didn't have to lie and I didn't have to admit that yeah, I've mustered my pitiful online detective skills to search for him a half a million times over the years. Haven't found anything; Joe Anderson is a very common name, and I can't even narrow the search to a particular country. Thousands of hits, even if I look for someone our age.

And I'm too proud and too stubborn to ask anybody else to help me. Partly because I don't want to have to explain the backstory to somebody who doesn't know it. And anybody who *does* know what happened would worry and look at me like I'm sick again. I couldn't stand that.

So I shove down the memories, bury them in work and laughter and friends and family, and I stay at the restaurant until closing. And then I drag my tired body upstairs to my apartment and drop into bed to lose myself in sleep.

But he comes to me in my dreams again. We're at the lake, sitting on our rock. I'm leaning back against his chest, and he's got his arms around me, tanned forearms resting on his upraised knees. His nose is in my hair, and he's been teasing me—I don't remember about what—but then his voice gets quiet. "I'm full with you," he says. "All my empty places fill up when I'm with you." And I don't ask because I know just what he means.

———————

I can pinpoint the moment this day turned to shit. It was when I glanced out toward the square, spied a guy who, from the back, looked like Joe Anderson, and promptly dropped a bowlful of pasta in the middle of the Kennedys' table, spattering every single family member with alfredo sauce, crabmeat, and broccoli.

Should've cut my losses and gone straight to sleep after work, but no, I'm a glutton for punishment.

Come over, Tom texted an hour ago. I'll order Chinese delivery.

One so-so meal and a less-than-adequate attempt at sex later, I'm frustrated and pissed and still thinking of that Joe-looking guy as I push Tom off me and reach for my clothes.

"Sorry," Tom says, not sounding sorry at all. He's gotten what he wanted. "Tax season really takes it out of me. You want me to…?" He gestures at my crotch.

I don't even want to know what he's suggesting. "No, Tom, I think I'm done here. This wasn't worth my trip." Normally I'd be nicer, more patient, but *dammit.* My time would've been better spent cleaning up the broken glass vase I knocked off my dresser on the way out the door earlier or mopping up the coffee I spilled on the passenger seat of my car.

All because of one lean, unruly-haired man who moved with Joe's loose stride as he crossed the street to the square tonight during dinner rush.

The closers are gone by the time I get home, but I must've just missed them. The floors are still damp from their final mopping. Instead of heading upstairs, I cross to the restaurant's front door to see the spot where Not-Joe was earlier.

The square is quiet and dark now, twinkle lights off, only the dimmer, old-fashioned pole lights still on. Nobody out there anymore. Certainly no Joe Anderson.

I'm too young for a midlife crisis, aren't I? Am I losing it again?

My fingertips find the grooves in the doorframe, grooves I'd first found eight years ago, just before I opened the restaurant. I was touching up paint, and there, a few inches below door-knob level, were three vertical gouges in the wood. To my giddy mind, they seemed like marks made by the claws of a tiny creature stretching up for the handle and admission to a new world just inside the door. *My* new world. My dream become reality.

I had christened that little creature Hope. Mentally welcomed her back into my life.

And now, years later, I still stroke Hope's marks whenever I have something I need to think through.

Tonight, I don't want to think it through alone.

It's barely past ten. Andi might still be at the shelter. They're doing volunteer training this week. She stays late for that.

I text and she agrees to meet me at Lindon's in ten minutes. I beat her there and have her favorite ale—Son of a Peach from RJ Rockers down in Spartanburg—waiting for her when she arrives. It's fun to watch Andi cross a room. She's gorgeous but downplays it for all she's worth, scraping her dark waves back into a single thick braid, leaving her beautiful face completely bare, hiding her amazing curves under severely tailored slacks, flats, and drab-colored shirts. Still, eyes always follow her. She can't tamp down her glow.

She cuts straight through the tables to where I'm sitting, drops into the seat across from me with a sigh, and downs half her beer in one long drink.

"Thanks for meeting me. I didn't feel like going to bed yet."

She tilts her head and studies me. "What's up?"

I blow out a breath. Make wet circles on our little table with my bottle. "I'm being haunted by the ghost of relationships past."

She squints at me. "You mean that guy back in high school?"

"Ridiculous, huh?"

She takes another swallow. "You finally hear from him or something?"

"Nah. But he's in my head again. In my dreams every night. It's driving me nuts." I study my beer, not sure I want to see her expression.

She waits, and when I don't speak, she prods gently. "Bad dreams? Good dreams?"

I steal a glance at her. There's no judgment on her face; she's just watching me. "Good dreams. That's the problem. Waking up makes me sad. Then tonight I thought I saw him on the square, so apparently he's taking over my waking hours too."

"Oh." She raises and lowers her brows. Makes circles with her own bottle. "I can see why you'd call that haunting."

"Yeah." I sigh. "I liked things better the way they were. Peaceful."

She nods slowly. "What's really bothering you about it? You seem kinda shook. Not like you."

"It was exactly like me for a whole year after he left." I finish my beer. "I can't do that again."

Back in high school, I had told her about the bad times. She saw me rebuild myself. Force health and strength back into the body I'd despised and starved half to death.

Her eyes are alert now. "You eating okay?"

"I think so." So far. But I'm afraid this mental bs will be followed by starvation bs, just like last time.

She meets my gaze steadily. "I think you'll be okay. Something else probably triggered those memories. They'll die down, or you'll figure out what it's about and how to handle it."

I frown into my empty bottle. "That makes sense. I have been pretty…frustrated lately. That's probably it. Reminded me of a time when I had somebody…" Okay, this is a relief. I'm not losing it. This is just some kind of temporary triggering. I can handle that.

She's grinning her I'm-about-to-be-a-pain-in-the-ass grin as she tilts back her own bottle and drains it.

"What?" May as well ask—she's going to tell me anyway. There's a reason I channel Andi for my daily affirmations.

She pulls out her phone, types something into it, and slides it across the table to me.

On the screen is a storefront. An Asheville sex-toy shop storefront.

She taps the screen with one elegant finger. "And if your…dissatisfaction…doesn't go away, well, we'll just take a field trip. See if we can't find you something to distract you from your troubles."

CHAPTER 2

Joe

I MUST BE OUT OF my freaking mind.

I peer through the windshield, looking for something—anything—familiar. Woollybooger's Roadhouse is still in business, its beer-guzzling bigfoot mural more faded than I remember. The gravel lot has a sprinkling of trucks and cars already, although it's not quite dinner hour. There are more buildings between it and the outskirts of Galway than there used to be. A Target, a gas and convenience station, a small neighborhood. The town itself seems less changed, brick and stone and wood familiar, the trees taller.

My breath and my heart are doing funny things in my chest. I could point my truck toward July's on the town square, floor the gas pedal, and not stop for signs or lights until I'm at the restaurant. Race inside and sweep her off her feet. Carry her away to somewhere where we can find our home in each other again.

Or I could act like a normal person with some sense. Follow the traffic rules, find my building, give some actual thought to how to approach her now that I'm here.

Because I'm here.

It wasn't untrue, what I told Mom before she died. I really had been restless for a while. I thought opening the second restaurant might take care of that, but soon they were both doing well in the hands of a great group of people, and I was itching to do something else. I came up with a plan to sell the restaurants to my employees and go back to school. Specifically, a social work program.

So the night Mom told me what she and Dad had done, I added Western Carolina's MSW program to my application list. Stayed up late into the night doing my most thorough web search yet for July. No obituary, thank god, and no wedding announcement either. Just a million news tidbits about her being on some board or other. I found the restaurant on Instagram and Facebook, but nothing personal under July's own name.

After Mom died, there was nothing keeping me in Colorado that didn't feel like a burden. I was ready to move on. And July deserves to know what happened, even if her response is, "I'm sorry, who are you again?"

But now, as I ease into Galway, I'm in pep-talk mode. Sure, this change was quick, but that's not necessarily bad. It's *decisive*. And maybe it wasn't wise to commit to this move before I talk to July, but I didn't have a way to reach her except through the restaurant's phone number. I did try calling, twice, but chickened out when I heard the chirpy, definitely-not-my-girl voice call out, "July's!" over lively, clattering background noise.

After two decades of believing she didn't answer my letters, maybe it's understandable that it didn't occur to me until this morning that I could've tried snail mail again.

So I can rationalize or explain away those things.

Buying a building three blocks from July's, sight unseen, though? *That* was nuts, even if it does have empty commercial space below and living quarters above. Don't know what I'm going to do with my MSW—just got a vague idea that I want to work with young people in trouble—but by god, I've got me a building to do it in.

At a stoplight I don't remember, I wonder what my army buddy Gabe would do in this situation. He used to laugh at my impulsiveness, say it was gonna get me killed if I didn't become the boss of it.

Gabe would lay low for a bit, get a feel for things. Make a plan.

It's thanks to Gabe that I got through school and made a success of the restaurants. It's due to him that I'm not coming to July empty-handed. That would've been just great, me knocking on her door saying, "Hey, July, it's me! Sure, I disappeared the day after we made love, and you haven't heard from me in two decades, and well, no, I'm not working right now, but I'm back, baby!"

Chances are she'll murder me outright when she sees me.

Assuming she remembers me.

I have lost my freaking mind.

I count down the street numbers, find my "new" old place, and park.

This would be a bad time to go look for her at the restaurant. It's almost dinner rush. Very bad time.

I fish out the key the Realtor sent me and make my way into my tired brick building. Been empty for a while. Smells like old mildew and dust. The big front window is cloudy with dirt. Cobwebs up high, bits of leftover office stuff on the floors. Plastic trash can, a couple of pens. The fluorescent ceiling fixtures flicker and blink slowly, noisily to life when I flip the switch. That's good. But there are holes punched (*kicked*?) in most of the walls. Shit.

Besides the main room, there's a small office, a restroom, and a storage closet on the ground floor. Up dark, creaky stairs is an equally dirty front room with two tall windows and a kitchenette with ancient fixtures. Behind that, a smallish bedroom and bath. The water pipes groan and spit out rusty water for a minute before it runs clear.

It all needs a good scrubbing, and it'll be night soon. As I step back out onto the street, I can't help glancing toward the square, where I imagine light and laughter and music spilling from the restaurant that was once just my girl's dream.

I'm halfway there, picking up speed, before I get hold of myself and skid to a stop. A young couple passes me on the sidewalk, glancing over, eyes cautious, skirting wide around me.

I can't go to her now. If she's there, she'll be swamped with work.

And I need a plan.

"So you're not here to apply for a grant?" Rose Barnes, the representative I'm meeting with from the Galway Brown Foundation, leans back in her seat with a frown. She's a short, round woman with flyaway hair and big brown eyes in a sweet face.

"No, I'm just at the information-gathering stage." I explain my schooling plans and my desire to work with kids in trouble. "I looked up youth programs in the area, but I couldn't get a feel for what other services might be needed. I'm hoping you can tell me what's here, what's in the works, what gaps still exist... Maybe I can focus my coursework on some of the gaps."

"That's...very proactive of you." She describes the nonprofits working with kids in Galway County. "I've got some materials I can copy for you. Just a sec." She squeezes past me in her little office and goes out to the reception area.

Some wise part of me scheduled this appointment with the foundation before I left Colorado. They fund a lot of nonprofits in this area. Made sense to meet with them right off, to give me something to think about no matter what happens with July.

And it gives me something concrete to do with my morning, because I still haven't come up with a plan for approaching her.

It's a miracle I kept myself from going into the restaurant last night. Walked by when dinner rush was in full swing. Place was crowded, drawing me close, fifty different conversations and laughter I could hear from the sidewalk. I glanced in the windows when I went by but didn't see her.

So I walked around the square, had a beer at Lindon's, went back to my building, and worked on cleaning the living quarters and lugging my stuff in from the truck.

It was weird walking the streets. Didn't see a single person I knew from my few months here before, and nobody seemed to recognize me. Felt kind of like a ghost floating invisible through his former haunts.

Rose Barnes comes bustling back in from the other room and thrusts a fistful of copies at me. "Here you go. This will give you some idea of what we have already. Most of these have websites listed, if you want more information on them." She settles back in her chair. "So you just moved to Galway?"

"Got in last night."

"Do you have questions about the town? Did you find a good place to stay?"

I half laugh. "Actually, I bought a building before I came. Empty retail space on the bottom, apartment on top. Needs work, but it'll do."

She perks up. "What kind of work?"

I haven't given that much thought. "It's got kind of a someone-might-have-been-tortured-under-this-bare-bulb vibe to it. And an old tub with no shower. Gotta have a shower. Also, it's only got a little bitty kitchenette. Appliances older than god."

She glances at her computer screen. "Got time for an early lunch? I can introduce you to my husband. He does reno work, and he knows everybody else in town who does too. We can find you somebody."

"Well...that'd be great. Thanks." I was right, remembering Galway as friendly.

So I get in my car and follow her...and she leads me right to July's corner of the town square.

"I'm taking you to my favorite place," Rose says with a big smile as I climb out of my truck and walk over to where she's parked, just two blocks from my building. "Hungry?" She glances down, and I realize I'm rubbing my stomach.

Having trouble getting my gut to stop doing nervous flips.

"Uh, yeah. Skipped breakfast." Half-true.

I peer in the restaurant's tall side windows as we walk to the corner. No July in sight, but I can sense her there, just like last night. My blood is humming in my damn veins, wanting to burst out of me and go to her with little messages from my heart.

Rose and I round to the front of the building, and I tug open the door with cold hands, pretty sure this is a terrible idea. I'm nowhere close to knowing the right words to say to ease July into seeing me for the first time in twenty years.

Seems to be our pattern, me doing things that will be hard on her without giving her any warning.

Inside there's music and laughing conversation and air scented with fresh baked breads and spices. My empty stomach would be enthusiastic if I weren't scared out of my mind.

"There's Angus!" Rose has been up on her tiptoes, scanning the room, and now she waves at a huge guy flagging us down from a booth on the inside wall.

Dude's a giant. Gotta be nearly six and a half feet tall. A wall of a man with a wild, curly beard. He gives Rose a sweet smile, ushers her into the booth beside him, and then turns to raise an eyebrow at me.

"Angus, this is Joe Anderson. He's new to town. I asked him to lunch thinking you could help him get his place fixed up. Maybe recommend somebody if you don't do it yourself." Rose settles in the booth, and his expression softens again as she drops a kiss on his enormous biceps. "Joe, this is my husband, Angus Drummond."

We shake. I scan the room again before I slide in across from them.

Angus squints at me, his eyes a surprising bright blue-green. "You look kinda familiar. Why's that?"

"Lived here a few months when I was sixteen. Liked it. That's why I wanted to come back."

He nods, points, and shakes one big finger at me. "Yeah… sophomore year? You had long hair?"

One of many things Dad had hated about me. "Tail end of sophomore year and most of the summer, yeah." A flash of movement catches my eye and I glance to the right and—

There she is. My beautiful Amazon. My lungs squeeze up like I just slammed into a wall.

She's still tall and strong and solid, still golden and laughing as she lowers a tray to serve the lucky bastards a few tables over. I hear snatches of her words: "...only bringing this out 'cause it's your birthday, Frank. How y'all doin'?"

I don't give a shit about Frank's answer. My senses devour *her*. Snug orange T-shirt and jeans skating close along her thick curves, her shiny all-shades-of-blond hair caught back in a swinging ponytail, her voice the warm honey I remember. I wonder if she still smells like soap and baby shampoo.

Once in school, before I met July, I heard some dipshit call her fat. Her friends—she's always had good friends—looked him up and down, and then turned to her. "You want to kill him or can we?" July's cheeks were pink, and she could *definitely* have taken the asshole apart with her bare hands, but she just said, "Not worth it. He could probably use an escort back to fourth grade, though..." and swept on by, leaving him sputtering.

Fucking magnificent.

"You know July?"

I'd forgotten all about Rose. She and Angus are watching me, his brow quirked again.

I suck in some air—apparently I also forgot about the body's need for oxygen—and consider my answer. "Used to, yeah," I say finally. "Haven't seen her in twenty years though."

Birthday Boy says something, and July laughs that laugh that always made me feel like I was warming myself by a fire. My gut twists. "God damn," I hear myself say, and realize that Rose and Angus are looking at July now too.

She must feel it. She turns, meets my gaze, and—

All the color drains from her face.

I'm calculating the distance and the obstacles between us in case she passes out, but before I make it to my feet, she's moving toward us, her eyes darting from me to Rose to Angus, something like betrayal in her expression.

Then I'm up out of the booth, reaching for her. Just in time I catch myself and drop my hands to my sides. "July." I breathe it out. Drink her in.

She stops two feet away. "What the *hell*, Angus?" She takes her eyes off me and shivers as if I'm the ghost I felt like, walking those streets last night. Fine blond hairs on her arms stand on end as goose bumps form on her skin. She clutches the big serving tray to her like a shield.

My heart twists. I'm the cause of her distress.

Angus turns wide eyes from her to me, and fuck, I do *not* want the result of this reunion to be my stomping death in the restaurant of the woman I love.

She swings back to me, a wealth of pain and shock in her pretty gray eyes, and my heart breaks right in half.

"July. I didn't mean to... Angus and Rose didn't know... I'm sorry."

"What are you doing here, Joe?" Her voice is low and flat and deadly, her face like pale marble.

No time to make this gentle. I'm going to lose her now if I don't just say it. "I learned something recently about what happened. I owe you an explanation and an apology. Things weren't what I thought, so I know they can't have been what you thought either."

She stares at me for a long minute, brow wrinkling, jaw tight, knuckles white on the tray. There's a clatter from the kitchen and she jumps, glancing that way. "Your timing sucks. I've gotta get back in there."

I reach to touch her, but her gaze practically withers my hand.

I jam it in my pocket. "Could I…? Can I come back later? After you finish here? Please. I think it will help."

"I don't *need* your help, Joe." But her eyes are tormented. She blows out a long breath. Shoots another look at Angus and Rose, and then says, "Ten thirty. Knock on the front door." And she's gone, through that swinging kitchen door like something's after her, leaving a few hungry splinters of my heart on this side.

Beside me I hear Rose stir. "Joe…"

And big Angus rumbles, "You've got some explaining to do."

July

Ohmygodohmygodohmygod.

I was not imagining things. The ghost I conjured up is standing in my dining room, solid as me, smelling woodsy and clean, just as lean and sexy as I remember him, those ever-changing eyes still full of sincerity and warmth.

Asshole. Dangerous, lying asshole.

Tina's saying something to me, but I go straight past her and Donna and two servers, into the walk-in, where I stand counting my breaths.

In-two-three: *I was right. He is here. Joe is here.*

Out-two-three: *What's he want? Why's he here? What's he want?*

In-two-three…

My phone buzzes in my pocket, and I'm still holding the damn tray I used for Frank's table's meals. That seems like hours ago. I shake my head hard, trying to reorient myself, and reach for my phone just as the walk-in door opens.

"You okay? What's going on?" Donna, her voice low and calm as always.

I straighten, clear my throat, and step back out into the kitchen. "Just, uh, had kind of a shock. Remember that guy I mentioned from high school? Guess who's in the dining room with Rose and Angus."

Donna's brows shoot up and she glances at Tina, whose eyes go wide.

"I need to refill some *drinks*," Tina says. She grabs the tea pitchers and is gone before either Donna or I can call her back.

"That woman's gonna be the death of me." Donna's eyes are on the still swinging door.

I love her. She can always make me laugh without ever cracking a smile herself. "Me too." I touch her arm on my way past her to the order board.

My hands are shaking, and I have to read the new orders three times before the familiar words penetrate my brain. Three quiches, one prime rib sandwich, extra pickled onions, two—

"Here." Donna presses a glass of water into my hand and nudges me aside. "Lemme do this today. You look like you need a break."

I grit my teeth. "It's the middle of lunch rush, D."

"Nobody's indispensable. Don't you have some paperwork or something to do?"

She knows damn well I do. She knows I hate to sit behind that desk in that cramped office while there are people here and more interesting things going on.

Joe Anderson is too interesting for my own good.

First time I ever saw him was at the old steakhouse where we worked the summer after sophomore year. I'd been aware of him for a few weeks at school—a lot of the girls were buzzing about some cute new guy—but I didn't see him until that day.

I didn't think he was that good-looking. He was skinny with long, wavy, light brown hair and a slightly crooked nose. But halfway through my shift at the cash register, I looked up and saw him. He had the guy who was training him on the grill laughing. Joe turned, gave me a half smile, and nodded. That's all.

And after that I noticed the light in his eyes. His capable hands. The way he caught on quick to everything anyone showed him. His kindness to our shyest, most overlooked coworkers. And when, a week later, he asked me out, I said yes, equal parts flustered and scared and excited.

I'd never reacted like that to a boy before.

Or since.

Why am I still shaking? I can't hold a knife like this. What the hell is he doing here?

Part of me wants to drag him upstairs and... Well, I'm not sure what I'd do once I got him there. I *want* that explanation he offered. I *deserve* that explanation. It's two decades too late to change anything now, but by god, I *deserve* it. And groveling. I deserve big-time groveling.

Donna's beside me, calmly plating orders, everything under control. "Go, babe. You're here too much anyway. Take the day off." She doesn't even glance up from turning orders over to two servers.

"I'll be back to help with dinner rush. Sooner if you need me."

"Not gonna need you."

I'm halfway to the office door when Tina comes back from the dining room. "That is one sexy man, July. Nice too. Seemed a little shook. Kept glancing back this way, even with Rose and Angus reading him the riot act."

Bless Rose and Angus. I should never've assumed they'd knowingly have anything to do with him surprising me like that. Rose didn't even live here when we were teenagers, and Angus probably didn't realize Joe was the reason I lost it way back when.

I'm useful as a tree stump, standing here watching Donna plate orders. "Okay, you're in charge." I head for my little office and ease into the chair. It feels different. Everything feels different.

Next week's schedule is half-done. I could work on that. Or on the produce order.

My phone buzzes again and I pull it out. Two missed texts from Rose:

July, I don't know what just happened, but I'm so sorry

and

I would never have brought him in if I'd known it would upset you.

That's my sweet friend. I type back, No worries. I'm fine.

Fine, fine, fine. Just stunned and numb, and I need to think. Need to do something else for a while.

Definitely not schedules or ordering though. I shove away from the desk and cut back through the kitchen to my private stairs, taking the steps two at a time.

Up in my apartment, restaurant sounds are muffled. I could change and go for a run, see if that brings any clarity. But for once I don't want to see anybody, and at lunchtime this area is packed.

I sink onto my couch and pull out my phone to text Andi. Guess which ghost just showed up at my place.

Five seconds later the phone rings. "Are you kidding me? Did you talk to him?"

The knowledge that he's downstairs, almost directly below where I'm sitting, gives me an uncomfortable buzz like I've had too much caffeine. I pop up from the sofa and pace as I tell her what happened. I reach the kitchen bar and swing back toward the front windows.

The creak of her chair is audible through the phone. I bet she's just put her feet up on her desk. She's as ladylike as I am.

"Remind me again what happened with you two at the end."

"It wasn't just the end that bothered me. It was having to look back at the whole summer with new eyes." I complete another circuit of the living area, picking up speed.

"Tell me." Her voice is calm. Probably the voice her clients at the shelter hear every day.

"We had two perfect months. Perfect. From the first time he asked me out to the last time I saw him. *Perfect.*" I'm going to wear out the floor if I don't stop pacing, so I plop down sideways and drape my feet over one arm of the couch. "That's what really got me when I was trying to make sense of it. There was zero sign of anything bad about to happen. He was always so sweet, so respectful. We talked for hours. I told him I wanted to open a restaurant someday, and he said he'd help me; he'd be my guinea pig for recipes. He'd cook with me or do my books or whatever I wanted."

Some of those conversations are as clear in my mind as if they'd happened yesterday. "He was a really good kisser, Andi. You know, in my expert sixteen-year-old opinion. When we finally worked up to sex, it was *so great.* Like, not perfect, but awkward and sweet and funny and nice, and...I never felt so close to anybody in my life. When he dropped me off at home, he made sure we were working the same shift the next day, and he said he'd pick me up so we could ride in together."

The tin ceiling above me blurs. "But he didn't show up. And he didn't answer the phone. I was late for my shift, and he was a complete no-show. And I never saw him or heard from him again."

Andi sighs. "Jesus, that sucks."

"And when I went to his address after work to see if he was okay, his neighbor told me he'd seen them, Joe and his folks, getting into their car late the night before. The neighbor said he'd hollered, 'See you later,' to them and Joe's dad answered, 'Not unless you plan on coming to Germany.' And I couldn't believe it, you know? Because I was sure Joe would've said something. But I waited and waited and waited, and just, nothing. Ever."

Even after all these years, the bleakness of that time can still close around me and choke out every warmer feeling.

"You gonna let him come back like he wants?"

"Yeah. I have to know what happened, Andi."

"Yeah. You deserve to know. Do you want company?"

"No. Thanks. I just want an explanation. I want him to look me in the face and tell me why he didn't warn me or say goodbye."

"You call me if you need me, okay? Even if it's late."

"Thanks." We hang up and I count my breaths until the tin ceiling tiles come back into focus.

CHAPTER 3

Joe

TEN O'CLOCK.

This flimsy folding chair groans under me every time I throw this old ball against an undamaged part of the wall. Probably should've tossed the chair out with everything else when I scrubbed the place down today after surviving Rose and Angus's interrogation.

Man, I thought Angus was scary, but Rose is freaking terrifying. A little round ball of crackling energy and intensity. I don't think she blinked those big brown eyes once while she was grilling me. Spooky.

What was I really doing back in Galway, and how did I know July, and why was she so upset to see me, and what had I been doing all these years, and why come back *now*? A bunch of good, valid questions. I answered some but then shut them down, saying July should hear it first. They stared at me so hard and so long after that I'm pretty sure they could tell what kind of beer I drank at Lindon's last night.

But I swore to them I am not here to make trouble and I won't hurt July, and that if she says she never wants to lay eyes on me again, I'll leave. I'll hire Angus to renovate this ugly, old building so I can sell it, and I'll find myself a place closer to campus in Cullowhee. I held their gazes, let them stare at me for another century or two, and finally they seemed to get that I was telling the truth.

July's people love her. Always did.

That's good.

The battered ball I found in the truck bounces off the wall with a *bap*! and smacks back into my palm with a satisfying sting. Distracts me from the high-pitched stress buzz in my brain. I throw it again.

In less than half an hour, I'll be talking to her. Just the two of us, alone together.

Am I doing the right thing?

I can't shake off the memory of her today, the flat, hard note in her voice. I'd never heard her use a tone like that. My July was always sunny. Happy. Kind.

What are you doing here, Joe? This time I hear it in my own voice. I'd convinced myself I was doing her a favor, coming back to let her know we hadn't failed each other after all. Convinced myself she'd *want* to know. She'd care. *I'd* care. *I'd* want to know. So she must too.

But if me being here has already hurt her…I don't know what to do with that. Maybe she was really happy with her life until I showed up to remind her of something bad. Maybe she hasn't spent years holding everybody she meets up to a perfect memory. Maybe that's just me.

Ten fifteen. The stress is eating away at my stomach now.

Maybe our time together wasn't even as perfect as I remember.

But the first time I saw her—halfway across a crowded cafeteria in yet another new school for me—she was sitting with a bunch of girls, holding up what looked like botched origami and laughing, her head tipped back, her gold-streaked hair sliding across her back like silk in the light, her friends patting her as if to console her. But she didn't need consoling. She was the sun, shining bright, everybody else in her orbit.

And when I saw her again at the steakhouse at the start of my new job a couple of weeks later, I knew it was only a matter of days, maybe minutes, before I'd be in her orbit too. I held out almost a week, just watching. She was always helping somebody when she wasn't busy at the register. Carrying a tray for a little kid, chatting up a lonely old person, helping the busboy clear tables. Always moving, always smiling, leaving a trail of warmth wherever she'd been.

And when I finally asked her out and was reeling from the miracle of her saying yes, I realized I had no money. I'd spent my savings on an old beater of a truck a guy at school wanted to get rid of, and my first paycheck wouldn't come until Friday. So I scouted out things we could do without money, and I ended up taking her to a private spot I'd found at Galway Lake. It was just a little clearing with tall trees all around. A big, flat, sun-toasted rock at the water's edge. The smell of pine and a long, glittering view down the lake.

I'd snuck Cokes from the fridge and a can of Pringles from the cabinet. The drinks were warm before we even parked, but July acted like it was a feast. I spread out a towel on that rock, and we sat and talked until it got dark and mosquitos were eating us alive.

"Next time maybe we should bring bug repellent," she said, a question in her voice as we climbed back into my truck.

"Next time I will *definitely* bring bug repellent," I promised her, and her smile lit me up.

I went up to the lake today, after I cleaned everything in this building that could be cleaned. I was overflowing with energy and nerves, and wanted to see if I could still find "our spot." It was there all right. Mostly the same, trees a little taller, still full of birdsong. Somebody had placed a wooden picnic table over to one side in the afternoon shade. Didn't seem right that it could be weathered and gray and splintery already, when what's in my heart feels so hopeful and new again.

I crossed the clearing and spent an hour on "our" rock, huddled in my jacket against the early spring chill, reliving our first swim, our first kiss, our first...everything.

I wondered if people who came to this place after us could feel the leftover magic humming in our rock, haloing the trees against the sky.

Ten twenty-two.

I catch the ball. Stand and lower it to the metal seat of the chair. Head for the bathroom to examine my reflection in the cracked mirror, trying to see whether it's a lucky man or a damn fool staring back at me. Splash my face, brush my teeth, wash my hands one more time before heading out. Lock the door and slide the long, old-fashioned key into my pocket on my way to the square.

The lights are off in July's, except for a low glow from the dessert case at the cash register. I round the corner and am at the door in five steps. There's no bell, so I just stand there in the doorway. Through the round window of the swinging door to the kitchen, I see brighter light. The door swings open, illuminating July's tall silhouette and the damp marks on the freshly mopped floors.

My inner buzz cranks up a notch, my breath stalling.

She pauses, maybe looking toward the front door to see if anyone is there. I raise my hand.

Her movements seem measured as she crosses the room. Not quite as slow as if she's dreading this, but definitely not the quick step of someone eager to see somebody they care about.

She flips the locks and pushes the door open, stepping back so our bodies don't brush as I come into her space.

"Hi." My voice sounds like I haven't used it since they added that picnic table at the lake.

"Hey. Something to drink?" Hers is cool. Noncommittal. She turns to lead me through the chair-stacked tables, and her ponytail swishes, leaving behind the faint scent of baby shampoo.

My knees weaken. I clear my dry-as-dust throat. "Maybe some water. Please."

She waves me to the booth closest to the kitchen and disappears back through that swinging door, coming out a moment later with a pitcher of ice water and two glasses. She pours for us as I slide in across from her and try to figure out what to do with my hands. My elbows. My face.

In this low light she could be sixteen again, still the girl who takes my breath away.

But her eyes come up to mine, and even in the near dark I see in them a world of emotion and experience that my girl hadn't known. "Okay, what are you doing here, Joe?"

―――――――

July

I'm holding it together so far. Pretty sure I haven't shown any cracks big enough for my anger and pain and fear to be visible. My voice isn't quite right, but it's not far off.

God, he looks good. Tired but so good my body and my brain

and my heart are a confused mess, wanting to crawl in beside him and touch him…and also chase him out of here with a cast iron skillet. My fingers twitch in my lap, and I press my lips together. His turn to speak.

He centers his water glass between his hands on the table and stares at it for a second. Then he lifts his eyes to mine, and in them I see enough to press me back against the seat cushion. His own pain, regret, sorrow, anger…and a light I thought at first must be reflected from the kitchen, but no, it's burning in him.

I suck in my breath and hold it, afraid to let any part of me stray into his reach.

"I spent a lot of years really, really angry with you" is what he says.

A roar rises up inside me, but before it can come out my mouth, he speaks again.

"Totally wrong. I know now." He holds my gaze. "I found out a few months ago, right before my mom died."

I never met his mom. Once when I asked him to invite his folks to a block party on my street, he said, "Oh, July, nah. They're… not real nice to be around." He didn't say more, and I didn't push. What can you say to that?

And now, when one of those parents has died, what do I say to *that*? "I'm—"

He waves me off. One corner of his mouth twists up, but it's not a smile. "Might want to hold off on condolences till you hear what they did."

I fall silent and he sighs. Looks down at his glass and moves it a fraction of an inch to the right.

"I'm making a mess of this. Let me start at the beginning. That night…that last night we were together?" He looks up, the light burning in him again, and I have to nod, even though I'm terrified of what he might say next.

"July, that night—that whole summer with you—it was everything to me. Everything. I know you must've thought afterward that it didn't matter to me, or I didn't love you, but it was *every*thing. You were everything." He looks back down at his glass, his mouth tilting up again, and this time it is a smile. "It took everything I had to drive away from your house that night. I mean, I felt like I had a future for the first time. A future I could look forward to, with somebody I loved in it."

He pauses, lifts his glass to make interlocking condensation circles on the table, and I try to make sense of words that don't make any sense. If he loved me, then why...?

"And then I got home, and my dad was sitting at the kitchen table with two beers in front of him. That was never a good sign." He huffs a laugh and pushes himself more upright in the booth. Meets my eyes again. "He told me to sit down. Shoved one of the cans toward me. Said, 'So you got yourself a girlfriend, huh? Drink up. Tell me about her.'"

His face twists. "Last thing I wanted was to tell him anything about you. I didn't even want your name in his filthy mouth. I sat there and drank that beer and tried not to say much. I started getting real sleepy. Last thing I remember is asking my mom why our suitcases were in the hall."

"I don't know what he put in the beer. Later he said it was Dramamine but could've been anything. I think I probably walked to the car and onto the plane, but I don't remember anything until eighteen hours later when we were in Germany."

I could swear he's telling me the truth, but how could he be? Who *does* stuff like that to their kid? I'm leaning toward him, my belly pressed to the table edge, my muscles locked. "Why?" is all I can squeeze out between my rigid jaws.

He shakes his head, those bright eyes sad and angry. "July, he never gave us reasons for anything."

Something in me thrills when he says my name in that low voice, even as terrible as this story is.

"I have an idea why, but it's a guess." He clears his throat, picks up his glass, takes a sip, thunks it back down. "I think Mom and I were too happy here. Evil son of a bitch couldn't stand it. Probably afraid he'd lose control of us. I was as tall as he was by then—nowhere near as big but as tall—and Mom had made a friend or two at work, and...I think he just couldn't have that."

Andi and Donna and Tina have told me bits and pieces about families with dynamics like that. The implications of his words sink in slowly as he watches me. My stomach rolls. "Did...? Was...?"

He nods. "Yeah. I was pretty sure you didn't know. I didn't want you to know."

My god, I *should* have known. I *should* have been able to tell if the boy I loved was being abused. "Joe, my folks might have been able to help! We could've—"

He shakes his head fast, cutting me off. "July, nah. No." He tilts his head, gives me a sad smile.

"*Why?*" How could that not have been better than leaving him in a house with a monster? Than letting him be drugged and dragged away from his home here? From me?

He reaches out and touches my hand where I'm gripping the table edge, strokes my skin once, burning me. When we were young and sprawled together on our rock at the lake, sometimes I'd touch him like that with a single fingertip. The tight skin of his belly would quiver, like a vibration, like something momentous was about to happen.

I feel that now. Something's rising in me, and I don't know what it is or what might burst out. I've got goose bumps all over. Makes me feel naked. I cross my other arm over my chest.

"I didn't want to leave my mom alone with him, and she wouldn't leave him. But also, I wanted to be your *man*. I wanted your family to see me as a good *man* for you. Not some pathetic kid who needed rescuing." He pulls his hand away and now I'm so cold.

I close my eyes and see my young Joe, his lopsided smile, his bright quick-change eyes. The long bruise down his spine I'd only found because I hugged him too hard one day and he gasped. *Tripped and fell against the door,* he told me.

He must know where my thoughts have gone. "That's not the thing I needed to tell you though."

I open my eyes. His expression is so bleak it makes me shiver.

"When I realized we were in Germany, I was... I couldn't believe it. I was in a rage, screaming at him in the taxi. He twisted my arm, leaned into me, got right in my ear, and said, 'You shut the fuck up right now. Germans don't mess around. A kid doesn't honor his father, he gets locked up for a long time.' I didn't know whether that was true, but Dad wouldn't hesitate to use it against me if it was. And he had our passports, and I'd never get away without that."

He slumps a little, as if just the memory defeats him all over again.

I'm pushing up from the bench to go around the table to him when I realize there's a lot he still hasn't explained. I freeze myself in place.

"So we got to our new apartment, and I found some paper and wrote to you. Tried to explain what had happened. I wrote to you every day. Sent you my address, told you how much I was thinking about you and how I'd find a way to come back as soon as I could. Worse come to worst, I could get away when I was eighteen. I'd just try to find some work and save up money for a plane ticket in the meantime."

Okay, this isn't right. I shake my head, frowning, trying to make sense of what he's saying. As awful as it was, it has seemed like he's been telling the truth up till now.

He's reading my thoughts. "I know. You didn't get them. That's what I learned when Mom was dying. She finally felt guilty enough to tell me." He shoves his water glass to the side and clasps his hands on the table, his knuckles white. "All the letters I put with our outgoing mail, every day for three, three and a half months? My folks got hold of them. Kept them and didn't tell me. Mom had them all these years."

He falls silent, looking at me with eyes that could break a stone heart.

And my heart is not stone.

I try to catch up. Try to take in what this means. "So for twenty years..." My words grind out at a glacial pace, which is how slow my brain seems to be working.

"For twenty years, you thought I up and disappeared and didn't care enough to even say goodbye." He nods. "And for twenty years, I thought you'd gotten all my letters and didn't care enough to write back."

Twenty years. He didn't voluntarily walk away from me. He didn't fool me and then blow me off as some gullible fat girl. He *did* love me the way I thought he did, and his parents stole him away and kept us apart for *twenty. Years.*

The world as I know it rears up and topples over sideways.

CHAPTER 4

July

I NEVER HAD A BOYFRIEND before Joe. Boy *friends*, sure, but when I got old enough to start going to parties where kissing occurred, my boy friends never seemed any more interested in kissing me than I was in kissing them. We played sports together. Did homework together. Watched shows and movies and played video games. We did not kiss.

So Joe was my first everything. My first date, my first boyfriend, my first kiss, my first...everything. And nobody that came after ever came close to inspiring as much of any kind of feeling as Joe.

Before our first date, Mom caught me staring at my swimsuited self in the hall mirror, taking inventory. Tall—too tall? Almost as tall as Joe. Good hair. Nice face. Clear skin. Realllly broad shoulders—broader than my hips, but did they make me look too much like a boy? And the muscles in my arms and legs... too much? Thick waist...I really wished my waist were much smaller and my stomach flatter. I was pretty sure I outweighed most of the people in my class and positive I outweighed Joe.

Mom came up behind me and put her arms around me. Leaned her cheek against my shoulder. "You look nice, honey." Of course she'd say that. She loves me. "I feel gigantic."

"You are young and strong and healthy and exactly the size you are supposed to be."

"Mom, I'm embarrassed for him to see me in a swimsuit. I'm not going to look like the other girls he's seen. I'm a giant."

"He's probably never seen a girl so pretty and strong and sweet and capable as you before." She looked me straight in the eye. "Which is why he asked *you* out, not them."

Part of me saw the sense in that. Part of me feared he just thought I was a sure thing. I'd heard the stupid things boys say about big girls.

But that wasn't how it seemed. He talked to me. He listened to me. He teased me. He didn't rush me, with anything. We didn't even get into the water that first date. Just sat on that rock and talked and laughed and made up silly warm-Coke toasts about our coworkers. He told me funny stories about other places he'd lived and asked me questions about life in Galway. He didn't say much about his own family—just told me he was an only child—but was interested in mine. Long before we kissed, he told me how much he enjoyed spending time with me. Let me know how much he liked me.

By the time he *did* touch me, I was comfortable and half-giddy in love and…so eager. For everything. And every single thing we did together seemed magical. And by that point, I believed with my whole heart that he loved everything about me the way I loved everything about him.

And then when he disappeared, once I finally pushed past the worry for him enough to convince myself that I'd know if he were dead or desperately ill, I had to come to grips with the fact that he just didn't seem to want to contact me. And my brain wouldn't let it go at that. Day and night, my head spun stories about why that might be so. Attempts at explanations that would mean I could still have hope. That I wasn't wrong about him. That he hadn't fooled me and used me and then abandoned me like a giant piece of garbage.

And over time, I'd run through all the scenarios I could think of. None of them was convincing. The phone stayed silent and the mailbox empty, and I had to face just exactly how wrong I'd been about every single thing to do with Joe Anderson.

And then I spent months bludgeoning myself with my wrongness, my freakish bigness, feeding myself a shame-only diet, wishing myself into disappearing. And I almost made it happen too because eating—or not—seemed like the one thing I could control in my life.

And for twenty years, Joe existed in two contradictory spaces in my head at the same time: the this-is-how-to-love space and the this-is-why-I-should-never-trust-love space.

Now, in this dark dining room, the upturned chair legs casting long, strange shadows across the floor, I look in grown-up Joe's eyes and try to understand how this could have happened. How it could be that not only did his parents fuck him over in every possible way, but that I did too when I lost faith in him.

He looks back at me, his bright eyes solemn, his crooked smile nowhere to be seen. The bump on his nose...I bet his monstrous dad did that too.

Joe's skin has the permanent tan of somebody who is out in all kinds of weather. He's clean-shaven, like when I knew him. I bet if I reached out and touched his cheek, my fingertips would still know him.

My memories of learning him are so strong I can almost feel the softness of his eyebrows and the thick nest of his hair. If I buried my nose in the warm skin at his collar, heard his quiet hum in response, my other senses would recognize him too. All the parts of me that used to melt and tighten and rise up to greet him are doing it again.

The Joe I gave up on—the Joe who really did love me, who really meant all those words and touches and kisses and promises—is back.

God help me, he's back.

And if my whole life and future rearranged itself in a massive and unfathomable upheaval before, when he left when I was a sixteen-year-old kid with a part-time summer job, how might things change now that he's back?

What are my responsibilities and to whom?

What do I want to happen? Who do I protect?

What can I handle?

Joe

Searching my suitcase for jeans, I come across the shoebox Mom gave me. The letters. Why didn't I take them with me to July's last night?

And why did I leave her?

I can still see the shattered slate of her eyes, huge and tragic, welling with tears that didn't fall because she wouldn't blink. My hands itched to reach for her, and my gut twisted more each second we sat there.

She stayed silent so long I was starting to think she *couldn't* speak. But when I asked if she was okay, she nodded once, fast, and cleared her throat. "I'm, um, having trouble processing this."

I get that. It was hard for me to rearrange my head four months ago too. And if I'd expected some big tearful, hugging reunion where we'd declare our undying love for each other, well, that was unrealistic to the point of ridiculousness.

So even though all I wanted was go to her and wrap us around each other, to feel her strength and her warmth and her softness again, the way I dreamed of for years, I eased out of the booth. "I'll give you some space, then, okay?"

Bad, bad decision.

She looked up at me with those big eyes and nodded. Didn't protest.

I moved toward the door and she followed, and I *still* didn't take her in my arms. Didn't touch her face or brush my lips over any bit of her smooth skin. "I'm just down the street if you want to talk, okay? Your friend Rose knows where." I dredged up a smile, remembering the interrogation. "Don't be mad at them. They're looking out for you. I was lucky to be alive after they got done with me." I had to clench my jaw then to stop babbling. To keep from reaching for her hand.

She watched me step out onto the sidewalk. "Night." Her voice was someone else's, tiny and unsure. Before I could answer, she pulled the door shut.

I left her there on the other side, old wood and glass and twenty years of thwarted emotion between us, and headed "home" to this dump. Spent the night tossing and turning on my squeaky air mattress.

What if she had questions for me? What if she needed somebody to hold her? What if she wanted that as badly as I did?

And what's she thinking now? Does she believe me? These letters might reassure her I'm telling the truth. And there's my plan for today.

I make a grocery run, eat a peanut butter sandwich, watch a few YouTube videos on patching walls, and when I'm pretty sure lunch rush is over, I take the shoebox to July's. Not sure how to handle this...maybe order something to eat and ask the server to give July the box.

But she's on break when I get there. Sitting in the booth we used last night, poking at a salad, looking as beautiful as ever, even with shadows under her eyes.

From across the room, I see her freeze when she notices me. She doesn't move as I cross to where she's sitting. Just gazes up at me.

And I can't read her anymore. There's an ocean of sadness in that.

I clear my throat, hold out the box. "I should've given you these last night."

Her eyes fasten on the box like it's got a cobra in it. She settles her fork on her plate and reaches out with shaking hands. "Is it...?"

"The letters, yeah. I mean, they were supposed to be yours." Fuck, this is awkward. I'll just leave them with her and go somewhere else to eat. Suddenly I'm not hungry anyway.

She clutches the box, holding it a few inches from her chest, and looks back up at me. "Want to join me?"

And just like that, the day brightens.

I nod, a too-eager jerk of my head, and slide onto the bench across from her. Our knees don't meet under the table, and I'm disappointed. This would be easier if we were touching.

She sets the shoebox beside her, next to the wall. "I should probably wait till later to read them."

I shake my head. "You don't have to read 'em at all if you don't want. I just thought you should have the choice. Throw them out if you'd rather." In fact, maybe I should've read them first, to see what sixteen-year-old me wrote. I was pretty bitter there at the end…

"Joe." Her eyes are as certain as I've seen them, and for a second, I see past our current awkwardness to the old bond between us. "I *want* to read them."

She fetches me a menu and relays my order to the kitchen herself. Slides back into the booth with water and iced tea for me. She pushes her salad aside, studying me, her eyes moving over my face like a touch. "This is weird," she says finally. "I want to catch up. I want to know everything, but…twenty years…where do we even start?"

How much of this woman is my July, the sweet, happy girl I knew and loved, and how much is someone I've just met? She's still kind. Still draws me like a magnet. Still has that sprinkling of pale freckles across her nose—a warm constellation I've mapped a hundred times with my lips.

She's waiting for me to respond.

I glance around the dining room with its exposed brick, funky art, bright tablecloths, and flowers in tiny vases on each table. "You got your dream. I'm glad you got your dream." *I'm sorry I couldn't help like I promised.*

She doesn't look away from my face. "What about you? What have you been doing?"

I half laugh. "I got your dream too. Met a guy in the army—my buddy Gabe—and he took me under his wing. Tried to teach me everything he knows. He knows a *lot* about cooking." Gabe was a lifesaver to me.

I swirl the straw around in my tea. "After my discharge, I went to school in Colorado, worked for an old guy in a restaurant. Ended up running it for him. When he decided to retire, he gave me a good deal on the building and equipment." And I changed things up. Made it my own. Got it noticed in a good way.

A smile blooms on her pretty face. "*Really.* So we've been doing the same thing these past few years."

It's physically impossible not to smile back at her. "Yeah. But I was getting restless. Started applying to social work programs. Then Mom gave me the letters and...anyway, I start classes at Western Carolina this fall."

She nods, her eyes measuring me. "And you bought a building down the street."

I wince. "Yeah, in hindsight that seems a little..." I scratch the back of my head. Presumptuous? "I happened across it while I was looking for apartments. Thought maybe after I get my degree, I can use it for some kind of youth program."

"I was hoping I'd catch you on break, July!" a voice booms and we both jump.

A stocky, blond dude is beside us, tie loosened, shirtsleeves rolled up, suit jacket nowhere in sight.

"Oh. Tom." July's voice is neutral. Careful. "Joe, this is Tom. Tom, Joe."

I nod at him. Dude looks me over, probably comparing the cost of my T-shirt and denim jacket to his professional gear. Doesn't say anything, and after a few seconds, it gets awkward.

"Would you like to join us?"

I've been away for twenty years and even *I* can hear the lack of enthusiasm in July's tone, but this guy says, "Of course!" and slides right on in next to her, crowding her up against the box of letters. *And* kisses her on the cheek. "Missed you last night."

Fuck. She does have somebody. And it's *this* asshole.

My joy over her asking me to join her evaporates.

But July rears back and looks at him like he's lost his mind. "What? Why? We didn't have plans."

Interesting.

A server arrives then with my food. I'd ordered a rice dish called Summer Chicken, and its aroma is nearly enough to distract me from the asshole. I taste it while the server takes his order.

July watches me. "Like it?"

With the blond dude distracted, it feels like just the two of us again.

"It's good. Really good." And man, it is. Complex. I can pick out some of the flavors, but it'll take me another few bites to figure out the rest.

She smiles. Warms me up from across the table without ever touching me.

"So." Blond dude turns back to us as if we've been waiting for him so our lives can resume. "Miguel's transferring to Rio."

July nods. "Yep, I heard. Good opportunity for him."

"Yeah, but it leaves *us* without a left fielder." He smirks at me. "Don't suppose you play softball? Outfield?"

July turns those gray eyes back on me. I can't read her expression. Does she remember how good we were that time we played together at her block party?

"I do, yeah." Pretty sure I keep belligerence out of my tone.

"He's good." July says it to him without pulling her gaze from me.

Dude—Tom—rakes me again with a glance, clearly unimpressed. "Wanna play in our coed league? Wednesdays and Saturdays." Sounds sorry he mentioned it.

I glance at July. That call's got to be hers.

"It's a good group," she says. Maybe encouraging me? Maybe meaning they're not all like Tom?

"Sure. Sounds fun." It'll give me a way to see her more. Get to know her again.

Tom settles in, monopolizing the conversation, managing to work in mention of a million inside jokes and past experiences with July.

I eat my Summer Chicken, eyeing my utensils, wishing I'd belonged to some special forces branch that teaches you fifty ways to kill with a spoon.

CHAPTER 5

Dear July,

I'm so sorry I couldn't pick you up for work. Did you get there okay? Are you okay?

Joe

I KNOW I SHOULD GIVE her some space. I don't know how long it will take her to read the letters or what she'll need or want afterward. But it's Wednesday, and I don't know whether those softball team practices start today or Saturday or next week...

So after a long run and another goddamn scrub-and-spray in my old tub and a trip to the home store for wall-patching supplies, I go back to July's for food and information. I get there in the lull between breakfast and lunch.

The waitstaff is starting to look familiar to me. One woman gives me a big smile and leads me to that booth near the kitchen, then leaves to get my iced tea.

July brings it out to me, and I'm stunned. She looks like she hasn't slept in days, her face pale, shadows under her eyes.

"Are you okay?" Stupid-ass thing to say, but I'm off-kilter.

"I'm *fine*," she snaps and then pauses, closing her eyes, looking like she might wilt to the floor in exhaustion. "I'm sorry. So many people have asked me that today, I know I must look terrible. But I'm fine. Just tired. And you're the last person I want to yell at." She perches on the bench across from me as if she's not sure whether to go or stay.

Don't know what she means by that last part, but I'm glad she doesn't want to yell at me. I want to run my thumb over the curve of her cheek. Hold her and let her rest. Do that skin-to-skin bonding thing like people do with babies. Warm her with the heat from my body. But...boundaries, Joe. "I just came in to check about softball. You really okay with me joining the team?"

Her smile starts in her tired eyes. "Yeah, I'd like that. Want to ride with me to practice tonight?"

This whole second-chance thing is a goddamn roller coaster. But, woman, I would ride with you anywhere. "Yeah. That'd be great."

We sit gazing at each other until the waitress comes to take my order. Then July stands, slowly. "Come back with your stuff at five forty-five, okay? I'll be ready to go."

I watch her all the way back into the kitchen. Takes me a minute to realize that the waitress is standing there watching *me*, a little smile on her face.

July's got a sporty blue Subaru Crosstrek in her own alley parking space. It suits her.

I toss my bat bag in the back and climb in.

Sitting beside her in a car is different from being across from her in a booth. Her scent—still soap and baby shampoo—surrounds me. Teases me. Every part of me leaps in recognition and joy. I'd loved everything about her when we were sixteen but she's even more beautiful to me now. The years have carved away some of the baby softness from her face, but I know the exact feel of those long, strong, smooth arms and legs. Her breasts, which I'm doing my damnedest not to stare at, are fuller now. I remember everything about how she used to look and feel and taste. My hands twitch on my knees, and I tear my eyes away so I can concentrate on what she's saying.

"I think you'll like the team. Especially my friend Andi." She signals her turn and pulls out of the alley, heading away from the square. "She's amazing at first base. She won a full ride to college."

I study her clean profile. "What about you? Did you play in school?"

Her smile fades, and she darts a quick glance at me before refocusing on the road. "Um, senior year of high school, yeah. My schooling after that was culinary and business hospitality classes here and there. No degree. Just what I needed to run a restaurant."

I'm hungry to hear about every minute of her life since I left. Why mention just senior year? I know she played sophomore year—she was in her uniform the first time I saw her—but why not junior year? Something in her expression keeps me from prodding.

She pulls into a four-diamond park on the east side of town. Two diamonds have practices already going on, and on a third, my pal Tom is walking the infield, dropping temporary bases at the proper places. A woman is putting on a catcher's mask, and a few other people are warming up their arms.

"There's Andi." July points to the tallest of the women. "Try not to drool when I introduce you two, okay? Obvious drooling pisses her off." But she's grinning as she cuts the engine.

Andi could be Sarah Shahi's younger, bigger, curvier jock

sister. "Joe." She's got a firm handshake and a cool, all-seeing gaze that sweeps over me as July makes introductions.

"Joe, go on out to left field. Let's see how you do." Tom's voice is brusque. He grabs his glove and trots himself to shortstop. Because of course he does.

Once the whole team arrives, we've got enough players to have three in batting at a time while the rest of us field. The team's pretty good. Tom's decent at short and July is poetry on third. Her arm is amazing. At first base, Andi catches everything aimed in her general direction, stretching full length for wild throws and scooping balls out of the dirt with equal ease.

I'm loosening up, not embarrassing myself in the field, and trying to keep my eyes off July's fine ass in front of me when a hot grounder makes it past Tom. I scoop it up a few steps behind him and throw to Andi.

"Hit the cutoff, Joe." Tom's face is red.

I imagine he didn't like me fielding the ball he missed. I get that. So I try to reassure him. "I will whenever I'm farther out."

If possible, his face gets even redder, his blond eyebrows bristling like pale little caterpillars. "You gotta do it every time."

"Dude, I was *right* here. I could've handed it to you. But that would've wasted time, and we might not have gotten a runner out."

"If you don't do it *consistently*, Anderson," he says, loud and slow like I might have trouble understanding, "nobody can trust you to do the right thing."

Was that a jab? Sounded like a jab, maybe for July's benefit. But it doesn't hold any truth, so it doesn't hurt.

He wants a pissing contest. Maybe whip out a ruler to measure our dicks right here. Asshole. But I'm brand-new to this team, and I don't want to embarrass July or any of the others. I shake my head. "Okeydoke. Next time I'll hand you the ball and let you throw it."

July's come over and she's frowning. "Tom, that's silly when he fields it so close in. You saw him make the throw. You know he can do it. Let him go for the out." She calls over to first, "Andi, was it a problem that Joe threw directly to you?"

Her friend waves her glove. "Naw, I was ready."

Victory. But I don't want to cause trouble, so I turn to Tom. "I'll get it to you if I'm more than a few feet back."

He ignores me, his face the color of a beet as he moves back to short and waves his permission for the pitcher to carry on. It's clear we will not be friends.

And later, when we all go to Lindon's for after-practice beer, he sits close to July and directs most of his comments into her ear. And when he sees me heading to the bar for another round, he asks her, just loud enough for me to hear, "Wanna come over tonight? I'll make it worth your while. Been a few days..."

She turns and says something too quiet for me to hear. He glances up at me and smiles as I pass.

I bring back two pitchers and, as soon as I can, excuse myself and walk home, gut churning.

I want her to be happy. I do. It doesn't have to be with me. But *that* asshole? Really?

———

July

I'm in dire need of sleep. No way could I rest the night I talked to Joe and learned what happened. Or the next night, with those letters.

All I could do, reading them, was picture my sweet, young Joe all alone in a strange country with abusive parents, writing the only person he thought he could count on but never getting any response. By the second letter, I was in tears. By the fifth, I could barely see his writing. By the twentieth, I was sobbing out loud, and by the time I finished the hundredth letter, it was 4 a.m. My eyes and throat were raw, my head throbbing, my heart shattered into a million pieces.

Night three of no good rest brings nightmares. In them, a big evil force has hold of Joe and is pulling him away. I'm trying to get to him, but Tom keeps showing up, stepping between us, talking about things that don't matter, making it so I can't reach Joe's hand.

I drag myself through my morning work on autopilot, my mind full of Joe's clean, fresh-air scent in my car, his eyes, his unruly hair—*Is it still as soft as I remember?*—and the flash of his smile whenever he caught my eye. It's impossible to play third base while staring out into left field. I swear, I let one ball go by just so I could turn and watch him field it with his effortless speed and grace, T-shirt riding up his lean side as he threw to first base.

And then my brain was fixated on that patch of taut skin I glimpsed. He's put on some muscle since I knew him, but he's still thin enough that I want to take him in and feed him. Lay him down and kiss and nibble all those intriguing new ridges and hollows. Hold him tight until he feels loved and cared for. I want all his passion and tenderness and his smile just for me, and then I want to cover his smile with mine...

I fumble a plate and almost lose the omelet off of it. Catch it just in time and reposition the orange-slice part of the garnish.

Last night was another missed opportunity. It was so nice walking over to Lindon's with him after we parked my car behind the restaurant; I hoped we'd walk home together afterward. Maybe sit in the gazebo on the square and talk some more. I wouldn't mind getting no sleep if I were with Joe.

But he slipped away early while Tom was pulling that possessive crap. I turned to Tom to tell him to stop that shit, that if he kept acting like we were together, next time I'd call him out publicly. He played innocent, but I saw his little smirk as the door closed behind Joe.

Andi walked me out later. "Talked to your boy Joe." Straight to the point. "I like him. I see why you fell for him. And he's a fine-looking man, isn't he? A little skinny, but you *do* own a restaurant..."

Now I put up an order for Sonya, and she asks if I want her to add the side to one of the dishes. Because I've forgotten. *Shit.*

I know which building is Joe's now. He had me pull up there to drop his bag off before Lindon's. After the third nightmare woke me up, I seriously considered going and knocking on his door. Seeing if he'd let me spend the night with him, just talking or...whatever. I pictured him pulling me inside. Locking the door behind us. Leading me up to his apartment, holding me on a couch, on a bed. Talking like we used to, him teasing and nuzzling me, making me laugh as we undressed each other. Joe looking delighted as he kissed the smile he raised.

A long, slow, delicious night of learning each other again.

Bacon sputters and pops and catches me on the arm. I jump back and try to refocus on what I'm supposed to be doing. This obsession is dangerous.

I watch for Joe to come in, but he doesn't.

The only thing I'm actually able to concentrate on is the young girl who asks if she can submit a job application. Usually I hire straight from Andi's women's shelter, but we've been shorthanded lately, and this girl has perfect timing. And I remember her from a couple of months ago.

She had come in with her mom. I brought out their food—because we were, as we so often have been lately, a person short that day—and the two of them were giggling in a booth over their terrible driver's license photos. They'd just moved to North Carolina, they told me, and had gone to get new licenses that morning. They asked me whose picture was worse. Both were god-awful—eyes closed, expressions like they'd just sneezed or maybe had someone vomit on them—so no way was I answering their question. I said, "I'm just gonna send out a couple of complimentary desserts, okay, as a welcome to Galway and an apology for your photographer, who clearly has some personal issues to work through." They both laughed, the mom looking not much older than the daughter.

But today the girl's alone, no smile in sight. I get her a glass of tea and have her fill out an application, and then I go ahead and interview her.

"Got any restaurant experience, Maisie?" I don't expect her to say yes. She looks young enough for this to be her first job.

"No, but I learn fast. I can do dishes and I'm learning how to cook and I have good manners…" Her brown eyes are huge and serious in her pale face.

"You're still in school, right? So you're looking for evening or weekend hours?"

She nods. "I can do anything after three thirty on weekdays. And anytime on weekends. And when school's out, I can work whenever you want. As much as you want."

She's beyond earnest. She seems almost desperate.

I study her. "Maisie, you okay?"

Her eyes widen even more. She nods fast. "Yes, I just...really want a job. And I remembered how nice this place was—how nice you were—when Mom and I came in. I was going to put in applications a bunch of places, but I wanted to try here first."

I tap her application on the table. She watches as solemn as a judge.

"Well, you have excellent timing. We're a little short-staffed, and it'll be warm enough soon to set up the patio tables outside, and then we'll be even busier." Something about her tugs at my heart. Makes me want to take her under my wing. "Usually I hire older women, but I'm willing to give you a try."

Her eyes light up, but she still doesn't crack a smile. "I'll work really hard. I promise."

"Good. Here's the most important thing: We're a family here. We treat each other right. We treat the customers right. No matter what might have gone wrong at home or in the kitchen, we treat people right here. Think you can do that, even when you're in a bad mood?"

She nods, never taking her eyes off my face.

"You got reliable transportation?"

"I ride my bike to school, and it only takes me a few minutes to get here from there."

I shake my head. "I don't want you riding home after dark or in bad weather."

She's speaking almost before I finish my sentence. "I can use Mom's car. She says we can work it out to get me to work. I'll just ride my bike when I have daylight shifts."

"Okay. One more thing. School comes first. If your grades

start slipping, you tell me you need to cut back on your hours. This is not more important than that, all right?"

She nods. She's perched on the edge of her booth bench. I'd bet she's got a white-knuckle grip on the seat.

"Let me get you a menu to take home, then. Learn as much of it as you can. Can you come in Saturday morning at eight? We'll go ahead and start training you this weekend. Be prepared to learn a little bit of everything."

She shoots up out of the booth, her energy filling the room. "Thank you so much! Saturday at eight. I'll be here."

"Wear comfortable shoes. Nothing with open toes, nothing slick on the bottom. Kitchen floor's usually wet. Jeans are fine, and plain T-shirts, no holes, no stains."

At last she gives me a hint of the brilliant smile I saw when she was with her mom. "Okay! Thank you!"

She takes the menu I hand her and practically skips out the door, lips moving as if she's repeating my instructions to herself.

And I go right back to obsessing over Joe.

CHAPTER 6

Dear July,

I'd give anything to be there with you now. Last night was so special...

Joe

BY PRACTICE SATURDAY AFTERNOON, I'VE resigned myself to a world where July is in a relationship with somebody else. I can keep going, but it grinds away at me like having a thin layer of sharp gravel under my skin.

I'd driven over to Cullowhee Thursday morning. Got myself a hotel room with a real shower for a couple of nights. My new campus is beautiful, nestled in the Smokies, surrounded by as much nature as I could possibly want. Too late for skiing and too soon for rafting yet, but I hiked the university trail system a couple of times. Maybe one day I'll do it on a mountain bike.

I wandered the campus, found the social work department, and introduced myself to the people there. Some of them gave me reading lists, so I went over to the campus bookstore and picked up everything I could find that might be useful. I explored the town, tried some interesting-looking restaurants, drove to Lake Glenville, and took a canoe out for a few hours.

I absolutely did not think about how much better it would all be with July. How we could paddle out to the middle of the lake and drift and talk and learn each other again. How I could hold her and lull her into getting some of the rest she seems to need so badly.

Didn't think about her going home with that smirking asshole, holding *him*, rolling around in his bed, teasing and laughing with him the way she might've with me twenty years ago. About the warmth of her smooth skin and the light she casts everywhere she goes. Did *not* imagine her going quiet, looking into his eyes before tilting her head to kiss his mouth with the tenderness she showed me so many times.

I mean, I *knew* it would be a miracle if she was still single when I came back. The odds against it were astronomical. Tom may be a dick, but he's not stupid, and if he didn't want her, there's probably a list as long as my leg of other Galway guys who would snatch her up in a heartbeat.

So I used my time in Cullowhee to calm my hopes the fuck down. I'll just go ahead with my plans for school. Fix up my building so I have a decent place to live for the time being. Decide later whether to sell it or open some kind of youth organization there. Wait and see what happens between July and Tom.

She didn't seem madly in love with him. Maybe they won't last.

But I'm going to leave the ball in her court. Not going to hang around begging like a half-starved pup. She knows I'm here, knows I'm single, knows where I live. If she wants me, she can tell me.

And then she can have me, because goddammit, I'm still hers, under-skin gravel and all.

I beat her to practice Saturday. Andi waves me over to warm up with her and the left center fielder, a little speedball named Hiromi.

"So, Joe, what do you do for a living?" Hiromi asks right off. "Wait—let me guess…"

"I'm thinking career criminal," Andi says beside me.

"Ooooh, like a cat burglar!" Hiromi looks me up and down. "Yeah, you're built for stealth. And speed."

She's not, like, purring or anything, but I'm pretty sure I'm blushing.

"Yeah, like that guy in that old Ocean's movie. The one who did that laser dance." Andi sounds perfectly serious and is almost certainly being a smart-ass. She just has that look about her.

I snort. "I'm not much of a dancer. Besides, that guy had moves no normal human could do."

"I'm a normal human," Hiromi says, tossing the ball to Andi and then suddenly arcing backwards, glove and all, into a flip. She lands on her feet in plenty of time to catch the ball Andi throws back.

Dirk, the right center fielder, coming toward us with another ball, sees all that. His eyes go wide, and he trips over thin air.

"Damn, Hiromi, you are freakishly skilled." Andi's shaking her head in disbelief. "You guys got any hidden talents? We could be the Savannah Bananas of softball. I can twerk."

Dirk turns his eyes to her, and I can see the heroic effort he makes to keep from looking down at her curvy ass. He's blushing furiously. Pretty sure the women have rendered him speechless. He might've swallowed his tongue.

The three of them actually have me laughing when July drives up.

She climbs out of her Subaru and I'm shocked. She doesn't look well rested or well loved or well sexed *at all. Ima hafta kill Tom.* She looks exhausted, the shadows under her eyes more like bruises now. When Tom calls her name and holds up a ball, she nods and hauls a bag out of her back seat and moves toward us like she aches all over.

"Dude, you okay?" Andi calls to her, and I know then that I'm right—this isn't normal for July.

July waves her off. "Just stiff. I'll work it out."

She does seem better as practice gets going. Her fielding is almost as sharp as it was Wednesday, her throws from third to first right on the money. She covers a lot of ground, and her batting is strong. She talks to everybody, teasing and laughing the way I remember her always doing.

She jokes with me too. I'm part of *everybody.*

Tom and I pretty much ignore each other. Well, if you don't count me carefully placing my own hits right up the middle, just out of his reach. Or to the left side. Just out of his reach.

July catches me grinning after the third one, so I hit the fourth right at him, so as not to be petty. He fumbles it. I have to fake a coughing fit to hide my laughter.

I'm not usually this much of an ass.

This is my dad coming out in me. *Fuck.*

I straighten up and try to act right. Swing for the fence, practice placing shots to the right side, down the lines. When it's somebody else's turn to bat, I take my position in left and concentrate on keeping my mouth shut and doing a solid job fielding.

At Lindon's afterward, I choose a chair between Hiromi and

Dirk. Tom sits next to July, of course, but he keeps his hands to himself. The only physical contact they have is when his shoulder brushes hers as he leans forward to say something to the catcher.

I can feel July's eyes on me as I get to know my teammates, but I don't know what it means. When I look at her, I can't read her expression.

"So, Joe, what's it like being back?" Andi leans across Dirk to ask. He doesn't seem to mind a bit. Pretty sure he's sniffing her hair, which is curling out of her thick braid.

I think about how to answer. "I still like Galway. Hasn't changed as much as I thought it might've. Good people."

That starts everybody talking about which teammates grew up here and which are transplants. Tom's eyes move from me to July as if he's just figuring out she knew me before. But she's busy talking to other people. Seems she's the link between most of the members of the team.

She's a little more animated now. Doesn't look so tired in the muted light of the bar. Maybe she really was just stiff earlier.

If I were Tom, I'd give her a long, slow massage to banish every bit of pain. Bad enough the asshole's got my girl; it's unforgiveable that he's not doing his job properly.

July

Joe fits right in with this team in this bar, just like he did at the steakhouse when we were young. He told me once that his family always moved around a lot. I guess he's learned to talk to pretty much anybody.

I was almost late to practice tonight, hoping he'd show up to ride with me, but that was silly because he knows the place, time, and team now. And he hasn't been around at all since Wednesday, so why would he ride with me?

The last couple of days have been tough. I've had a hard time concentrating at work. Burned myself twice, messed up a couple of orders, and haven't been able to focus on my paperwork. Still not sleeping much. I keep waking up from nightmares of trying to reach Joe as something carries him farther and farther away. Those are mixed in with dreams of being with him at the lake, of touching him as he looks at me with that light in his eyes. Having him whisper in my ear, his words delicious, his fingers finding and worshiping all my secret places, his warm breath stirring the fine hair at my neck.

It isn't easy seeing him laughing and joking with Andi and Hiromi and the whole group, with zero need for me or my help or my input.

I don't know why I'm feeling like this. I'm not a jealous person. God knows he's had a rough enough time that he deserves this. And I mean, maybe he really just came back because he liked Galway before, and he explained his disappearance just because it was the right thing to do as long as he was here.

But I must've gotten my hopes up for something more. Must've thought he'd come back for *me*. Silly. I guess it's good that I see otherwise now, before I set myself up for a bigger fall.

Because I've been messing things up. Important things. Responsibilities. And that's got to stop. I've got too many people depending on me. And as of today, one more.

I'd forgotten Maisie was coming in for her first shift this morning, and when she turned up five minutes early, something must've shown on my face, because Donna and Tina sized up the situation and took her under their wings without me having to ask. Maisie will be trained right if they do it. Not so sure I can say the same if I train her.

I need to get myself under control and my ass in gear.

———————

But over the next few days, my Joe obsession grows along with my mistakes. I accidentally leave lettuce and tomatoes off the produce order and have to make an emergency run to Ahmed's Market and pay three times as much. I forget Sonya's going on vacation and underschedule us for the whole week. I put salt instead of sugar in a giant batch of custard. I forget to buy my sister, Jen, a baby gift and only manage to show up at her shower because my brother comes to get me.

Every night I drop into bed more tired, have more dreams about Joe, and then I wake up too soon and go right back to making mistakes.

I'm letting people down right and left. This is no way to run a business. No way to treat my family or my employees, who are having to cover for me and redo my botched work. Wednesday morning, after an entire week of me being unreliable, Donna comes in with a daily to-do list on a giant chalkboard. "To help us train Maisie," she says diplomatically as I watch her screw it to the wall next to the walk-in. But I know it's for me and my no-longer-working mind.

At practice, I watch Joe's lean body as he runs and fields and throws so easily. I listen to him tease back and forth with the team while I can't think of a single thing to say. The breeze riffles his hair and the light flashes off his smile and his eyes, and I know it's going to be another sleepless night.

I'm hoping his shirt will ride up again so I can see the thin trail of hair down his belly. His waist is way smaller than mine, dammit. His butt in those sweats looks so perfectly cuppable...and the flex of muscles and tendons in his arms makes my mouth water. I feel ravenous for him and heartbroken that he isn't here for *me*. I'm so tired my mental filters have taken a break. When he and I collide as we're going for a pop fly, I land on top of him, my breast in his throwing hand. I don't know if he realizes his thumb is moving on my nipple. His eyes are so intense, so close... Lust crashes over me like a giant wave. Fuck everything. I want him right now. A few minor adjustments and I could be riding him...

An actual growling sound comes from my throat. I'm a quarter inch from kissing him, forgetting where we are and that we're surrounded by people, when Tom runs up yelling, "Don't forget to call the ball, y'all! Somebody's going to get hurt!"

Tom grabs my hand and pulls me to my feet, yanking me back to my senses before I can embarrass myself. I move back to third base, not looking at Joe, feeling weirdly like crying.

I haven't cried since the year he left.

Haven't felt so broken, so wrong in all ways since that time.

I can't go through that again. I don't know if I could survive it, and way more people are counting on me now. I can't let myself get lost in this.

I was just a kid then. I'm an adult now. I'll find an adult way to handle it this time. I'll do better.

Nobody can be as good as my memories of him. I just need a reality check and some adequate sex, followed by a good night's sleep, and I'll be fine. Back to normal, problem solved.

Even if he didn't come back for me, he's single right now. Probably wouldn't mind a night together, no strings, right?

So after practice, as we're all leaving Lindon's for home, I catch him and ask if he's been to the roadhouse yet. If he'd want to go with me tomorrow night, if he doesn't have plans.

His eyes widen a fraction and his gaze shoots to Tom, who's on my other side, talking to Andi.

"We're not a couple," I grit out.

Joe's smile, when it comes, is slow and warm and knee-weakening. "Okay then. I'd like that."

We arrange to meet at my car in the alley at eight tomorrow night. I go home, pace for three hours, sleep for six, help open the restaurant, and right after breakfast rush, I sneak over to Naomi's Lingerie across the square to do some shopping.

CHAPTER 7

Dear July,

I'm sorry I couldn't say goodbye. My dad probably knew I'd run if I'd known what he was planning.

Joe

THAT DRESS IS...DAMN.

The July I used to know was always in a steakhouse uniform or a swimsuit or shorts and a T-shirt. Grown-up restaurant July wears jeans and a T-shirt and a crisp apron. Softball July wears clothes suitable for sliding into base or diving for line drives.

This dress makes me forget my words. A little white top that clings to her breasts, bares her smooth shoulders and strong arms and a hint of cleavage and something lacy; a wide belt over a soft blue skirt that flutters around her ankles, giving me glimpses of pink-painted toenails peeking from leather sandals...all places my fingertips and my mouth want to map and rememorize oh so slowly.

Ever since she asked last night, I've been counting the seconds to this chance for us to get to know each other again. Now I'm not sure I'm even going to be able to speak.

I've always known what to do when I'm out with a woman and she slides me a long, slow look and a smile like that. Sixteen-year-old July hadn't mastered that look. She'd just reach for me with mischief and laughter in her eyes. Whisper to me and run her hands through my hair. Kiss me and kiss me and kiss me. Hold me and talk to me for hours. We'd worked up to everything slowly—only ever had full sex once, that last night, so we never developed secret cues or private signals about it. I don't know if I'm reading this—her—right tonight.

So I slide into her passenger seat and ignore her tanned shoulders a few inches from mine and the bare curve of her calf under the fluttering hem of that skirt. I try not to remember the feel of her in my hand, of her eyes and her body on mine, and that fucking sexy little growl in her throat when we collided last night. I try to talk to her, to bring back that easy way we used to have of being together.

She used to tell me stories of her life and confide her dreams for the future like it was no big deal. No risk in sharing. But tonight as we drive to the roadhouse and find our way to a booth inside, she has more to say to the people who hoot and holler to see her dressed up than she does to me.

I try for her attention when we're settled across from each other in our booth. "Tell me how your life's been, July. You know about mine." This is my chance to link the then-and-now Julys in my mind.

But just as her eyes finally meet mine, the server arrives to take our order. And then someone brings drinks and townspeople I don't know stop by to say hi, and then our food comes and the lights drop and the music cranks up and she's tugging me out on the floor.

We make a half-assed attempt to learn a line dance, mostly screwing up and laughing at ourselves, but then the DJ plays "Tennessee Whiskey" and July moves into my arms and I'm back to not being able to speak.

Hallelujah. Finally, I'm holding her again, close enough to feel her heartbeat, to hear her sigh, to have her fingers tickling the back of my neck and her soft hair teasing my nose. I'm with my July.

And I close my eyes and wrap my arms around her a little tighter and just sway with her. Breathe her in and sway. I may not know what she's thinking anymore—yet—and I may not know all her little signs and cues, but I've got this. I've got another chance. I can wait for her secrets. We can talk later. Right now I just want to feel this hope. Soak in this closest thing to joy I've felt since the last time I held her.

It's hard to let go of her when the music speeds back up. My feet drag like a stubborn little kid's as we head back to our booth.

But it's all good. Now I can look in her eyes, listen to her warm honey voice, enjoy all her expressions over our meal.

"Tell me about this building of yours." She picks up a fry and nibbles it. It has to be cold by now. My steak is.

I huff out a laugh. "It's in pretty rough shape. I've done some cleaning, but it needs work."

She shoves her plate away, food basically untouched. "Show me."

"You're not hungry?" Okay, we can talk somewhere private better than in this crowded, noisy place.

She shakes her head. I push my plate aside and reach for my wallet, but she's already laid money on the table for our bill. She raises a finger when I start to protest. "My invitation, my treat."

We've got our whole future to eat steak together. Next time I'll buy. So I toss cash down for a tip and follow her out the door.

"It has potential," she says after I've walked her through the place and gotten her settled with a beer on the secondhand love seat someone down the street had put out with the trash yesterday. Glad I wrestled the lumpy thing up here now; our only other choices are the flimsy metal folding chair downstairs or my squeaky air mattress in the back room.

No thinking about mattresses. Tonight's not for that.

This place doesn't seem nearly so depressing with July in it. After I patch the walls, I'll paint. She can choose the color. I'll get some real furniture, maybe a TV. I can have her over, cook dinner for her...

She moves her purse to the floor so I can squeeze in beside her with my own beer.

"Thanks for asking me out tonight." I clink my bottle to hers, trying not to be done in by her nearness, her clean scent, the firm, warm press of her thigh all along mine. A million questions run through my head. *What did you think when I disappeared? Were you okay? Did you hate me? Could you feel that I was out there loving you?* The one I blurt out is, "What was it like for you after I left?"

Her gray eyes meet mine, and for the first time tonight, I feel her full attention on me. "Aw, Joe," she sighs, dropping her head to my shoulder. "It wasn't fun. I don't like thinking about it."

I twist to see her better, to ask more, but she takes my bottle and sets it on the floor beside hers. Turns back and gazes at me for a long, intense minute. And then she reaches for my hand. Strokes her thumb across my palm and raises it to her breast. Pressing, holding it there to her softness.

I didn't expect this, this fast, overwhelming *onslaught* of feelings and reactions and instincts. I'm hardening but something's not—

And just as I lift my surprised eyes to hers, to make sure she's wanting what it seems she's wanting, she dips her head in—*for a kiss?*—and starts to swing her leg over my lap to straddle me, and then, oh god, her nose pokes me in the eye hard, and as reflex jerks me away, her knee catches me right in the groin, and my world explodes in pain stars and the sound of air leaving my lungs in a high-pitched whimper.

I double over, trying not to throw up—that's never a good thing to do mid-date. Around the edges of jagged stars, her voice creeps in, panicked and horrified. "Oh god, Joe, I'm so sorry! What do you need? What can I get? Ice?"

I shake my head, afraid to open my mouth. Her fingers flutter over me, nervous moths on my back, until the pain starts to subside.

I don't know what just happened. We've barely spoken tonight. Every time I've tried to get her to talk to me, we've been interrupted or she's distracted me. Sex with her tonight...it would be everything I want and nothing I want at the same time. My heart squeezes.

Something is wrong. This is not us. Something is wrong here.

July

He was trying to talk to me. I was so focused on my plan that I didn't pay attention.

So focused on myself that I didn't pay attention to *him*.

When I made my move and he looked confused, I ignored that. There was as much alarm and concern on his face as anything else, but I told myself, *Nah, it's excitement.*

When we were young, we'd just reach for each other. No need for words. We'd wrap our arms around each other, and he'd whisper, "Click." The first time he said it, I asked why. He shrugged and hugged me closer. "We just...go together. Like...two halves of a seat belt. Makes me feel more secure."

But tonight there was no click. Zero clicking. And I feel anything but secure.

And now we're quiet as he recovers from my clumsiness. I'm mortified and full of regret, my eyes blurring on the smudged, discolored wall of his living room.

Finally he straightens. Looks me in the eye and raises one hand to my hair, touching me so carefully. So gently. "July." His voice is low and uncertain, hopeful and cautious at the same time. "What just happened? What was that about?"

I close my eyes, trying to keep tears in and my utter fucking stupidity out. The least I can do is give him the truth. "It was... an attempted exorcism. Sexorcism."

I didn't know a person could go so still. If I couldn't see his pulse in his neck, I'd think he'd turned to stone.

"A...sexorcism?"

It feels like I'm imposing on him, crammed in against him like this. Taking up too much space. Probably crushing him into the cushions of this ugly love seat. I climb to my feet. I can't meet his eyes now. I am the world's biggest coward, the world's stupidest person.

I *so* did not think this through well enough. "I thought... Joe, I've been obsessing ever since you came back. Messing up everything I touch. Feeling like I'm losing my mind. I thought maybe if I...if we..." I gesture between us and force myself to look at him. "I thought maybe this, tonight, would help me get it out of my system."

His eyes widen a fraction and I see it: the light dying. He turns his face away and clears his throat. "And..." He clears his throat again, but his voice still comes out sandpaper rough. "Did it? Am I out of your system now?" He turns back to watch me answer, the corners of his eyes crinkling as if he's bracing for a blow. I've never seen an expression so bleak, even when he was reliving being forced to go to Germany.

I imagine it's how he looked the day he gave up on me ever answering his letters.

And the dying of that light echoes the death of something inside me...any belief I had that I am basically a good person. Someone he could want or love again. Shame rushes in to fill the void.

Did it work? Good terrible question. Again, I owe him the truth. "I don't know."

He swings his head toward that fugly wall again and climbs to his feet, moving like he's aged thirty years in the time we've been here. "Your plan was, what, to use sex with me to...be done with me?"

I can't honestly tell him no. I hadn't known for sure what to expect. What I wanted.

At my silence, he shakes his head. Says, "I'm glad you just kneed me then. Less painful."

He bends to scoop up our mostly full bottles and takes them to the kitchenette. Upends them in the sink. Then he glances at the door and pats his pockets as if searching for his keys.

I guess I'm leaving now.

That seems like the best and worst idea in the world.

I have never hurt anyone like this in my life. It feels like we're both being impaled on the same two-pointed blade. To me the pain is so fresh and sharp I almost expect to see my blood splashing out on the floor, but Joe's suddenly become a different person. Or a robot. All his light and life and energy and grace are...just gone. Everything that made him Joe. Made him wonderful.

I've done that.

I clutch my purse to my belly. "I'm sorry, Joe. You—"

He interrupts me. Raises a hand, shakes his head. "Just..." He's never cut me off before. He moves to the door, holds it open for me. Studies the floor as I come closer.

"You don't have to walk me back." Mine is the tiny voice of a person who knows she's committed a wrong so big she can barely fathom it. I've broken this sweet man. Somehow he survived abuse and a massive betrayal by his hellish parents, only to come back and have me...do this.

His answer is rusty and resigned. "Yeah, July, I do." For the first time ever, my name sounds ordinary on his lips. Just another word. Nothing special.

He walks me back down the street to my corner—that's a million steps when your conscience swells, burning, in your throat and on down through your body to pool with the weight of lead in your feet—and stands silent as I go alone the rest of the distance to the restaurant door. With shaky hands I fit the key in. When the lock clicks open, he gives a weary half wave and is gone.

My fingers find the grooves on the doorframe, but tonight the claw marks are no help at all. Maybe Hope isn't a sweet little creature eager for a new, better world. Maybe Hope is a monster.

I wake up on my couch, ravaged and raw and exhausted in the gray morning light, but as the day gets underway, I know what's going on around me. I can do my job. At the same time, I'm hyperaware of the connections between the people around me—strong, fleeting, fragile connections, some obvious and some invisible.

We carry a special birthday pastry out to Ramona, the fire chief's tiny daughter, and she sings along with us, her dark eyes shining, her little puffball ponytails bobbing. She carefully gives her baby brother the first bite, and he beams. People all over the dining room are smiling and clapping as we go back to the kitchen. Tina is thrilled her newest pastry creation was a success, and Donna is bursting with pride for Tina. Threads of kindness and joy and love connect them with each other, with Ramona's family, and with all of us in the kitchen and dining room.

Even Maisie smiles, and she's the most fiercely focused trainee we've ever had, listening intently to every instruction, trying so hard to get everything right that her hand shakes with the effort.

She's pouring a tray of iced teas to take out to the dining room. Sonya's beside her, talking to Tina, waiting for me to plate four orders for one of her tables.

"Wonder if they're ever going to figure out who it was that died in that bus crash in Asheville," Sonya comments.

Tina shakes her head. "I heard they're gonna offer a reward for information if nobody comes forward to identify the body. Maisie, hon, add a little more ice to each of those. It melts so fast in fresh tea…"

Maisie fetches a big scoop from the ice machine and tries to divide it between the glasses, her hands shaking again, her face way more serious than the situation calls for.

I put Sonya's orders up.

"Maisie, I need you to sign one more payroll form." I nod her toward the office, and when she follows me in, I tell her, "Listen, don't worry so much, okay? You're doing great. Everybody likes you, and soon you'll have this job down pat. You're good, okay?"

She looks at me with those enormous, serious eyes and manages a tiny, wobbly smile and nod before she ducks back into the kitchen.

I follow more slowly, hoping I've woven a comfort thread into her day.

Comfort. Joe. I wish for the millionth time I'd done everything differently last night. Skipped the outfit, skipped the roadhouse, skipped inviting myself to his place. I could've cooked him dinner, and we could've sat on my couch, watched the comings and goings on the square, and talked. I think that's what he wanted—just to talk. Maybe that would have calmed me down better than a botched sex attempt. And it sure wouldn't have ended with me hurting him. Trying to use him.

My stomach rolls. There were threads attaching us too—past love, current interest, curiosity, hope—until I hacked them apart.

I plate the next two orders and try not to resee the light dying from his eyes.

I'd been so worried about what would happen to me and my business—and all the people who are my responsibility—if I couldn't get my Joe-obsessed head out of my ass that I never stopped to consider what he might want or need.

I was so scared of breaking like I did before, of being unable to function, that I didn't remember how people always help me through tough spots. Then and now, people have always helped me through.

Joe didn't have anybody then. He came back here knowing only me. And I've just severed our threads.

CHAPTER 8

Dear July,

My dad's been a fucking asshole my whole life. Sorry for my language. I love you and hope you're okay. I'll get home to you as soon as I can.

Joe

I CAN'T STAND THE SIGHT of that fucking love seat. It's the first thing I see when I step back into the apartment.

I grab it, hearing myself growl like a wild animal, and drag it, bumping, downstairs. Leave it by the curb of the still-dark street. If there's a merciful god, it'll be gone by noon.

Back upstairs, I avoid the area where the love seat was, afraid if I look too hard, I'll see the shards of my stupid dreams lying there where they crashed.

I don't know how long I stand at the window, staring out over the deserted street, before I realize July's scent is on me. Part of me wants to crawl into that fucking bathtub and scrub it away. Another part wants to curl around it so it won't disappear like my hope.

I'm a fool. I am every bit as stupid as my dad used to say I was. What kind of dipshit drops his whole life to move sixteen hundred miles on the basis of an old memory? What kind of functioning adult believes that two lovestruck teenagers can be separated for twenty years and still be compatible when they meet again?

Why did I even trust that my memories of July were accurate? Sure, she'd been the one sweet thing in my life...for exactly two months. Yeah, maybe she did love me with her sixteen-year-old heart, but the adult woman is a stranger to me.

And I am—was—a distraction to her. Worse—I was something so bad I had to be driven out like a demon. My reappearance was wrecking her great life.

A teenage crush can't overcome that.

For her, this night wasn't a new beginning or a reason for hope. It was a means to an end. And sex wouldn't have been making love—it would've been her using my dick like a barge pole to push me away. To get the dipshit with the messy feelings away.

Christ. I'd handed her those feelings—my heart—in an old shoebox.

I gag and barely make it into the bathroom before throwing up what little I'd had to eat.

Afterward, I slump down to the cracked tiles and just lie there. Not sure for how long. Maybe I doze. A siren somewhere jerks me back to alertness. I'm still shaky and queasy, but I can't stay here, and I don't have any place else to be. I pull on running gear and hit the predawn streets, walking at first, then picking up speed until I'm running flat-out.

My feet take me to the outskirts of town, up the road into the mountains, and onto the narrow turnoff for the lake spot that was once mine and July's. I don't want to be there, don't want to see it, don't want to remember, but my legs churn faster and faster until I burst into the clearing, gasping for breath.

Hands on my knees, it takes me a minute to register the flurry of movement from the direction of the picnic table. A wild-haired young guy is on the table, struggling to get out of a sleeping bag, his eyes wide on me.

"Oh, shit! I didn't mean to scare you. I've never seen anybody else up here." I back away, pointing to the rock at the water's edge. "I was just going to sit there and look at the lake. Will that bother you?"

He stops struggling. "No...that's okay. I must've fallen asleep here. I need to go home anyway."

Yeah, dude. You accidentally *fell asleep in your sleeping bag.* This is a kid in trouble. He's bigger than me but looks like a young teenager with his baby face.

I nod and head to the rock, sitting so that my back is to him. Behind me I hear rustling and crinkling, as if he's shoving his bed-roll into a plastic bag. Then footsteps retreating into the woods, then nothing.

Takes the edge off my pity party. Yeah, I'm a thirty-six-year-old dumbass with no firm future plans and an ugly-ass, older-than-shit building, but at least I've got a roof over my head.

I scour my mind for the information Rose Barnes had given me on Galway-area organizations serving at-risk kids. Can't for the life of me think how *I* could help him—*if* I ever see him again—without scaring him or making him think I'm some kind of predator.

Not that I'm likely to see him again. It's time for me to get the fuck out of this town.

My much slower run home ends with me sweating and exhausted, unfit for human company, so of course Angus and Rose are leaning on his work van outside my building.

Rose smiles. "There he is! Still got time for us this morning?" I'd completely forgotten we set a date. Can't remember what it's for. My head the day I met them had been too full of my fool dreams about July. But what the hell. Got nothing better to do, except for packing my truck to move to Cullowhee.

I ignore the question and unlock the door. "Sorry. I should've gotten home in time to take a bath before you got here."

"That was one of the things you said you needed, right? A real shower?" Rose flips open the notebook she's holding and turns it to a fresh page.

"You've cleaned the place up." Angus is standing in the middle of the main downstairs room. Light actually comes in through the big front windows now, illuminating the damaged walls, but at least nothing grits or crackles when we walk across the floor.

"Yeah. That's *all* I've done so far." Guess I ought to be honest with them. "What were we going to do today again?"

Angus snorts and Rose rolls her eyes. He nudges her with one elbow. "Told ya."

Rose purses her lips, her brown eyes crinkling at me. "Angus said you wouldn't remember. Said you had your attention... elsewhere."

Seems like centuries ago.

"Yeah, well. Today I'm all yours."

Apparently we'd arranged for them to come over to discuss what needs doing in the building. At this moment I could not possibly care less. We can burn it to the fucking ground for all I care.

"So show us around." Rose gestures with her notebook. "Tell us what you want and Angus can work up an estimate. If you don't hire him for the work, you'll know what a fair price would be from whoever you do hire."

"That's...really nice. Thanks." I should've remembered. Should've given this some thought. "I guess...I need to have the place rewired. Add more outlets." I scan the downstairs. "Not sure how I'll be using this area yet. Don't want to do much to it yet except patch and paint. I can do that."

Angus makes notes on a spiral pad he's pulled out of his back pocket. "Talk to us about upstairs, then."

We go up and look around.

"Geez, Joe, this is depressing as shit." Rose is gazing at my open suitcase and inflatable air mattress, the only two things in the bedroom. "And that kitchenette looks like a fire hazard."

I can *almost* laugh.

Angus grins. Reaches out a big hand to squeeze the back of her neck. "Damn, Rosie, tell him what you *really* think."

There's pure adoration on both their faces as they gaze at each other.

I blink away. Squint at the wood floor. "So replace the tub with a shower. Redo the kitchenette. Uh..." I'm drawing a blank. Who gives a shit what else I do to the damn place?

We stand in silence while they wait for me to say more. I got nothing.

"Building was on the market a long time," Angus says finally. "Updates will help it if you ever decide to resell."

I shoot a glance at him, wondering if he can tell I've already got one foot out the door, but his beard hides half his face, and his eyes are unreadable. "True. Sorry I'm not more help. Got any suggestions?"

They exchange a look and Rose lifts her notebook. "How about I ask you some questions about what you like? Angus and I can come up with some simple ideas for how to make the place nicer to live in now and easier to sell later."

"Okay."

She spends twenty minutes firing questions at me—color and style and lighting preferences, how I plan to use the front room of the apartment, what kind of mood I'd like for each area—and scribbling notes, and then I walk them back downstairs.

Angus pauses at the front door, his big body filling the frame. "Rosie's real good at this. I'll get back with you in a couple of days with an estimate and her ideas. Call if you have any questions." He fishes a business card from his wallet.

Then they're gone and I'm alone again.

———

July

"This explains so much." Rose stares toward me from across my little dining table, but I think she's seeing something else. "He seemed so different this morning..." Her eyes dart to mine and she clamps her mouth shut. I don't think she'd meant to say that out loud.

Beside her, Andi is quiet, looking back and forth between the two of us.

I'd invited them over for dinner. Rose agreed immediately, as did Andi. The kitchen crew downstairs laughed and shooed me away earlier when I told them to holler if they needed me. Disrespectful, the lot of them.

Today the loveliness of pretty much everybody in my life makes me ache with awareness of just how alone Joe is.

"Different how, Rose?" I'm afraid to hear it, but I've got to.

"Different like...dull." She waves a hand vaguely. "He seemed...dulled. Even his eyes. Not that he looked us in the eye much. Angus noticed too."

Andi frowns. "Joe's got bright eyes. Like a mischievous kid." I always loved that about him.

Rose shakes her head. "Not this morning."

It's all I can do not to let my head thump face-first into my pasta. Not to wail.

Andi studies me. "So when you say you hurt him, what do you mean exactly?"

I'm going to throw up. *No. No, I won't.* I have to be accountable. "I asked him out. Took him to Woollybooger's, then invited myself back to his place to seduce him."

"We did that last week! Well, I mean, it would be hard to say who was seducing who, but Woollybooger's was really fun and—"

I don't know whether Andi kicked Rose under the table or Rose saw something in my expression, but she cuts off abruptly. Says with a completely straight face, "Sorry. I mean, oh my, yes, that *does* sound awful for poor Joe."

I sigh. "I went to kiss him and accidentally poked him in the eye with my nose. And then accidentally kneed him in the crotch when he ducked away."

Andi winces and leans back in her chair. "Damn, girl. You're usually more coordinated than that."

Rose stares at me like I've taken leave of my senses. "Joe

doesn't seem like he'd hold an accident against you. And he seemed physically fine this morning."

I shove my plate away so I can rest my elbows on the table. Drop my head into my hands. "No, that's not what upset him. He's hurt and pissed—understandably—because I was trying to do it for bad reasons, with no regard for him. He was trying to talk to me. To get to know me again. And I was trying to use him."

I pick up my napkin and place it on the table. "I'd been so stressed over how much I'd been thinking about him and how much I was messing everything up everywhere...I was afraid I was backsliding."

Andi knows what I mean, but Rose cocks her head. "Backsliding?"

I hate having to talk about That Time again. "When he disappeared in high school, I lost it, Rose. For a whole year. I questioned everything I thought I knew. I lost faith in myself, couldn't handle basic everyday things. I was depressed, stopped eating... almost had to be hospitalized." I'd been the girl with the blessed, easy life full of love and support and privilege. Everything had always gone my way. And when Joe disappeared, I broke. I'd only known him for two months, and I broke.

Rose cups my arm and squeezes. "I'm so sorry."

A tear drips to the table when I blink down. Pathetic. I don't deserve to cry. "Last night, he tried to get me to tell him what was going on. He was holding me so nice. He sounded so confused. Concerned. For *me*." The urge to vomit is back. I straighten, push my hair out of my eyes, and look my friends full in the face. "I told him it was a sexorcism."

Silence.

"Pardon?" "A what?" They speak over each other.

"I told him I'd thought sex might help me get him out of my head so I could stop screwing up."

Andi winces again and Rose leans back in her chair, closing her eyes for a few seconds.

We sit in silence as they digest that. Then Andi puts her hands palms down on the table in front of her. "Okay, well, I can see how that would hurt. Is it possible you're overreacting a bit though?"

I meet her dark eyes. "If it were anybody but Joe, maybe."

"Why's Joe different?"

"Because I'm the only person he really knew when he came back here. And I just tried to use him. I was so wrapped up in myself, I didn't think about him at all until it was too late."

They sit looking at me, waiting for me to explain more or better. *Jesus, isn't that enough?*

"Because he seemed so *alone*. And now I've hurt him and he's even more alone, in a town that might as well be new to him. Not a soul who loves him. He's always been alone. I'm afraid he's going to go off into the world and be even more alone than ever. His folks are dead. He sold his business. He came back here for some reason—maybe because he'd liked this town and felt like he could belong here—and I just made it awful for him."

Rose and Andi both have experience with being alone, so I try again. "What if he leaves town for good and goes off somewhere? Who's going to care about him? He's *alone*."

Andi's lips quirk in a tiny smile. "Yeah, I'm picking up on that theme." She turns to Rose. "You saw him this morning. Did he say anything about leaving town?"

Rose shakes her head. "Not in so many words. But he didn't seem very interested in making that god-awful building any more livable."

Andi faces me again. "So maybe he's thinking about leaving, maybe not. We don't know. We've got our first game tomorrow. Let's see if he shows up. See if he says anything then."

"I'm doing some sketches for him tonight." Rose tells us about her ideas for Joe's place as they get up and help me clear away the dishes.

I stop them as they head for the stairs a few minutes later. "Why aren't y'all telling me how bad I suck?"

Rose's eyes are warm. "I've got no personal experience of you sucking."

Andi shrugs. "To be honest, I'm kind of relieved you have some human flaws. The whole Wonder Woman thing wears pretty thin after a decade or two."

Before I can think of a reply to that, they're gone. But their friendship and support and honesty keep me from being alone, even though the restaurant crew waves me away when I go down to see if they need me. So I change my clothes and go for a run to see if I can outdistance my guilt and shame.

CHAPTER 9

Dear July,

I found the U.S. Embassy. Told them what happened, but they said my own parents couldn't have kidnapped me if I'm a minor in their care.

Joe

TIRED AS I WAS, I still only get a crap night's sleep, in and out of dreams. Nightmares. In one, my dad is burying something in an unfamiliar backyard. Shoeboxes. One with my letters to July, one dripping with blood from the heart he's ripped out of me. I yell and run across the yard to stop him. He turns and looks up, grinning...and he's July.

The nightmare that hauled me out of bed for another dawn run, though, started out good. I answer a knock at my door and July's there, her smile soft and secret. Sweet and just for me. She steps in and looks around and says, "I like what you've done with the place," and everywhere her eyes touch, something beautiful blooms. Bright colors, comfortable furniture, flowers in pots. She reaches for my arm, slides her hand down to entwine her fingers with mine, and leans in. Warm, so warm, smelling like shampoo and powdery soap. Her breath tickles my ear as she whispers, "Come on, let's go upstairs." I go willingly, and when we're up there, she turns me to face her and smiles and says, "Where shall we start?" and my heart skips and I say, "Start?" and she laughs that warm, bubbly, sharing-something-just-with-you laugh I remember deep in my bones. And then she says, "Yeah, silly, with the packing. I brought boxes. Let's get you on the road so I can get back to my life." And I jerk awake gasping. Roll off the squeaky mattress and fumble in the dark for my running gear.

There's a cold mist over the lake this morning. No sign of the kid or his sleeping bag. I cross the clearing to the big rock and watch the sun creep up over the trees.

I need a plan. I could leave today, head over to find an apartment in Cullowhee, but I should probably wait to talk to Angus. Maybe hire him to do just enough to get the building resold. But I could start patching up the walls. Packing. It's not like I've got much, and most of it's still in boxes. The shitty little stove conked out the first time I tried it, so even my kitchen stuff's not put away.

I think about calling Gabe, but my phone's got no bars up here. Just as well. It's way too early, and he's probably got something fun going on with his husband this weekend anyway. Their bright Hawaii home seems like another world.

When the sun finally breaks through the mist to touch the water, I slide off the rock and head back. Clean up in that goddamn clawfoot tub and pull on yesterday's jeans. I'm just shrugging on a soft flannel over a fresh T-shirt, wondering where besides July's I could get a good breakfast, when somebody pounds on the front door.

Please don't let this be my July nightmare coming true.

It's not. It's Rose Barnes, waving a notebook as she balances a drink tray and paper bag in her other arm.

Her brown eyes skate over me from my damp hair to my bare feet. "Oh, good, I'm glad you're up. I know it's early." She shoves the bag at me—heavenly smells rise from it, bacon, eggs, croissants—and steps in.

I follow her gaze around the empty storefront room. "Sorry. Still no furniture."

She shrugs, settles the drink carrier on the floor, and plops her round, little body down cross-legged beside it. "No biggie. I can help with that if you want."

She's brought three drinks, two cold and one hot. She unwraps a straw, pokes it into one of the cold ones, and takes a sip, then notices me watching. "I didn't know what you like. I brought you iced tea and black coffee. There's sugar and cream in the bag if you want it."

The coffee scent winds its way into my brain. I settle near her on the floor and take the cup into my hands, inhaling it, letting it warm me.

She opens the bag I've abandoned and pulls out two foil-wrapped packets. "I hope you like breakfast sandwiches. These are the best. Tina's homemade croissants plus July's crispy bacon? It doesn't get any better than that."

My stomach rumbles in response to the fragrance, and I try to remember the last time I ate. It almost doesn't bother me that the food came from July's—I didn't have to see her.

Rose pulls out a packet of strawberry preserves, opens her sandwich, and carefully squeezes the preserves onto it.

I watch in horrified fascination.

She glances up and sees my expression. "It's delicious. Here, try it." She holds out her sandwich. When I don't reach for it, she says, "If you don't like it, I'll eat that one. If you like it, keep it and I'll fix the other one for myself."

Not knowing how to politely refuse, I take a tiny bite and, fuck, it's delicious. "Damn. I did not expect that. I'm keeping this one."

She laughs and doctors the second sandwich. Takes a bite and chews, a slight smile on her lips as she surveys the empty room.

I'm halfway through my sandwich, wishing there were three or four more in that bag, before I manage to speak. "I appreciate this. Good morning. What's the occasion?"

She nudges the bag toward me with her foot. "There's another one in there for you, but you have to jelly it up yourself."

Hallelujah.

She puts down her own sandwich, wipes her fingers on a paper napkin, and flips open her notebook. "Here's Angus's estimate." She tosses a stapled itemized list in front of me. "He's working this morning, or he would've come with me. Says he'll email you a copy too, and you can email back any questions."

The estimate looks reasonable to me. Cheap, compared to Colorado prices for work I had done there. "Thanks." I poke in the bag for the other sandwich. "You sure you don't want this? Split?" When she shakes her head, I apply strawberry magic to it.

She looks at me sideways, her eyes bright, a dimple forming in one cheek. "Now for the fun stuff."

"Mm?" No idea what she's talking about, and my mouth is too full to ask.

She pulls out several rough drawings and lays them in a row in front of me. Simple lines, just the barest suggestion of rooms, but

I get the idea. "Upstairs living area," she says, her fingertip on a sketch of open bookshelves on an exposed brick wall. "I'm thinking a bright sofa here with armchairs flanking it." She points to the next sketch. "Dining area." A clean-lined table that would easily seat six in front of another brick wall. "Maybe some quirky artwork here." Next sketch. "A restauranteur needs a real kitchen, right? So I've made yours into an *L*, with room for full-sized appliances. You could hang pots and pans from a rack over this island. For these front rooms I'm seeing greens, ranging from yellowish to a deeper blue-green. Bright but not too bright. Soothing but still interesting. A few plants here and there, comfortable window seats..."

"Now here." Her finger lands on the second to last drawing. "I'm thinking mostly cosmetic changes. Fresh paint, refinished floors." She's sketched in a rough bed, nightstand, and dresser. "Maybe dark walls with white trim? Nice mood lighting and another green plant. A reading chair. But if you want more natural light than that alley window gives you, you could maybe put in a couple of transom windows here, high in the wall the bedroom shares with the living area. Pull in light from the big front windows but still keep it a private, separate room."

She slides the last drawing in front of me. The bathroom, with my clawfoot nemesis gone and a clean glass-walled shower in its place. "Another alley window. We could make this room white, to reflect as much light as possible. I can see a driftwood-colored slatted bench with shelves above it for towels, another green plant in front of a long, framed mirror opposite the window. White tile everywhere."

"Jesus." I pictured it all right along with her and I would not have recognized the space as mine. "That sounds perfect, Rose." I could live in a place like that.

But not in Galway, right down the street from the source of my best and worst memories.

As I'm trying to figure out how to tell her how much I appreciate her effort but no thanks, my phone buzzes.

Group message from Tom. We're down three players for today's game. Flu. Need everybody else to show up on time. Y'all in?

Fuck. The softball team. I can't not show up.

"Everything okay?" Rose's voice has an edge of concern.

I glance up from my phone. "Yeah...just something I'd forgotten." My teammates' responses flood in, and I find myself typing, I'm in with them.

Then I stuff the phone into my back pocket and look down at Rose's sketches. I can't justify leaving the team. And it's not like anybody in Cullowhee needs me—classes don't start for months yet. If Angus can make this dump look like Rose's plans, I can maybe stand to stay for a little while. I'll just...avoid the restaurant. Focus on my other teammates at the games and practices.

I can bury myself in painting and repairing downstairs and working my way through the reading lists the professors gave me. Maybe figure out some way to help the kid at the lake if I run into him again.

Just need to make sure I stay away from July as much as possible. Wouldn't want to mess up her nice life.

I can probably do this. It'll probably be fine. I've been through worse.

I suck in a big lungful of air and sigh it out. Face Rose. "When can Angus start?"

July

I'm elbows deep in a clogged dish sink when Rose texts me that she thinks Joe isn't going to leave town right away.

I call her as soon as I unstop the sink. "How do you know?"

Her voice has an extra level of barely suppressed Rose energy. "He hired Angus to do some work. Says he'll do the downstairs himself. I asked if he wants me to help him shop for furniture, and he said maybe, he'd let me know."

I squeeze the phone between my chin and my shoulder as I scrub my hands and arms. "Good. This is good, right? Maybe I can, I don't know, find some way to make things better for him. Without bothering him. Maybe I can connect him to more people. Give him a community."

"That's a great idea. I'll try too."

"And Angus?"

"He'll help."

"Without letting Joe know."

"Goes without saying. Don't want to wound his Man Pride." She hangs up laughing.

Ouch. She's not wrong, but it's me—not his pride—that's the source of his most recent wound.

I work up until the last possible second before heading to the ballpark. Not sure whether he'll be there, but I don't expect it to be easy either way. He'll show and we'll have to face each other, or he won't show and I'll know that's one more thing I robbed him of.

He's there, warming up with Dirk and Hiromi. I find a parking space and change into my cleats. Andi pulls up and I go to meet her.

"Hey. Favor."

She's not even out of her car yet, but she nods. "Sure. What you need?"

"Rose is pretty sure Joe's not going to leave right away. Would you consider helping him bond with the team? I'd do it, but I think he needs a break from me."

She reaches into her back seat for her bat bag and slings it over one shoulder. Glances over at our team, then back at me. "Sure. I can do that."

"Thanks."

We join the others, pull on our gloves, and warm up our arms. Joe doesn't *not* look at me, exactly, but his eyes flick across me fast and his "hey" seems carefully neutral. I knew this wouldn't be easy, but it's a whole new, unexpected kind of hard. I've known the pain of Joe's absence, but I've never felt the pain of his *presence* before.

I keep several people between us so he doesn't have to talk to me. We finish warming up, Tom confirms the lineup, and then it's our turn for the field. I take my bag into the dugout, all the way to the far wall, leaving Joe a clear escape route and a broad choice of where to sit.

He's a machine on the field today. Total focus, brilliant play, no errors. When it's our turn at bat, he drills line drives in the holes and turns on the speed for extra bases.

I realize I'm staring, drinking him in, when Hiromi mutters beside me, "That man is something, isn't he?" Her eyes, like mine, follow him from first to third.

"Yep, he's good." Like I don't know what she means.

We win, of course, and then I've got a dilemma. Join the team at Lindon's and risk scaring Joe off, or say I can't go and risk the group deciding not to go either?

"Just a quick one for me," I say finally, just loud enough to be sure Joe hears. "I've got to get back to work."

And at the bar, I make sure to sit so there are three people between us, and after one beer, I head out, leaving Joe to make friends. He was really good at that when we were young. I go back to the restaurant, shoving down a wish that I was sitting beside him, sharing a pitcher and stories and laughter, leaning into him enough to feel his warmth and his breath in my hair.

I've thrown away any chance I had at that. I need to remember that and suck it up.

Donna and Maisie are in the kitchen, with Donna showing the girl how to garnish today's catfish special. "Put the greens like this and then top them with a spoonful of this…" To me she says, "Thought you'd go to Lindon's after the game."

I shrug and look at the order slips on the board. "I did for a minute. Wanted to come see if y'all needed help."

"Nah, we're good." Donna turns her attention back to Maisie.

I head into my office. Got some planning to do for when we open the outside patio seating in a few days. But first I call my brother, who happens to be stroller shopping with Jen.

"Hey, July." Brendan sounds exasperated. "Tell your sister to step away from these cheap-ass things that aren't safe enough for our future niece or nephew. Tell her I can afford to get her a decent stroller."

I laugh. "I am not getting roped into this discussion. Hey, would y'all stop by here on your way home?"

"Sure. You okay?"

"I'm fine. Just got an interesting story to tell you."

An hour later we're settled in the booth nearest the kitchen, splitting a piece of Tina's incredible Italian cream cake. I've just finished telling them about Joe being back in town and what his parents did.

Brendan stops eating halfway through. "Shiiiiit. That sucks."

"Poor Joe!" Jen's eyes are wide with sympathy. "You know, I always hated hating him after he left. I hated having to think he was a jerk."

You and me both, Sis. "Yeah. I could kill his parents. But they're both dead already. Joe's going to start classes at Western Carolina for social work." I fiddle with the saltshaker. This next bit's tricky. "I'd like to help him meet people. But...we had a... falling out. So I don't think he wants to spend time with me. I was thinking, you know, if you happen to run into him, maybe you could let him know you're happy to see him? Happy he's back?"

Jen studies me, her eyes narrowed, her big brain working. "What do you mean?"

Brendan glances from her face to mine and stays quiet. He can tell something's up too.

I'm no good at this shit.

I lower my voice to just above a whisper and lean in. "I hurt him, and I don't want him to go off all alone. I think he could be happy here if he gets to know more people. I'd just...like you to help if you can. Without letting him know."

"You hoping to start over with him?" Brendan's words come out slow, careful.

"No." I shake my head firmly. Gotta nip that in the bud so there'll be no matchmaking attempts to make both Joe and me miserable. "Not going to happen. But I hurt him, and I don't want to be the cause of him leaving again."

"How'd you hurt him, July?" Jen's voice is soft. She's got a big enough heart to feel sorry for both of us if I let her.

"I don't want to talk about that. But it was bad. Will you help if you see him? He's living just down the street."

They look at each other, carrying on one of their wordless conversations that always used to drive me nuts.

"Yeah, we'll help." They say it together.

My freakish, wonderful little brother and sister.

They'd loved Joe once too.

CHAPTER 10

Dear July,

The motherfucker (who I will refer to as MF from here on out) has my passport so I couldn't leave even if I had money for a ticket...

Joe

"YOU'RE SURE YOU CAN MAKE this place look like Rose described it?"

I'm standing in the kitchenette area with Angus, holding Rose's sketches.

He had interrupted my busy afternoon of cursing and patching holes, interspersed with flashbacks of the good old days and the painful recognition of my foolishness in thinking July'd still be like that—or that we'd still be like that together—now. I'm a fucking idiot, mourning a girl and a relationship that probably only ever existed in my head. Her name, her smile...she had me believing she was warm all the way through. It's impossible to reconcile the sweet girl of my memory with the woman who wanted to use me like a blow-up sex doll.

Angus's voice brings me back. "It'll look worse before it looks better. Gotta do some demo and the wiring first, then the plumbing. I can start the demo today." He studies me with bright turquoise eyes. "Kitchen won't be done for a couple of weeks. That okay?"

Haven't been eating much, but I know some carryout places now. I'd rather have July's food, but nope, not going there. "Yeah." I toss the drawings on the cracked countertop and look for a change of subject. "Rose do design stuff as a side gig?"

He snorts. Opens his toolbox, pulls out a tape measure, and pokes around for something else. "Nah, she's never done that before. Except for her house. Our house."

"Seriously?" Hard to believe. "She could. Her ideas are great."

"Woman's a wonder." His voice is gruff with pride. "She can do pretty much anything she sets her mind to."

"I don't remember her from high school." Short, little fireball like that, I think I'd remember. "She younger than us?"

He sets a crowbar on the counter, then goes into the living area and unrolls a big sheet of plastic to cover the floor. "Yeah, but she didn't move here till last year."

That surprises me, given her apparent tightness with Angus and July. "You know her from somewhere else?"

He doesn't look up from his work. "Nope. She just came to town and...here we are." He smiles down at his hands, a private smile not meant for me.

Huh.

He straightens and turns. "I'm about to make a mess in here, tearing out these walls to get to the brick. Might want to close the bedroom and bathroom doors."

"Want some help?"

He shakes his big shaggy head. "Nah, thanks. Got a method. Do better on my own."

Hell, I'm not going to stand around and watch him work. But I'm tired of patching holes, and I'll be damned if I'm closing myself in that dingy bedroom for the rest of the day. "I think I'll head to the library, then. Here's the spare key. You got my number if you need anything?"

He nods and is already fitting a mask over his face and earbuds into his ears by the time I get to the stairs.

At the library I show proof of residency and get a card. A librarian helps me look up local organizations working with young people. There's not much, just the Galway County Youth Home, the foster care system, and a suicide hotline. Gay-Straight Alliance groups at the city and county high schools, and a PFLAG group affiliated with those. A community center near downtown that hosts sports and dance and exercise classes.

I download articles on working with at-risk kids and spend the rest of the afternoon in a snug corner, reading and taking notes. I browse the library shelves and find a few social work–related books I can check out. I don't know how late Angus is planning to work today, so I stay at the library until closing time and then head back around the town square, a stack of books under my arm.

The lights are still on at July's, but the dining room is empty. My stomach growls, reminding me that I haven't eaten since a peanut butter sandwich at breakfast. I'm thinking about where to go for dinner—a roadhouse steak sounds good, but the memories are too fresh—when I notice an odd little procession approaching. Five guys, all older than me, walking single file, not talking to each other. Like they're together but not together. All carrying bags or backpacks. The lead guy has military posture and Albert Einstein hair. He goes straight to July's door and knocks.

These guys looking to make trouble for her? I move a little closer, trying to see better. Inside the restaurant, the kitchen door swings open and July trots across the dining room. Her voice floats across the green to me as she pushes open the door to let them inside. "Hey, Devon. Evening, guys." When they're all in, she flips the bolt to lock the door.

What the hell?

I lean against a storefront, still almost half a block away, and watch, fascinated. The restaurant is lit up like a stage, and I can see everything as the men place their bags on the floor in a row not far from the door.

July seats them in the booth and table nearest the kitchen. She talks to them for a second—they don't seem to say much—and then ducks back into the kitchen, coming back out a moment later with a fistful of mugs and a coffeepot. Pours for everybody, and then leaves and comes back with water glasses and a pitcher. She pours a round of water and then talks some more. Looks like she's listing things on her fingers. Each guy in turn says a word or two, except one guy who seems to speak for himself and the man beside him. July listens, nods, and goes back to the kitchen.

Nothing much happens for a few minutes, but no way am I leaving without knowing she's okay in there. The guys take turns getting up to go to the restroom. By the time they're done with that, July is back with a tray that's got to weigh fifty pounds. It's loaded down with filled plates and bowls. Sandwiches, pasta, soup, bread... I watch her lay a feast across their two tables. Then she refills their coffee, touches the Einstein guy—Devon—on the shoulder, and disappears again. Five minutes later she's back with a tray of desserts. Pie and cake. They demolish it all and then climb to their feet, stretching and making their way slowly back over to where they'd laid down their bags.

July's back with a tray for the dirty dishes and a big plastic bag of her own. She sets down the tray on a nearby table, reaches into the bag, and pulls out a fistful of narrow packages. Toothbrushes, maybe? She holds them up for the guys to see, and one guy raises a hand. She passes him a package and reaches back into the bag again, this time coming out with small, dark, soft-looking bundles. Socks? Two of the men nod and she hands them each one.

Then they all move over to the door, scooping up their bags. July lets them out, and they leave the way they came, single file, not speaking, with Devon in the lead.

Not a penny exchanged. No coins, no paper, no cards.

Whatever that was about, it turned out okay. July clearly didn't need me to stick around. How many more ways do I need to get that message?

But I stand and watch as she relocks the door and begins to gather up their dirty dishes. Two trips, it takes her. Then she comes back out with a cloth, wipes the two tables down, and finishes stacking the dining room chairs.

Another woman, as dark as July is fair, comes out of the kitchen with a mop bucket and begins to mop the floor, but July stops her. Takes the mop, hugs the woman, and waves her away. I watch her finish the floor, there in the dining room alone, her movements steady and smooth and economical, her hair gleaming gold under the lights. Finally she wheels the bucket away, flipping off the lights as she goes.

It's chilly and my library-book arm is stiff. Still, it takes me a minute to pull myself together enough to go on my way.

Who were those guys? What was that about?

I do not know the first thing about this July stranger.

———

July

"Here, taste this." I spear a chunk of potato from my newest vegetarian experiment and hold it out for Donna.

She reaches for the fork and takes a bite. "Oh, that's better. Joe?"

I nod. "Took the first version to him last night. This morning's note said, *Hit it with some smoked paprika.*"

"Boy's got a good tongue." She shoots a stern look at Tina, whose eyes are laughing as she carries a tray of sourdough baguettes to the walk-in, the words "'Bout time July found herself a man with a good tongue" floating behind. Donna closes her eyes and shakes her head.

"Woman's gonna be the death of us," I mutter, and Donna laughs.

"Really though, July, keep getting his input. We don't want to get stale."

"Donna, your cooking's never going to get stale. But I will keep asking him."

I'm trying a new way of involving Joe in Galway. Two nights ago, I packed carryout boxes with two new dishes I've been experimenting with. I took them down to his building, hung the bag on the knob, and pounded on the door. When he appeared in the hallway, I pointed to the bag and took off. Inside the bag with the hot food, I'd placed a note that read: Remember how you promised to help me taste test stuff for the restaurant? Your thoughts on flavor, texture, and serving suggestions appreciated. Yeah, I'm not above holding him to past promises to get him to engage.

The next morning, we found he'd pushed the note under our front door. No personal message, but he'd written on the back:

Spinach dish: Good flavor. Maybe add water chestnuts or slivered almonds for texture.

Chicken: Perfect. Wouldn't change a thing.

So last night I took him another dish, and tonight I'll take another. And tomorrow and the next night and the next...

Rose said she and Angus think Joe forgets to eat. That hit me square in the heart. Me taking him food doesn't make up for what I did, but if I work really hard every day and make sure Joe's got dinner every night, I can help him and sometimes rest okay myself for a few hours.

Maisie pushes through the swinging door with another tray of dirty dishes, two other servers right behind her with three new orders, and all of a sudden, we don't have time to joke or experiment anymore. This week's been brutal. We opened patio seating and the weather has figured out it's spring, and we've been slammed. All hands on deck every day, and still we're not able to catch up for more than five minutes at a time. Finally yesterday, quiet Maisie spoke up to say she had a friend who was looking for work and would I consider hiring him to wash dishes?

I was just tired and desperate enough to agree to talk to him.

"Sam's here, July. Should I bring him back?" She's filling tea pitchers as she talks. Girl learns fast.

"Got any place for him to sit out there?" I plate a sandwich, two salads, and the pasta of the day.

Tina swings by with baskets of hot rolls and a pitcher of ice water.

Maisie shakes her head. "All the tables are full. Inside and out."

I blow out a breath. "Bring him back. Have him pull my desk chair into the office doorway so he can see what goes on here in the kitchen. I'll interview him when I can."

I'm vaguely aware when Maisie leads a large young man with a baby face past me, but then I forget everything but the work. Two servers come in with new orders, and a third with more dirty dishes. We're running out of places to stack them.

"We're getting low on glasses." Tina sets down the emptied water pitcher and dashes over to the dishwashing area. Fills a rack with dirty glasses, sprays them off, and sends them into the dish machine. Then she fills another rack with glasses and a third with plates she's scraped into the trash at lightning speed. Sprays those down and sends them into the machine too. Donna plates three desserts and an hors d'oeuvre, and then spins around to catch the rack coming out of the clean side of the dish machine. She shakes off the excess water and transfers the clean, hot glasses to trays, carrying them to the drinks station.

Out of the corner of my eye, I see the boy—Sam—craning his neck to watch them. He sits tapping his foot, observing this ballet of people seamlessly shifting from task to task, from food prep to dining room to dish station and back, and then the next time I look over, he's scraping dishes himself, loading them onto trays, spraying them down, and sending them into the machine, seeming not a bit intimidated by its hiss and steam. Sends in three trays, then goes around to the other side to unload the clean ones coming out of the machine. He must have seen the silverware caddies and figured out how to do those himself, because the next thing he sends through is a rack of forks and knives and spoons. Donna meets my eye, her brows raised and mouth pursed. She's impressed.

Three hours later the dinner rush is finally over, and we've made a dent in catching up. Tina has gone home, and the closers have started their stocking and cleaning duties. Sam is soaked, head to toe. It's a wet, dirty job anyway, and we didn't think to give him an apron.

I lean back against the counter and look him over. He's tall and heavyset with round cheeks, pretty blue eyes, and hair that's well trimmed if not stylish. "Well, Sam, you've earned yourself dinner and a half day of pay today anyway, whether you take the job or not. If you want it, it's yours. You did well. Thanks."

Maisie comes in just in time to hear me, and she gives Sam that big, glowing smile I haven't seen since the day she was here with her mom.

Sam smiles at her and then at me. "I'll take it. Thanks."

I fix us both a sandwich and sit down with him to fill out the necessary paperwork while we eat. I give him the same spiel I gave Maisie when I hired her, about how we treat people, how to dress, and so forth. I don't think there will be a problem with Sam. Donna and the others will probably adopt him just like they did Maisie. Spoil him and tease him and train him right.

I chug my water and stretch as Sam completes the last form.

God, I'm so tired. Achy. I've been fighting a cold. And I've been here fourteen hours today so far. But it's been a satisfying day. A good day.

I'm pretty sure I didn't do anyone any harm today.

Now I just have to pack up the leftovers for Andi's shelter, leaving out enough for Devon and however many guys he brings tonight. Get them taken care of. Figure out what to make for Joe. Deliver that. Check on the closers to see whether they need help. And when that's all done, maybe I'll actually be able to sleep.

CHAPTER 11

Dear July,

I don't fucking know what to do. Please write me if you can think of a way to get me back there. Maybe your folks might have an idea? I hate to ask but I'm pretty desperate...

Joe

I'M BACK FROM MY RUN, fresh out of the damned tub when Angus comes in carrying his toolbox and something wrapped in aluminum foil. He's already finished demolition on the front room and kitchenette area, so there's no countertop. He tosses the foil packet to me.

I gesture at the empty space around us. "You work fast." Then I pry open the packet, and oh my god, cinnamon heaven wafts out.

"Rosie's homemade cinnamon rolls. She and Tina from July's have a friendly rivalry. Everybody wins." He settles his toolbox in a corner and opens it up.

The rolls are still warm, with just enough gooey icing sliding down between the layers. I pry off a big chunk, stuff it in my mouth, and have to close my eyes and steady myself against the wall. "Da-a-a-a-amn."

"Rosie thinks you don't eat enough." Angus circles the room, measuring with his tape and making chalk marks where new outlets will go. "Thinks you need fattening up."

"Why's she being so nice to me?" I say it lightly, but I have been wondering.

Angus doesn't look up. "Probably got a crush on you."

I choke on my second too-big bite. "Pardon?"

Now he looks up. Has himself a real good laugh.

Two can play this game. "She's awful cute. And nice. If she cooks like this all the time, I'm in."

He bares his teeth in a truly frightening grin. "In your dreams, Toothpick Boy."

I laugh around the rest of the roll.

Unfortunately, my dreams are full of someone a lot more confusing than Rose.

Angus finishes what he's doing and straightens. "Need to start demo'ing the bathroom today. You won't be able to take a bath for a few days. Rosie said you should come over for dinner tonight, stay in our guest room."

That's a hell of a kind offer. No way do they do that for all of Angus's clients. I don't know what's up, but I can't accept. "Tell her I really appreciate it but I can't. Got softball tonight. Usually go out with the team after." I look down at my bare feet. "I'm clean now. I can make do with a sink bath for a couple of days. But thanks."

"Okay. Lemme know if you change your mind. House is just four blocks from the square."

I put on shoes, but halfway down the stairs, I stop. "Hey, Angus!"

He pokes his head out of the bathroom. "Yeah?"

"You gonna break up that tub?" I'm envisioning sledgehammer action. Violence. Tub-maiming. *That* part of the demo I will gladly do myself.

He reads my mind and...there's that scary grin again. "Sorry. Porcelain over cast iron. But I got a buyer willing to pay enough to cover your new shower."

"Oh. Damn."

His laugh follows me down the stairs.

I finished patching the holes yesterday and bought painting supplies. Rose had suggested pale neutral colors down here. "Nothing trendy—just make it look bright and clean," she'd said. So I got a creamy color for the walls and white for the trim. I get started on it, surprised to find it's kind of therapeutic. Not swinging-a-sledgehammer-at-a-hated-bathroom-fixture therapeutic, but...

Halfway through the morning, a guy pulls up in a pickup truck and backs it right onto the sidewalk beside the dumpster Angus has been filling. I let him in and watch as he, Angus, and another guy slowly maneuver the tub out of the bathroom and down the stairs. I try to squeeze in on Angus's end to help out, but he shakes his head, his massive shoulders and arms bulging as he supports the same weight as the two other men put together. Dude's a Clydesdale.

They load it onto the back of the truck, I go back to painting, and damn, Rose was right. This big, empty downstairs room looks completely different now. I'm just starting on the little office room when Angus comes down.

"Looks good down here. I'm meeting Rosie for lunch. Wanna come?"

No way am I intruding on the newlyweds' lunch. "No thanks. But hey, I've been meaning to ask, you know anybody named Devon? He's got all this wild, white hair. Walks like he might've been military."

"Yeah, he's a vet. Good man. Why?"

I shrug. "Just wondered. What's his deal? I saw him with some other guys, all carrying bags."

Angus nods. Studies me with those aqua eyes of his. "There's a homeless encampment, couple miles from here on the creek. Devon's kind of unofficially in charge."

"No shit. Huh."

"He's got serious leadership skills. Just can't stand to be under a roof for very long."

I nod. I've known guys like that.

He turns toward the front door. "I'll be back in an hour. Sure you don't wanna come?"

"I'm sure. Tell Rose thanks for the cinnamon roll. Tell her I'm proposing next time I see her." I never say shit like that. Something in me just wants to poke at Angus. Gentle-like, so he doesn't kill me.

It feels good to want to smile.

One corner of his mouth quirks up. "Do and die, boy. Do and die." He waves and is gone.

He's got me thinking about food. I'm hungry again, and what I really want is July's Summer Chicken. The idea of going over there messes me up though.

My brain used to have a steady supply of images of my girl the way she was when we were young. Laughing in the sunshine.

Making her little brother and sister and me taste her latest experiment in their family kitchen. Racing out to the buoy in the middle of the lake, water droplets flashing like magic off her fingertips. Coming into my arms in my old truck, her eyes bright with mischief and what I'd believed was love, her skin smooth and warm, her lips soft on my neck. On my mouth.

But the old images are overlaid now with flashes of her on that love seat, her expression determined and unfamiliar. Detached. And pictures of her with Devon's bunch, after hours in the restaurant, serving them free food and a smile and warm socks. Swaying with that mop in the dining room after everybody'd gone. Glimpses of her outside my door in the dark, hanging another bag on the knob for me, waving before she darts away again.

Which one of those women is the real July? How could those pieces add up to one person?

For the life of me, I can't figure out what those nighttime food deliveries are about. I mean, clearly she doesn't want to have to actually talk to me or spend time with me... But if she wants to exorcise me from her life, that's a weird way of doing it.

If I'm going to be eating her food every day, I ought to at least be paying for some of it. Her sidewalk dining area is open now. I can eat there, at a little table up against the wall, out of view of anyone in the restaurant. That shouldn't bother her or distract her.

Maybe I'll do that tomorrow.

Softball's another matter. We've got practice tonight, so that means another two hours of standing behind her in the field, trying to focus on anything else but her. Her grace. Her body. The way she laughs and teases everybody, making sure to include them all. Except me—she's quiet and careful with me. So I stand in left field trying to pretend I'm there for the love of the game. Trying to pretend she's just another player, just another person with no control over my body or my heart. Trying to pretend I am not confused every second of every day and night about every goddamn thing in my life.

July

The noise is unfamiliar and annoying, and it will. Not. Stop. I pry open my eyes and squint at the ceiling of my bedroom. Gray light seeps in around the edges of the window shade.

Shit, the alarm! When was the last time I actually slept until the alarm went off? I stretch for my phone on the nightstand. Everything hurts.

Last night's practice was the worst I have ever played in my life. I'm mortified, remembering.

Tom had arranged a scrimmage game with another team, which is normally all the fun of league play without any of the pressure. But last night I could not do anything right. I couldn't cover my normal amount of ground at third. Joe had to field my misses again and again and again. I went for a line drive and somehow—I don't know how—fell flat on my face. I couldn't bat worth a damn—flied out to left center twice, and for the one grounder I hit, I couldn't beat the throw to first. When I finally got there, I was wheezing and coughing and bent over, almost puking right there on the basepath.

Andi brought me some water, and both teams yelled at me to sit down. I spent the rest of the scrimmage on my ass in the grass, watching Joe play my position. Beautifully, of course.

I went with them to Lindon's afterward but only stayed for a few minutes. I couldn't drink because I'd taken cold medicine, and the night just seemed weird anyway. All evening I felt Joe's eyes on me, but I could never read his expression.

The old Joe was an open book to me. I could glance at him and see *I love you, I think you're wonderful, I'm so glad you're with me, I want to kiss you,* and a million other things on his face.

I miss that Joe.

But the team loves new Joe just fine. He has no problem teasing and laughing with them. It's just me that brings out the unfamiliar quiet gravity in him. So really, I was doing him a favor, leaving early to give him more time to have fun with them.

Lying here past the alarm now does no one any good. I drag myself up—maybe I shouldn't have had that other dose of medicine last night—and could swear I hear my bones creaking. I always take a shower at night before bed, but this morning I'm so woozy I need another.

I give myself two minutes under the spray: one minute of hot water to pound away my aches, and another of cold water to wake me up. Then I dry off, twist my hair up into a ponytail, and get dressed.

Downstairs, Donna has beaten me to work for once. "Hey, sleepyhead."

Tina's been baking for an hour or more already. "Whoa!" She pauses on her way past me to the walk-in. "July, you're not looking too good."

"Ha. You should have seen me on the ball field last night." I pour myself a mug of the strong coffee Donna just made, blow on it enough that it won't boil my insides, and suck in a long swallow.

There's a knock at the back door. I let in the produce guy and check that order. Then the dairy delivery arrives, and I check that, put everything away...and I am already dead on my feet. I refill my coffee and try to remember what's next.

"Rose called." Tina slides another pan of cinnamon rolls into the oven. "Said she's running late but she should be here in a few minutes."

That's what I'm supposed to be doing. Rose is hosting some kind of brainstorming session with the mayor and several Galway nonprofits this morning, and I'd promised to provide a continental breakfast for them. "You bake extra for her?"

Tina gives me that grin/scowl she does so well. "Of course." She nods toward a big box on the counter near the door.

"I've got the fruit." Donna is cutting pineapple and adding it to a big platter with strawberries, blueberries, and sliced kiwi. "Just need to make the meat and cheese tray."

I ought to be able to handle that, even in my pitiful condition. I swing around toward the walk-in and the room spins. There's a loud *whack!* and then I'm staring up at Tina's horrified face.

"I have become the least competent person in the world." My words sound faint, even to me. Can't play ball, can't remember my own job, and now, apparently, can't turn around without falling down.

"Oh my god, July! Donna, we need ice in a towel." Tina drops to her knees beside me.

Somehow I'm on the floor between the counter and my prep island, my back pressing uncomfortably against a cabinet door handle. Then Donna's there with the ice. She holds it gently, so gently, to my hairline, and still it hurts like hell.

"Ow, ow! Let me do that. It's dripping in my eye."

"Hon, it's not the ice that's dripping," Tina says, and Donna adds, "Put some pressure on it, July. Scalp wounds bleed bad."

"All right. Just let me sit here a minute. Can y'all finish up Rose's order?" My head is throbbing, and now I see the blood dripping off my wrist. "Shit, I'm making a mess."

They yell at me when I move to get up, so I keep my ass right here on the cold floor and try to think what to do. Probably call somebody in. I'm not going to be able to cook while I'm a biohazard. If I could just think straight for a minute…

"Oh my god, what the fuck happened?" Rose has arrived, along with the language she's always trying to stop using. She rushes over to me, and I ward her off with my nonbloody hand.

"It's okay. I'm just going to sit here for a minute until it stops bleeding. Tina and Donna have your order almost ready."

"Screw my order! You need to go to the ER!" Despite my efforts, Rose has taken the ice bag from me and is peering at my scalp. "This isn't slowing down. You need stitches at least."

"It'll be fine, Rose. You've got your mayor thing. Tina'll help me in a minute. I've got some butterfly bandages somewhere in my office."

"Nah, July, she's right." Now Donna's looming over me, staring too. She glances at Rose. "I called her sister. She's on the way."

What? When did she do that? Is time passing without me noticing?

"Probably should call somebody in for me, Donna, till I get this cleaned up."

"Already did. Got you covered today. Don't come back."

Shit. I *am* missing stuff. "Bossy." I scowl up at Donna, but it makes my head hurt more so I stop.

"Don't move your face!"

"You're making it bleed worse!"

If you think having sinus pressure and splitting open your head is bad, you should try it while sitting on the floor with a bunch of people looming over and yelling at you. My head is pounding, and the lights are too bright. I close my eyes, but that makes the room spin, so I shade them with my clean hand.

"Oh my god, July!" This last voice belongs to my sister, Jen.

Guess I'm going to the emergency room.

It'll probably seem like an oasis of peace and quiet compared to this place.

CHAPTER 12

Dear July,

I think of you every minute. I miss you so bad. I'm sorry I'm not there. I hope you're okay.

Joe

SINK BATHS ARE ONLY MARGINALLY more annoying than clawfoot tub baths.

Angus and I grunt at each other in passing as I hang my towel on the bedroom doorknob to dry and head out to July's. Going to try the hiding-in-a-patio-corner idea for breakfast and see how that feels.

But when I get there, Rose is coming out the front door with two big paper bags and blood on her hands, looking more upset than I have ever seen her.

"Whoa, Rose, you okay?" I touch her arm.

She says, so low that I have to bend to hear her, "July's on her way to the ER. She fell and whacked her head in the kitchen."

"Shit, is she okay?" I'm mentally reviewing the town map

in my head, trying to remember the quickest way to the hospital from here.

"I think so. She was talking okay. Just probably needs some stitches. I hope they screen her for concussion too, while she's there." Her voice trails off and then comes back stronger. "But that leaves the kitchen way understaffed, and they've been slammed lately with the patio open. I'm trying to figure out how to end my meetings early so I can come back to help out."

Shit, what was I thinking, that anybody would want me to go hold July's hand in the hospital? I'm the last person she'd pick. Still, if I'm here, might as well make myself useful. "I could help in the kitchen. It's what I used to do."

Rose's brown eyes widen. Maybe even tear up. "That would be perfect, Joe! Go on through to the back and ask for Donna. Tell her I sent you because of your experience."

I go in through the front door. Breakfast rush is underway, not an empty table in sight, a steady flow of people picking up carryout orders. The servers are moving quickly. They're so professional that if I didn't know something was wrong, I wouldn't guess.

Back in the kitchen, one tall woman is cranking out orders from the overloaded order board. Her hands are blurs, she's so fast, but her air is calm. "Who are you?" She barely glances up at me when she says it.

"Donna? Hi. I'm Joe. Rose sent me to help out."

She pauses long enough to look me up and down. "Food-taster Joe?"

"Yup."

She points me to the aprons and sets me to work.

Within five minutes, we've got a system. I make omelets,

crepes, bacon, all the basics, and she does sauces and sides, and plates everything, giving it the July's touch before sending orders out to the dining room.

I haven't cooked in weeks, but it feels natural. Feels good. Donna reads my mind, or I read hers, and on her other side, a flirty, little woman named Tina I remember from my first day here is doing magical things with baked goods. At one point I catch us all swaying together to a great cover of Stevie Ray Vaughan's "Mary Had a Little Lamb" piping through speakers to the dining room.

I'm not even embarrassed when Donna catches my eye and smirks. "Who is this? They're great."

"Local band. Blue Shoes. Friends of July's."

Of course they are.

This has *got* to be the most popular place in town. The breakfast rush barely tapers off before we're into a booming lunch service. "You going home?" Donna asks Tina a little after eleven, and Tina says, "Rose said she's coming back to help. I'll stay till then."

I've pieced together that Tina and Donna are partners who share a big place with some of the other servers and their kids. Somehow, despite working and living together, everyone still manages to get along.

Rose comes in, and when the lunch rush finally slows, Donna and I take staggered breaks.

"Servers are impressed with you." Rose has taken over July-ifying my orders while Donna's on break. "They didn't think anybody'd be able to keep up July's load. They were coming up with contingency plans to fix whatever you might fuck up."

I snort, but I feel proud. Happy for the first time since the attempted sexorcism. Useful. Appreciated.

Donna comes back just in time to hear her. "You know you can't use that language when Maisie and Sam get here, Rose."

Rose's turn to snort. "Donna, I *learned* that language from high schoolers." She sighs. "But you're right. I should rein it in. I think seeing July on the floor bleeding freaked me out."

"You and me both." Donna drops her dishes in the cleanup area and comes to take over for me, waving me on break. "Get yourself something to drink and tell me what you want me to send out to you."

"Summer Chicken, please." I down a glass of ice water and then fill it with tea before heading out to the booth the staff uses for breaks. What the hell is taking so long at the ER? My head is full of terrible images of July hurt now.

She seems so invincible. Indestructible. It's pretty clear I'm not the only one who thinks so.

Last night's softball weirdness makes more sense now. Her coughing fit was the only clue that anything was wrong. I thought she was just having a bad night. Everybody does now and then. She didn't make a lot of errors; she just didn't cover her usual amount of ground. And her throws to first didn't have their usual zing. And when she fell going for that one line drive...I didn't know what the hell that was about. But she kept hustling, kept trying, and when she couldn't beat out the throw to first and she doubled over coughing, it was all I could do not to go to her. Wrap my arms around her. Rock her a little, feed her Andi's water myself.

Which is a fucking ridiculous thing for me to have wanted.

Sonya brings out my Summer Chicken, and I inhale it and go back to work. The afternoon is just as busy as the morning. I'm already tired by three when July's sister, Jen, comes into the kitchen.

Everybody stops what they're doing to hear her report.

"She's okay. They cleaned up her head, gave her those liquid stitches. X-rayed her, screened her for concussion. She checked out okay on those but when they heard her cough, they x-rayed her lungs, thinking she might have pneumonia. She doesn't—just bronchitis and a double ear infection. They said the ear infection's probably what made her fall. I got her settled upstairs. Made her promise to go straight to bed and not try to do anything else today. She's got a couple of prescriptions she's not supposed to take on an empty stomach. I told her I'd take up some food."

"I'll do it." The words are out of my mouth before I know I'm speaking.

Donna, Tina, and Rose exchange a look I can't read. Before I can ask, Jen says, "Joe! You're here!" and throws herself at me.

I haven't seen her since she was twelve. Now she's, what, thirty-two and hugely pregnant, but I'd know her laugh and her sweet face anywhere.

It feels damn good to be hugged.

"If you don't mind taking it up for me, that would be great. I've got some work to catch up on. Tell July I'll check on her later and to text me if she needs anything." She looks me up and down and hugs me again. "I want you to come over for dinner soon. You haven't met my husband."

"I'd like that." It's true. For a month of my life when I was sixteen, I'd felt like I had a little brother and sister too, by sharing July's. I missed Jen and Brendan. Got a lot of catching up to do.

She leaves and I turn to fix something for July, but Donna's beaten me to it. She hands me a tray with chicken soup, a steaming mug with a tea bag in it, a dish of fresh fruit, and one of Tina's crusty sourdough rolls. "Make sure she's really okay alone up there."

"Yes, ma'am."

"And tell her not to show her face down here tomorrow either. Woman needs rest."

I nod obediently.

I've never been up in July's private apartment. Donna unlocks the door to the stairwell, and I start up into the fresh-air-and-clean-laundry-smelling space, balancing the tray, equal parts trepidation and...excitement?

I'm a dumbass. She's not going to be happy to see me. I'm a dumbass.

July

I knew the ER visit would take forever. Jen and I don't normally get to spend big chunks of time together, so I hate that I'm too out of it to be good company. Of course, when I mumble something about it, she says, "You're right, July. It's real bitchy of you to pay more attention to your head wound than to me. Selfish." Girl always was a smart-ass.

When they're finished with me, Jen drives me home. She helps me shower without getting the surgical adhesive wet. "Finally I've found advantages to not having your height or your blond hair!" she mutters, dabbing at my head with a clean washcloth.

"Yeah? What's that?" I close my eyes, let the tile wall hold me up.

"Won't land as hard, 'cause I don't have so far to fall. And brown hair hides blood better."

Before she heads downstairs to get me something to eat, she tosses me a nightgown Mom and Dad sent from Florida on my birthday. I lean against the wall to put it on, but it's got some kind of itchy lace around the neck, so I yank it back off. I'll put on a tank top or something. I go to step into the bright orange bikini panties she's gotten out for me, but of course I lose my balance again. They warned me at the hospital not to make sudden moves. I catch one foot in the elastic, almost go down, stagger several feet into the bedroom trying to regain my balance, and fall face down onto the bed. *Ow, ow, ow.*

The stairwell door opens, and I hear careful footsteps coming up.

"Jen, I need help with one more thing, please." My voice is muffled by the quilt.

The footsteps speed up. She'll mock me, and then she'll milk this story for all it's worth at our next family gathering. I don't care. I just want to crawl under these covers for a few minutes.

"What do you need? You okay?"

Well, *that's* an unexpected voice from the doorway. Then dead silence.

Isn't this just peachy? "I'd be okayer if you were Jen." I can feel a blush creeping over my entire body, including my giant naked ass. Or maybe it's just fever.

I hear his footsteps retreat fast, and then from the hall, Joe says, "July, I don't know what, uh, to do right now."

Shit. Does he think I somehow lured him up here for the excellent view of my butt? He's seen it before. And I didn't ask him to come up. "Do about what exactly?" Apparently, exhaustion makes me testy.

"No, I mean, I want to help, but I didn't expect... I mean, what would you prefer I do at this moment?" He sounds flustered, which would be kind of cute if this weren't such a mortifying situation. I haven't seen him flustered since the first time he saw my boobs, when we were sixteen.

"I would like for you to go back downstairs and for us both to forget this ever happened."

"But you need help with something." He sounds worse off than I do, for god's sake.

I groan and push myself upright. Too fast, of course. The room spins and I flop back down, coughing so hard I shake the bed frame. When I can breathe again, I scrabble at the quilt and manage to drag part of it to cover my rear end. "All right, you can come in without me mooning you."

He comes back and steps past me to set a tray on my nightstand. "Okay. How can I help?"

"Well, if you were *Jen*, like I *expected*, I would have you grab a tank top from that drawer over there and help me sit up to put on my underwear." I wave the orange bikinis I'm still clutching. "But you're probably not comfortable with that. Where *is* Jen?"

"She had some work to catch up on." He crosses behind me again to my dresser, pulls open the underwear drawer and shuts it fast, then opens the second drawer and takes out a pale blue tank. "Okay, stretch your arms above your head."

When I do, he slides the tank past my hands and down my arms and very gently over my aching head. He fetches my robe from the back of my door and slides my arms into it too. "Now I'm gonna slip my arm underneath you and help you sit up, okay? I won't look. I'll just hold you steady so you can belt your robe. Then when you're ready, I'll keep you from falling while you put on your underwear. Real slow, okay? Don't do anything fast."

"Yes, doctor."

The mattress dips at my waist, and I feel his hand slide under me, then his forearm, then the curve of his inner elbow. "When you're ready, push up, okay? I'll help." His skin is warm and he smells...like my restaurant.

"Joe, why do you smell like the restaurant?"

"I...uh, came in to eat, and Rose told me you were hurt. I offered to bring the tray up. Donna fixed it for you."

I tense against his arm. "Oh, no, I need to talk to Donna!"

"No, you don't. She said to tell you not to show your face down there today or tomorrow. She's already got you covered."

I want to argue, but instead I have another coughing fit. Joe rests his other hand between my shoulder blades and rubs little circles there, through my robe. It almost distracts me, but not quite.

I opened the restaurant eight years ago, and I've never taken a full sick day, much less two in a row. I've also never felt this physically bad. And I've sure never had such balance problems. "Guess they don't want me staggering around with a sharp knife."

"Makes sense." There's a hint of a smile in his voice. "C'mon, let's get you up. Ready? One...two...three...careful now." He hauls me up and turns so that I'm sitting with my back pressed against his side, almost on his lap, his arms tight around my waist.

I can't see him, but it's oddly intimate. The heat of his body warms me. His breath in my hair tickles my neck. His roughened hands help me tug the tank down to cover my chest and ribs. There's a hitch in his breathing, just for a second.

"Can you...do what you need to do?" His quiet voice in my ear sends me back to another time and place.

Oh. He means, *Can I put on my underwear?*

I hold it in front of me and press back against him as I raise one foot to the first leg hole. The room sways but Joe's got me.

Very slowly I repeat the process with the other foot. His biceps bunch against my sides. His hold doesn't waver.

I drag the panties up to where they meet the bed. "I need to stand up for just a second."

He stands with me, bracing me from behind, and I ease the undies the rest of the way up.

I'm giddy with accomplishment. Or with his nearness. One of the two. "Hallelujah! I never thought underwear would be such an ordeal!"

"Neither did I." His voice is rough as he lets go with one arm and leans past me to pull the covers down. "In." He holds my forearm as I maneuver myself onto the bed and between the sheets, my back against the headboard, which feels almost as solid as Joe did.

"Thanks." My earlier irritation seems petty and ungrateful. This is really, really nice of him.

"Glad to help. We're not done yet. Here, take a big drink of hot tea. You've got to get some of this food in you before you take your meds, Jen said." He's all business now, settling into my bedside chair, reaching for the pill bottles on the nightstand, reading the directions aloud to me as I break off a piece of sourdough and dunk it in the soup. I'm not really hungry, but I do remember the doctor saying that.

Besides, I need to get my strength back, not starve it out of me again. And the warm liquids are probably good for my chest. "I'm going to drink my soup, Joe. Don't look."

There's definitely a little smile lurking around his lips now. He doesn't look at me as I take the bowl in both hands and drink several swallows. After I've eaten some more of the roll and a few bites of fruit, he hands me my medicine doses, one by one.

"Nobody's babied me like this since my mom."

His eyes meet mine and I'm dizzy all over again. Some of the light is back in him. His irises seem to change color as I watch. And then he looks away. "Okay, got your phone? Set a timer. Four hours for this med and six for the other. Somebody will come check on you later."

He goes into my little kitchen and comes back with my water bottle. Sets it on the nightstand beside the fruit and the rest of the roll. Then he watches until I've gotten in sleeping position. "Call me if you need anything, okay? I'll be around." His voice is rough again.

"Thanks, Joe." I close my eyes. I can't remember him leaving.

CHAPTER 13

Dear July,

I tried to get a job so I can save for a ticket back, but no one will hire me because I don't speak the language and don't have the right paperwork...

Joe

I LEAN ON THE WALL outside the restaurant kitchen just to breathe and get hold of myself. This is nuts. She'd obviously wished I were Jen or...anyone but me. I'm not sure I even like her anymore. So why does it kill me to see her helpless? To feel how shaky she was when I supported her?

There's zero mystery about why the sight and feel of her naked on the bed would affect me. Anybody with a pulse and an attraction to women would react that way to her curvy backside. To seeing the tanned public parts of her framing soft, pale private parts.

Her vulnerability now wipes away some of the sting of the sexorcism night. Maybe that cold, determined stranger *wasn't* the real modern-day July.

When I finally push through the swinging door to the kitchen, there are two teenagers there: a big-eyed girl and a much larger boy who seems familiar.

"Maisie, Sam, this is Joe." Donna points at me from the oven area. "He's filling in for July today."

"How is she?" The girl's face is anxious.

"Okay, I think. Dizzy. But she ate about half the soup and some of the other stuff. Got her meds down. She's going to sleep now." I drop the tray off at the dishwashing station, where the boy—Sam—is tying on an apron.

Then it hits me. Where I've seen him. Sam is a neater, cleaner, shorter-haired version of the young man I startled at the lake. The sleeping bag boy.

I keep an eye on him as Donna and I fill orders and restock for the dinner rush. He's good at his job, steady and efficient, and within an hour, he's caught up on the mess from lunch and is helping the servers clean tables. He looks healthy and strong. I guess whatever problem had him sleeping on a picnic table has been resolved.

By five o'clock we're slammed again.

Donna and I shift back into high gear, cranking out orders for the evening servers to deliver. Tina comes in to make dough and then checks to make sure we're okay before she leaves again. She lays her hand on Donna's arm. "How late you plan on staying, babe?"

Donna glances at me. "Till closing, I guess."

I look back and forth between them. Should have occurred to me before that she would not normally work a shift this long. "When would you usually leave?"

She looks down at the order she's plating. "Three thirty or four. Usually July and Maria do dinner, but Maria's out of town at a funeral."

Takes me a minute to process this. "Wait, so July usually works straight through all the shifts?"

"Right?" Tina's nod is emphatic. "She works way too much! Donna and I tell her that all the time."

"I mean, she leaves sometimes, for a run or a board meeting or softball." Donna's loyalties are obviously torn. She shakes her head. "But she probably averages twelve to sixteen hours a day."

"Why the hell doesn't she hire somebody else?" My voice cracks with outrage.

"She loves it." Donna's voice is matter-of-fact. "It's her baby."

Beside her, Tina snorts. "She needs somebody real to love." She darts a glance at me after Donna shoots her a look I interpret as warning. "But you didn't hear it from me." She stands on her tiptoes to kiss Donna's cheek and then leaves.

Donna sighs, and from behind us the two kids chorus, "Woman's gonna be the death of me."

She points a sauce spoon at them. "You two are on thin ice." They just laugh and go to work.

"Donna, if you'll stick around with me till the dinner rush starts to slow, I can take it after that. I got nowhere to be tonight." I study the order board, toss two sirloins on the grill, and set some onions to caramelizing. Make sure we've got enough baked potatoes. "Oh, and I told July you already had her covered for tomorrow. I can do it." I mean, what else am I going to do? This place is a damn sight better than breathing paint fumes in my construction zone of a building.

She nods slowly, sending two more orders out to the dining room and one to the patio. "Might take you up on that." She checks on the vegetables she's roasting. "Couple things you ought to know. I can do 'em if you don't want to. At eight when we lock the doors, we package up the day's leftovers for the women's shelter."

"The place Andi works?"

"That's the one. But we make sure we keep enough for—"

It hits me and I say, "Devon," just as she's saying, "Some guys who stop by just after eight."

She frowns and tilts her head. "How do you know Devon?"

"I've just…heard about him." I wipe down my counter. Jesus, how many people does July take care of in this town? "I can do it. Just get me through the rush. Tell me everything you think I need to know."

She stays till 7:30, instructing me on all the touches July's puts on each dish on the menu, and then she pulls out her buzzing phone, looks at it, and shakes her head. "Asking me if *we're* okay. *She's* the one with the head wound and the bronchitis and the double ear infection." She says her response out loud as she types it: We're fine. You rest. "What time's her next dose of medicine due? I'll take her something up before I leave."

"She probably just took a dose of one of them. I left her some fruit and bread up there before. Other med's not due till around nine. I can take her something after I take care of Devon's guys." Don't know why I keep offering. I'm sure July would rather see Donna. But Donna's got family to get home to, and I…want to check on July again. So sue me.

Donna studies me in silence for a long minute and then says, "Okay. I'm trusting you, Joe. I like you. But if you so much as make her frown, I will hunt you down and take you apart like a chicken carcass."

I feel my eyebrows shoot up to my hairline. "Okay then." I believe her. And I have seen the woman's knife work. "I respect your loyalty. And I would never willingly hurt her."

She nods, gives me one last look as she takes off her apron, and heads to the door. "The closers will be fine. Make sure Maisie and Sam leave at eight. It's a school night."

"Yes, ma'am."

Things go pretty smoothly after that. When the closers tell me they've locked the door, I finish up the pending orders and pack up most of what's left for Andi. I'm waiting when Devon arrives with his group.

I open the door. "Devon. Guys."

Devon stands looking at me from the sidewalk, not saying a word.

"I'm Joe. Filling in for July. She's sick. Fell and whacked her head. Got some stitches."

His eyes sharpen on me. "She okay?"

I nod. "Just supposed to take it easy for a few days."

He studies me another long minute and then leads his guys in. I do everything I saw July do the night I watched from outside, including offering socks and tooth care stuff from a big bag I found in the office. They don't talk much. Devon watches me like a hawk the whole time.

After they leave, I relock the door and turn everything over to the closers. Whip up a spinach and goat cheese omelet. Toast with butter and honey. Then I load a tray with the food, a mug of hot tea, and another one of Tina's rolls. When the closers assure me they've got everything under control, I use the key Donna left me and let myself into July's space.

Her phone alarm is chiming as I go up the stairs, but she's just beginning to stir as I set the tray on the night table and swipe the alarm off. "Joe. You're back."

I can't read her tone, but it's definitely not thrilled.

"Yep. Brought breakfast for supper."

She told me once, all those years ago, that her mom used to serve breakfast for supper whenever she or the other kids were sick. Now a slow, sleepy smile spreads over her poor bruised face, and something inside me breaks loose.

"Mm. Yummy." She levers herself up slowly, cautiously, until she's leaning against the headboard. She takes the plate from me, and I have to close my eyes at her expression when she tastes the omelet. "Oh my god, Joe. This is heavenly."

I turn my attention to safer things, rereading the medicine instructions and preparing her next dose. Refilling her water bottle. Writing out the dosage times for each medication and checking off the ones she's already taken.

She cleans her plate, watching me without speaking until she takes her med with the last bite of toast. Then she licks a drip of honey off her thumb—I manage not to groan, just barely—and picks up the mug of tea. "Why you doing this, Joe? Why you up here? Everybody else scared to come up?"

"No, course not." Why would anybody be scared of her? She takes care of the whole damn town. Her other questions, though, I don't really know how to answer. I study my hands. "I got more free time than pretty much everybody in the world right now. Less on my plate. Seemed like the thing to do."

She starts to frown and winces; the movement must pull at her stitches. She straightens and moves slowly, carefully, to the edge of the bed. Swings her legs around, swaying slightly, until her feet touch the floor. She waves me off when I reach to steady her.

"I'm fine. I'll just go slow. I've gotta brush my teeth or I'll dream they're rotting out of my head."

I watch her move gingerly to the bathroom doorway, and then I load the tray with dirty dishes and carry it to her kitchen. I haven't really looked around before. There aren't any lights on in the main room, but the streetlights on the square illuminate it some. Her little kitchen area is white and gleaming. The living area has a simple round table and chairs and a seating arrangement in front of tall windows. The layout is similar to my own upstairs, but it's already nice. Simple. Comfortable. Clean.

I hear water shut off and July making her way back to the bed. "Thanks, Joe. I'm gonna sleep some more now. I can't believe how tired I still am."

"You're coughing less already. That's good." I can't make myself head for the stairs. But I can't expect her to stay awake to talk to me.

And she doesn't; she's already under the covers when I peek in, her eyes closed and her bedside light out.

I go get the tray to leave but...she never reset her alarm for the next medicine dose. Shit. I stand in her darkened living room, trying to decide what to do.

Her long couch looks comfier than my air mattress. I could set my phone alarm for her next dose. Watch TV real quietly for a little while. The alarm will wake me up if I doze off.

The sofa welcomes me. I find some kind of animal documentary and turn the sound down low, dozing off and on.

My alarm goes off and the next dose goes fine. Sometime after that I wake up to find July standing over me, quilt wrapped around her. "I thought I dreamed you," she says, her voice groggy. Before I can formulate a response, she settles herself beside me on the couch, her head on my shoulder, her arm and thigh pressed to mine, and tosses one corner of the quilt over me too. Another minute and her breathing slows in sleep.

And I stare at the flickering TV, thinking about how many nights I've lain awake wishing she were beside me. Thinking this is a really fucked-up way for that to finally come true. And I'm a really fucked-up guy to enjoy it.

July

Joe and I are at the lake, sprawled on our rock, watching the last traces of sunset fade from the sky. We just finished a long shift at the steakhouse, and we still smell like the restaurant kitchen, but I don't even care. The bugs will descend on us soon, but I don't care about that either. I've been starving for this, for the quiet space that forms around us when we're alone together.

I feel like I've been waiting for it forever.

He lets go of my hand and rolls toward me, wrapping his arms around me. I hold him, listening to his heartbeat, feeling his slow, even breathing and the warmth of him all up and down my body. He traces little patterns on my back with his fingertips. Hearts, I think. Brushes his lips over my ear. Settles my head against him better.

This is exactly what I always thought love would be like. Being with Your Person, not having to talk all the time, just happy to be in their presence. Happy they want to be in yours.

"What you thinking about?" His voice has that raw edge that usually means he's about to kiss me.

"Artichokes," I lie.

"Yeah." He nods. Sighs. "Me too."

We last five seconds before our laughter bursts out, overcoming us. I have to sit up and wipe my eyes.

"I love when you're goofy," I whisper when he pulls me close again.

"Yeah?" He rests his nose on my forehead. "I love you all the time."

I tilt my head back to find the warm glow of his gaze. His eyes are the only color in the graying twilight. Green, gold, and brown. "Me too."

He doesn't smile as he tilts his head toward me. His face is solemn as he skates his lips softly, so softly down my nose. Across one cheekbone, then the other, his movements slow and almost completely silent. He's memorizing me with his mouth, his tenderness undoing me.

My eyes slide closed as he cradles my head in his hands and kisses my jaw. My other senses compensate. I'm aware of every rustle of our clothing, every rasp of skin on skin. The smooth, still-warm surface of the boulder beneath us. The clean taste of his mouth when he finally finds mine. The slide of his tongue. The curve of his faint smile, the soft sigh he gives when I kiss him back.

There's nothing extra about my Joe. He has exactly what he needs: bone, sinew, teeth, a little bit of muscle, and just enough skin to stretch over it all. How a body so spare, so whittled, can feel so good, so safe to me, I don't know. Under my hands, he is a lean, solid support I curl around, his biceps bunched and taut, his hair soft and baby fine in my fingers, his words blurred and warm against my skin.

He dips his head to my throat, kissing the hollow there, and I feel his hand at the sliver of bare skin above the waistband of my jeans. I want more of him, more of his touches, more of his sweet, hungry kisses, more of his skin on mine. I reach up and open buttons. One of mine, one of his, one of mine, one of his. I wrap my arms around his neck and arch into him, murmuring his name into his hair.

He bends me back over his arm, his mouth following the open neck of my shirt down between my breasts, his tongue tracing along the edge of my bra, over the swell of my skin. I press into him, and he drags his hands up over my ribs, stopping just short of cupping me. "July, is this okay?" His whisper echoes my heartbeats.

Yes. "Yes!" *There. Now!*

His hands cover me, half inside my shirt, half out, and we both go still.

I know he must feel my nipples pebbling under his palms. I can feel every tiny movement, every bit of friction, even through my clothing. I want the fabric gone. I want nothing between me and his touch, his mouth, his warmth, his breath on my skin. I slide one hand free from his hair and undo the front clasp of my bra.

It opens under his hands, and he freezes for a moment...and then his fingertips move on me, so softly I can barely feel it, but I do feel it, because I can feel everything. The brief whisper of breeze from the lake. The heat of his gaze. The calluses on his hands. My own spine arcing into his.

Impossibly slowly, he brushes aside the fabric and bares my breasts to his eyes. "July," he breathes a long sigh, raising his gaze to meet mine. "So pretty." He touches me again, flattening his palms against my nipples, moving just a little, and it feels so good I cry out. His eyes fly to mine. "Okay?"

I nod and touch his face. Trail my fingers down his cheek.

He presses with his palms again. Cups his hands around me and squeezes lightly. Scrapes his thumbs across my nipples, and when I cry out again, he leans forward and licks me. Drags his tongue over my nipple and sucks it into his mouth.

The pleasure overwhelms me. I clutch him to me, writhing, wanting to fuse with him. Wanting him to keep doing what he's doing forever, and I moan...loud enough to wake myself up.

I am in my living room on my couch in the dark, as I have been so many times before. But this time I am not alone.

Joe is...oh my lord, he is doing wonderful things to me. I don't know what made him change his mind about wanting me, or why he'd pick the middle of the night to act on it—surely he must have thought I was awake. Joe would never make a move on a sick, sleeping woman—but it feels too good to stop.

Through his jeans, his cock is a hard ridge against my belly. I ease my hands up under his soft T-shirt. Slide one down into his loose waistband to close around him. Squeeze and stroke and...

His soft groan and curse as he palms my ass and thrusts against me is the sexiest sound I've ever heard. His fingers slip between my legs, slicking over me as he thrusts again, and I am frantic to get rid of the barriers between us.

Unbutton, unzip, push aside soft layers, wrap one leg around his waist...and with his next thrust he is inside me, hard and thick and just as perfect as any of my dreams. He's riding me like he's wanted this every bit as much as I have, and that idea, the heady feeling of that, combines with every perfect thrust to fill me to giddiness.

"Joe!" It's a moan each time I rise to meet him. A heartfelt, superstitious chant, because I don't want this spell to be broken.

And then he jerks awake, wide-eyed, his gaze ricocheting around the room as if he doesn't know where he is.

Oh no. No, no, no. Again, he wasn't wanting this. Me.

He looks down at my breasts, at my nipples wet from his mouth, at his cock buried deep inside me. At my eyes, that have to be echoing the "Joe, please…" that falls from my lips, because he closes his own. Makes a sound like a whimper, or the prayer of a damned man.

I see him swallow, see his jaw clench, and then he's moving again, slowly at first, his thrusts punctuated by breaths I can feel under my hands and against my face. Filling…and taking away. Filling…and taking away.

"July," he whispers, his biceps bunching, his hands clutching the cushions on both sides of me. He lowers his face to my neck and breathes in and thrusts deeper. "July."

In the weak, gray early morning light, the rest of the world seems silenced, shrunk down to us on this couch in this living room. To our perfect fit and friction, and our heat that must surely tint the air around us with fire colors. To our bodies rising and falling, the sounds of flesh and cloth and heartbeats and our raspy, desperate breathing.

In my arms is a man I've wanted all these years but only got to have like this once, clumsily. A stranger I don't know but who knows what my body needs so much better than any other man I've been with.

I tighten my grip on his lean waist and move with him, answering, "Joe!" because I'm right there at the edge and I need it to be him I'm holding as I topple this time…

…and I don't topple so much as burst, tiny sparks cascading at the edges of my vision, every single bit of me clutching and releasing and clutching at him again, and at my cry his eyes open, wild, and he moves fast and hard in me, one hand stealing to my ass as he pumps and pumps and then stiffens, pressing so deep I feel every part of him as his head tips back and he lets out a choked cry and pulses inside me.

I wait for his warm, welcome weight to settle on me. For his arms to come around me. I wait for his words, blurry and warm with praise or love or mischief in my ear...I wait for any one of a dozen lovely Joe things.

But he raises himself up off me, sliding out of me, seeming to not want to touch me any more than he absolutely has to.

Having him withdraw his physical self from me is chilling.

Having him stand over me to tuck himself away and fasten his jeans—and seeing horror touch his shadowed face as he realizes we didn't use a condom—freezes me from the inside out. "Ohhh fuck." His whisper isn't sharp, isn't angry, but at the utter despair in it, fissures and fractures spread through me. "What the *fuck* is wrong with me?"

I imagine myself crumbling to dust. A giant pile of dust. Enough dust to swirl and seep through the floorboards and contaminate everything in the restaurant below us. Maybe the whole world.

I'm a big woman. I know a lot of guys don't like that. But I've never had anybody who's seen me naked—who's been inside me—actually be repulsed by me.

The part of my heart that had felt so alive, so giddy a minute ago shrivels. Maybe I should offer him a bleach wipe, to kill off my big-girl cooties. Offer to boil some water so he can take a sterile bath.

I push myself upright very carefully, tugging my tank top down, pulling my open robe shut and retying the belt, scooting to the far edge of the couch before looking at him.

He rakes his fingers into his hair. "Are you okay? Fuck. I'm sorry. Did I hurt you?" His voice is a scrape. "I was dreaming about something else. When I woke up I should've... I shouldn't've... I'm so sorry." He meets my gaze, a mess of emotion in his eyes.

I don't know whether he's sorry he initiated this or sorry because he thinks *I* did. Whether he thinks I took advantage of him. But asking about that would make me seem guilty. And I'm not, not this time. So I clear my throat to dislodge the boulder there and go with a different question. "Dreaming about something else, or dreaming about someone else?"

"No, it was about us. Just maybe not...now. We were at the lake, in the water."

"And it bothers you that we did this?" I toy with the tie of the robe, wrapping it and unwrapping it around my finger. Looking at him would be impossible.

"Well, you're sick...and injured, and it's not...where we are now...or who we are now, is it? And what if you get pregnant? I didn't use anything. I'll get tested, okay? So you know I'm healthy."

I sigh, sinking back into the couch, feeling a million years old and, despite my day of rest, completely wrung out. "I have an IUD. Won't get pregnant. I'll test too.

"But tell me who you think we are, Joe, please? 'Cause I don't know anybody else who's gone through this. I woke up and you were... We were... I thought you were into it." *Into me.* Beyond the obvious literal sense. I raise my hands and let them drop. "I don't know what we're supposed to do or not do. I know my attempted sexorcism sucked, and I'm so sorry. But beyond that... tell me. Tell me the rules."

He leans back beside me, facing the silent, misty square. His words come out haltingly. Carefully. "I think...we did things right when we were young. Everything was full of feeling because we'd gotten so close before we did it. We did everything out of love. But now we're, like, strangers. We've barely talked since I've been back. This feels like hooking up." He gives a one-shoulder shrug and glances at me, his eyes dark. Mournful. "I don't wanna hook up with you, July."

Yeah, I gathered that from the way you sprang up off me afterward. I stare at my hands where they lie face up on my knees. He sounds every bit as defeated as I feel. It's all I can do not to cry. "Well, if we're strangers and you don't even want sex with me, why are you here, Joe? I didn't ask you to come here." Let him wonder whether I mean "come back to Galway" or "come to my apartment." I'm raw and it's a little of both.

I jump when he picks up one of my hands. "Please don't think I don't want you. It's just...sex is not enough. And I'm afraid it'll wreck anything else we might've had. Get in the way of rebuilding a friendship. It would seem like an insult to what we had before." His eyes—hazel again—pin me in place. "Don't you remember how it used to be?"

I force my gaze to the window, to the square, my thoughts drifting back in time. In the morning hush, I can admit it. "It was different."

But I'm not ready to dwell on that or to talk about it yet. I start to push to my feet. "I've got to get to work. I'm gonna be late."

"Nope. Donna was serious yesterday. You're not to go downstairs. They've got you covered. Can't have you falling and bleeding all over the place or being Typhoid Mary." He stands and walks to the kitchen. "You're late for your next dose of medicine though. My bad. Helping out with that was my excuse for sleeping on your nice couch."

A coughing spell seizes me, but it doesn't seem as bad as yesterday. I follow him slowly to the island and sink onto a barstool, watching him fiddle with my bottles and tiny plastic cups. "Why are you up here with me, Joe, really?"

He barely glances up from what he's measuring. "I don't know for sure. I wanted to help. And I was the logical person."

"I'm having trouble seeing why, on account of us being strangers and all." Petty of me to throw that word back at him, especially when he's doing me a favor I don't deserve.

He pushes the medicine toward me along with a banana he's snagged from my fruit bowl. "I live so close, and...we have a history. And I care what happens to you."

I look down at the little cup for a moment, and then I peel the banana and eat it. Chase it with the meds.

He fills the teakettle and turns on the burner. Rifles through my cabinets until he finds a mug and a tea bag. "Do you feel any better today? You seem more alert. Steadier."

"I'm not achy, except here." I touch the swollen area near my cut, wondering what glorious colors I'm going to see in the mirror this morning. Wondering what color my heart would be if I could see *that* right now. Not all aches are physical. "I'm not dizzy. Not as hot. Just exhausted."

He nods. When the water's hot, he pours and passes me the mug, and I spend some time dunking the tea bag in it before looking up at him again. "You sure they have the restaurant covered today?"

"I'm sure. They were very clear on that. Threatening, actually." That little half smile almost makes him look like my young Joe.

I snort without humor, weary just thinking about how much older than that sweet, smart-ass boy I am. "Then I think I'll go back to bed."

CHAPTER 14

Dear July,

MF's been a smug, happy asshole since we've been here, but I know how things work. Pretty soon the tension'll start to build again, and then it's only a matter of time before he goes off on us...

Joe

I LET MYSELF INTO MY building, feeling as empty as this echoey downstairs space. Like somebody took a melon baller and scooped out my guts. For a few minutes I had her back...and then I woke up.

It's like I lose July all over again every time we touch.

What kind of asshole has sex with a sick woman he doesn't even really like? Looks in her fever-heated eyes, hears her say, "Please," and can't stop?

Upstairs Angus has kitchen cabinetry in place, and a note for me that countertops and appliances will go in today. In the bathroom there's another note saying I can start using the new shower tomorrow. *Halle-freakin-lujah.*

I wash up, making a terrible mess with shampoo suds when I try to rinse my hair in that little sink, but at least I'm clean when I'm done. I throw on a plain T-shirt and jeans, and head back to the restaurant.

Tina's already been baking. Donna lets me in the back door, still holding her purse. She tosses it into the office and grabs aprons for the two of us.

"How was July last night?" they ask, together.

Oh yeah. Nobody knows I was just up there.

"Okay, I guess. Sleeping a lot. She ate all the dinner I took her though." I check to make sure our prep stations are stocked. They are. The night crew did their work well. I keep my head in the reach-in long enough to add, "I think somebody else should check on her today."

Donna pauses with a stockpot in her hand.

Tina stops rolling out dough and turns to stare at me. "Was there a problem?"

Damn. If I thought Donna was scary with a knife, Tina is freaking terrifying with her impressive biceps and her rolling pin. The women of this town are a united, formidable front when it comes to July.

I deserve whatever kind of justice they might hand out. Not going to answer that question though. "It just...doesn't seem to cheer her up to see me the way I think it would to see you all." I glance through the orders that were placed yesterday for pickup this morning. I'm telling the truth, but it doesn't feel like it. I sigh. "July and I don't really know each other anymore. You all are closer."

I feel them standing down. See their tiny nods, their glances at each other. "Okay," Donna says. "I'll take up some breakfast later." She pauses beside me on her way to the stove. "We need an entree special for lunch and supper. Got any ideas?"

I recognize this for what it is: a gift. A sign of trust and approval of my work yesterday. I appreciate it, I needed that this morning, and I'll take it. "Yeah. Yeah, I do."

Tina turns up the music and we get to work. The servers come in, the breakfast rush starts, and we're swamped for the next few hours. Midmorning there's a brief lull, and Donna takes July some fruit with a big piece of quiche. Comes back down saying, "That's a nasty bruise she's got, but she says she's not in pain. Not shaky. Still got a little temperature. Argued with me when I said she can't come back till she's been clear of that for twenty-four hours."

Tina snorts. "How long did it take her to try some I'm-the-boss shit?"

Donna grins at her, lighting her whole face. "'Bout two seconds after I said the twenty-four-hour rule."

"You fire her?"

"Oh, you know I did."

They high-five in passing as Donna gets back to work.

Sonya pushes through the kitchen door to collect an order for her six top. "We got a couple more flower deliveries for July," she says to Tina. "Here's the cards that came with them."

"We don't have any more vases, do we?" Tina frowns. She'd texted July about the first few, and July'd said to tell the servers to split them up into bud vases for the customer tables.

Sonya laughs on her way back out with a loaded tray. "Ran out of those an hour ago. Now we're just putting whole arrangements on the tables."

Tina takes the cards to the office and grabs her purse. "I'm outta here, babe." She kisses Donna's cheek. "I'll come back at three unless you need me earlier."

I put the finishing touches on my proposed special for the day—fusilli with pepper jack bechamel and assorted peppers and mushrooms, blistered shishitos on the side—and hand a spoonful to Donna to taste. "What do you think? Give 'em a choice of meat if they want."

She takes a bite and chews, her eyes drifting shut. "Ooh, that's got some *nice* heat on it. Good flavor. Let's do it. I'll have Sonya add it to the specials board."

Breakfast drifts into lunch, and we're busy the whole time, cranking out menu items and my peppery special. Maisie and Sam come in around the same time as Tina, all of them laughing and joking with us.

It feels like my Colorado restaurants' backstage areas. Like home. Like family.

The kids aren't due to clock in until four. They go out to the staff table with me when I take my break. Donna shoves two plates of my special at them. "Here, Maisie, you should taste Joe's special in case anybody asks you about it tonight. You have some too, Sam."

I get the feeling she feeds them a lot.

"Ooh, this is good! Spicy!" Maisie says after a bite of the pasta. She pokes a shishito with her fork. "How hot are these?"

"They're not hot." Sam sets the stem of the one he's just eaten on his plate.

I've been wondering since yesterday if he recognizes me from the lake. Probably not, given that I woke him up. Should I mention that I've seen him before? He seems okay now. Maybe best to let it lie.

Maisie takes a cautious nibble of the tip of one shishito. "Mm, that's really good! I can't believe it's not hot."

They clean their plates and ask me about how July is doing. I tell them what I know. Tell them about the flower deliveries, pointing out the arrangements on all the tables.

Maisie nods. "I'm not surprised. She's the town mom. Always remembering everybody's special occasions... It was weird not to have her here last night, popping out to chat with people. Teasing us in the kitchen."

Sam nudges her. "Making sure we take sandwiches home after our shift."

She smiles at him. "Yeah, the women here really do like to feed us, don't they?"

He nods and pats his belly. "They sure do." He stacks their empty dishes and pushes them aside, then pulls out a notepad and flips it open. Correction: a sketch pad.

"Whoa!" I blink at the color blazing from the pages. "Sam, did you do those? They're great!" I'm not a big reader of graphic novels, but these look really well done. Professional.

Before Sam can answer, Maisie says, "He's going to be a famous graphic artist. Maybe do graphic novels. Or bigger stuff. Murals."

Sam blushes beet red. "Maisie. That's a long way off. And I got a lot of work to do to get there."

She shrugs and picks a shishito stem off her plate, finding a little more pepper to nibble off of it. "You will."

Sam gives me a *women!* look and shakes his head, but he leans into her a little after that, and she leans back, right up until we go back to the kitchen together.

They're an odd couple, the tiny, pretty girl and the big, quiet boy. Not a pairing anyone would expect. I can't tell whether it's platonic or romantic, but they are tight. Like puppies seeking warmth and comfort.

I wonder if people used to think July and I were a mismatch, she with her sunny, golden self and her perfect family, and me with my problem home life and my feeling that I've always been an old man.

I glance over at Maisie and Sam. She's tying on an apron and fake shoving him, laughing, out of her way as she heads to work in the dining room. Man, was I ever that young?

It hits me then: July and I were exactly that young—sixteen—when we were together.

Kids. No matter how grown-up we felt, no matter how many grown-up things we did, no matter how big, important, and forever our love felt, we were literally just kids.

And now we're adults. I may never understand the sexorcism thing, but this morning July was injured and ill, and she was not to blame for what happened on that couch. It was my mouth on her breasts, my dick looking for home inside her.

And she's right; she didn't ask me here.

And it's not her fault I can't stay away.

July

To my horror, it's two more days before I'm able to go back to work. True, I feel lousy—and not just emotionally, because as far as I know, humiliation and rejection don't cause fevers—but staying upstairs in my apartment is torture. It's a nice place, comfortable, but I hear life and people downstairs. Out my windows I see folks I know moving around the square, laughing and talking and going about their days. Up here I feel cut off, even with my whole family video chatting me and Andi and Rose texting and Donna and Tina bringing me food, refusing to talk about the restaurant.

"Tell you what," Tina says, when I've asked for the fiftieth time. "We'll promise to let you know the minute we need you if you'll promise to rest and stop worrying and get well until then."

They don't need me? She's speaking the truth, I can tell...but it's not exactly comforting. Who am I if my own baby doesn't need me?

I chew on that for a while before concluding that this emptynester stuff sucks.

Joe doesn't come back. The look on his face said it all. Sixteen-year-old Joe had wanted to be with me; thirty-six-year-old Joe does not.

There's no reason for me to feel shame this time. I won't. He doesn't have to like me or be attracted to me. He can feel however he feels, and I'll just...move on. Act like I have some dignity. If he doesn't want to stay around here, doesn't want anything to do with me, I'll just...keep my head up and let him go. At least I'll know what happened to him this time.

I sleep as much as I can Friday after Donna reminds me of that damn twenty-four-hour fever rule, and maybe it works because Saturday morning I'm fever free, something I gleefully text to both Donna and Tina along with a photo of the digital thermometer reading.

Tina texts back Yay! and a string of emojis I'm afraid to examine too closely. Donna's text says, Well done. If it stays down all day, perhaps you might be eligible for rehire.

I'm determined to be the first one at work tomorrow.

I bar them from bringing me food or checking on me today. Instead, I get up and fix myself scrambled eggs and toast, and squeeze myself some fresh orange juice, feeling like my arms have lost half their strength while I've been marooned up here. I hate that more than anything, but it's another sign I need to pay more attention to what my body needs.

I throw in a load of laundry, including my sheets and towels, wince at my reflection in the mirror, and then I venture out to the living room to reclaim my couch.

It looks the same as usual; I took my quilt back into the bedroom yesterday morning. Now I circle the sofa slowly, pausing to open one tall front window and then another, wiping my finger across the top edge of the wall-mounted TV to see if it needs dusting, and then I scoop up the remote, press power, and drop onto the couch. My couch. The couch I chose before Joe came back to Galway. The couch I'll still have when he leaves.

I settle my butt right down on the center cushion and watch TV for an hour. In broad daylight, my memories of yesterday's gray dawn are no more substantial than my dreams, and by the time I've watched two cooking shows, my apartment is my own again. No lean, hard, bright-eyed ghosts seducing and then abandoning me.

I take a nap in the afternoon and wake up feeling like if I don't get out of this place, I'm going to start screaming and never stop. Tom knows I can't play ball today—he actually texted to see how I was doing—so no one's expecting me at the game, but I sneak out to the alley to my car and drive to the ballpark anyway.

There's one empty parking space out near the right field home run fence, where no one's likely to notice me. I pull into it, cut the engine, and watch the game.

It's weird seeing my team adjust for my absence. We start out behind due to fielding errors, with miscommunications and hesitation from players who have been shifted to different positions than usual. It's all I can do to not grab my bag out of the back and hustle down there, I want to help so bad. Want to pull my weight. But then they hit a rhythm. The stronger players like Joe and Andi and Tom stretch to cover a little more ground than usual, and the less-sure players gain confidence. I can't hear what he's saying, but I see Joe encouraging everyone, teasing them, making them smile. By the fifth inning, we've pulled ahead. I'm so proud I have to roll up my windows to keep my cheers from alerting them to my presence.

But it hits me as the game ends with us winning by one. The restaurant doesn't need me. The team doesn't need me. The person I once considered my soul mate doesn't want me. Who am I, even, and why am I here?

I start the car, back out quietly, and head for home.

Upstairs in my apartment, I clean my kitchen and my bathroom. Put away the laundry. Fix myself a sandwich and sit in front of the TV until it's dark enough that I can go back to bed.

It's still dark when I creep downstairs Sunday morning. Tina doesn't work on Sundays; she makes all the dough the day before and I bake it later. So no one is here before me today. I flip on the lights to a bright, shiny, meticulously clean kitchen. Same as every morning.

I ease open the swinging door and peer into the dining room. Again, clean and tidy, as usual, with one difference.

There is a flower arrangement or green plant on every single table. Three more on the counter near the register. Two big ones flanking the front door. What the hell? It looks like a funeral parlor.

Geez, people, I wasn't that bad off.

There aren't any cards with the arrangements. I check the kitchen. Nothing there either. I unlock the door to the office, and there, on my always-messy desk, what was probably originally a tidy stack of envelopes has avalanched sideways so that a couple have fallen to the floor.

I scoop them up and ease into the chair behind the desk. *Get well soon, July! We love you, July! We miss you!* Card after card, from everybody, the mayor's office down to the youngest T-ball team I sponsor. The Galway High Cooking Is Chemistry field trip bunch. The red-hatted Ladies Who Lunch club and the Thursday Night Guys. PFLAG and the women at the shelter and the dairy people and the folks at the free clinic. Even cranky old Miz Ames, and she hates everybody, except maybe Rose—I haven't quite figured out that relationship yet. But I'm blubbering like a baby by the time I reach the one that really gets to me.

No envelope for this one. It's a single sheet of paper torn from a spiral notebook, all the tiny little ripped-paper fragments removed from the edge. In pencil, all caps, is the message, *July, feel better soon. Love ya.* There are six or eight signatures, some legible, some not. The clearest is Devon's.

I had thought the most beautiful bouquet in the dining room looked like wildflowers. Now I know.

Donna and Tina find me here, still sniffling and wiping my eyes, a few minutes later.

Tina stoops to hug me. "You're here!"

I hug her back. "You're here too!"

Donna is her usual low-key self. "Doing okay?"

I wave her off and sniffle one last time. "You know that empty spot at the far end of the square near the library?"

They nod, looking at me like I've lost my mind.

"Let's donate a bench. Have 'em put a plaque naming it the Friendship Bench."

"Oh. That'd be great!" Tina glances at Donna, then back at me. "I just came in to see if I needed to do the baking today. You want me to stay?"

"No, I'm good. You go do your usual Sunday things." I'm not at full energy, I can tell already, but Sundays we close at two. Pretty sure I can hold out till then.

"Okay." She reaches into her purse. "I should text Joe not to come then." She pulls out her phone and starts typing.

That gets my attention. "Where you going with Joe?" Not that it's my business. Then again, since when does anybody mind their own business around here?

"She means not to come here. To work." Donna eyes me as if realizing...something.

"What?" My voice comes out flat and short.

Tina frowns as she hits send and slips her phone back into her purse. "You didn't know? How did you not know?"

I put both hands flat on the desk. Push myself up out of my chair. "Know what?" I already know what they're going to say.

They speak over each other.

"Joe—"

"—filled in for you—"

"—while you were out."

I sink right back into my seat. "Let me guess. This was Rose's idea."

Donna faces me. "Rose's and Joe's. It was a good one. Look around. Everything's fine."

Everything's juuuust fine now that Joe's here.

Great. I rub my temples. "How'd you pay him? He on the payroll now?" This is my fault. I shouldn't have kept us understaffed. Should never have thought I was invincible.

Especially with Joe around. I should know better.

"He wouldn't take any money," Tina says quietly.

"What?" I shouldn't raise my voice. None of this is their fault.

"Said he doesn't charge friends for help." Donna tosses down her purse and reaches for an apron. Ties it on and heads for the door, giving Tina a hug on her way past.

I tie my own apron on more slowly and follow, setting to work on the cinnamon rolls.

I don't know why this seems so bad to me. I think about it all through morning prep, all through breakfast and brunch and lunch. I greet people and smile and laugh and talk and wave through the door Sonya holds open so the dining room customers can holler, "Welcome back, July!" in some kind of freaky but really sweet unison. I think of it as I listen to Maisie and Sam chatter about how "Joe said" this and "Joe did" that. I think of it midafternoon as we finish closing and I drag myself upstairs. As I strip and climb into the shower and let hot water pound down on every part of me except my liquid-stitched forehead.

Then I pull on my robe and settle on my bed, exhausted, staring at my phone.

Joe, I text, finally. Why didn't you say anything about filling in? That's...too much. I don't know what to say. Don't know how to thank you.

Almost immediately the three dots appear. Then disappear.

Then appear again. It's a full two minutes before his reply comes through. No big deal. I had fun.

That's something my old/young Joe would have said. I text back, Joe. You saved my staff. My customers. Maybe my business. It was a big deal. Tell me how I can thank you. Then, afraid he'll think I was propositioning him, I add, Gift card? Free meals forever?

Three dots again, on and off and on and off and on for an eternity before finally he replies, I could use a running buddy.

CHAPTER 15

Dear July,

I don't even know if you've gotten any of my letters yet. We don't have a phone or computer here, and MF controls all the money, so that's why I haven't called. Do you have an email address? I don't but I could get one...

Joe

"I THINK YOU SHOULD HAVE a cooking channel. You're better at explaining stuff than a lot of the people online." Maisie slides a look of pure mischief my way. "And you're cuter. You know. For an old guy."

I shake my head, biting back a laugh. The kids came in after school and joined me in the booth where I had joined Sonya on her break an hour earlier. Maisie's been pelting me with questions about spices and sauces and knife work.

"You should listen to her, Joe." Sam glances up briefly from his newest sketch. "She watches all the cooking channels. She'd know."

Interesting. "You want to be a chef, Maisie?"

"No. I just like to cook. I like seeing how Donna and July and Tina and the people online do things." She watches Sam add shading to a curve in his drawing. Her mood has shifted but I'm not sure why.

The swinging door from the kitchen opens and July comes toward our booth. Falters just a second when she spots me, then keeps coming.

I haven't seen her since her apartment Friday morning. I've purposely pushed back the memory of waking up inside her, making love to her. Nothing to celebrate there. It would have taken a goddamn saint to stop when I realized...and I have never been anything close to a saint.

I stayed away from the restaurant Sunday after Tina texted that they didn't need me. Came by Monday, planning to eat at one of the outside tables, but Tina waved me in to eat with her during her break. Same Tuesday, only it was Donna instead of Tina. Today I just came on in without being asked. It feels more like home than my apartment, even though my apartment is starting to look pretty good. Finished the last of my painting yesterday.

So my last contact with July was that text Sunday afternoon. Still don't know why I asked her to run with me or whether it was a mistake. It took her forever to text back a simple okay, followed by Give me a few days to stop coughing.

"Hey, y'all." She stands beside us now, more awkward than I've ever seen her, a menu in her hand. Her forehead bruise has faded to the palest yellow, and some of the stitches seem to have fallen off already. She looks healthy again, her color good, her hands steady. Maybe just a hint of tiredness beneath her eyes, but she looks...good.

Not as good as when she was underneath me, her head tipped

back, early morning light silver on her throat and on the breasts
I'd obviously been sipping from, her warm pussy squeezing me,
but...

Shit.

Less fantasizing, more acting like a running buddy. With
manners. "Want to sit?" I slide over to the inside wall, hoping
she won't look down at my fly.

"Oh, um, okay, just for a sec." She perches on the edge, a
million miles away. "Just wanted to show you this, Maisie, but
it's good you're here to see it too, Joe." She lays the menu on the
table and flips it open to display a new *Daily Specials* card clipped
inside. "Check out Tuesday."

Maisie, Sam, and I all lean in to look. I see it, blink, swallow,
and blink again to get rid of the moisture in my eyes. The card
says, among other things, *Tuesdays: Smokin' Joe's Pepper Pasta.*

"Aw!" Maisie's voice holds a smile.

"Nice." Sam's nodding in my peripheral vision.

I'm having trouble speaking. Have to clear my throat.

"Donna suggested we add it. Tina named it." July sounds
surer now. "We all thought it was a good idea. Our way of saying
thanks."

Only time anybody's ever done anything like this for me was
when my Colorado staff named the skinny cartoon fox on our
restaurant logo "Joey."

"That's real nice," I say when I can finally speak. "Thanks."

Her gaze rests on me, her gray eyes seeming to see everything
the way they used to. "You're welcome. Thank *you.*" And then,
thank god, she changes the subject. "Tonight's softball," she says
to the kids. "I'll be gone for a couple of hours during supper, so
watch for extra ways to help out, okay?"

Then she turns back to me. "If I don't hack up a lung tonight, I'm ready to try running tomorrow."

I nod.

She stands, scoops up the menu, and heads back to the kitchen, patting Sam's shoulder in passing.

The kids watch her go, glance at each other and then at me.

I ignore the speculation in their eyes. I don't really have any more idea of what's going on with me and July than they do.

My dick can just chill the fuck out.

July was fine at softball last night. Only had one brief coughing spell, and that's because she stretched her double into a triple. The woman can't not hustle. She doesn't go to Lindon's with us afterward—says she needs to get back to work—but tells me she's good to go for running.

So here I am, waiting in the kitchen for her as she finishes up with Devon and his guys in the dining room. She wouldn't let me help with closing, so I just stand out of the way in the office till she pushes back through the swinging door.

"Okay. Give me one sec to change, and then I'm ready." She tosses her apron in the laundry hamper by the door, disappears, and is back in a flash dressed in her running gear. Blue leggings, sneakers, and a pale gray tank. Her body looks powerful and graceful, and it's impossible not to remember how she feels in my arms. In my mouth. Around my...

Goddammit.

I follow her to the alley, where we stretch. "We should circle this area. In case you start coughing or get worn out." When her gray eyes flash at me, I add, "I mean because you've been sick."

She opens her mouth, closes it, and sighs. "That makes sense."

"You set the pace."

She nods and sets out, her stride smooth, slow, and easy at first and then gaining speed as she finds herself able. I'm a bit taller but we're a good match, running-wise.

We don't speak for a couple of blocks, but finally I have to say something. "I saw Jen the other day. She looks...different. Good."

July glances over at me and laughs. "Yeah. She didn't look nearly so pregnant when she was twelve, huh?"

That opens a crack in the ice. I ask about her folks—retired early and moved to a condo in Florida—and her brother, Brendan, some kind of project manager consulting whiz.

"I'm glad they're all doing okay." I mean it. I really liked them back in the day.

She flashes me another glance. "They were glad to hear you were okay too. They missed you when you went away. We all missed you."

We go another block in silence while I wonder whether to bring up that period or not. The few times I've tried asking her about it, she was pretty evasive.

But I have to know. "Was that time as hard for you as it was for me?"

She doesn't look my way, but her brow furrows. "I don't see how it could have been, Joe. I wasn't the one suddenly dropped in a strange place where I didn't know anybody and couldn't speak the language." Her voice grows quieter. "And I had a really supportive family around me."

True, but...still an evasion? I try again. "So you didn't have a hard time, then?"

That gets her. Her eyes widen as she turns them on me for a second. "I didn't say that."

I count four strides before she speaks again, and then I can barely hear her.

"It was the hardest thing I've ever been through."

There's a story there. An important one, I'm sure of it. But she doesn't elaborate, and after another half a block, she changes the subject. Thanks me for being so good to Maisie and Sam. "They think you're pretty great." She flashes me a half-strength July grin. "I'm getting a little sick of hearing about it."

That makes me laugh. "Now that's funny. Because to me they went on and on about how you're the town mom, always taking care of everybody. They're crazy about you. Everybody is."

She fixes her eyes on something up the street. "Not everybody."

And we're back to silence. Back to me wondering what we're really talking about.

July

"Ms. Tate? July?" Sam corrects himself as I give him the evil eye from my position halfway under my desk.

I retrieve the pencil I dropped and straighten, turning to face him where he stands in the office doorway. "What's up, Sam?"

He casts a fast glance toward the door to the dining room.

What's that in his expression—worry? "You wanna come in and shut the door?"

"I can't stay long." He steps into the office but leaves the door open. "I just wanted to ask if you could schedule me and Maisie so that we have the same days and hours? Or real close to the same hours?" He glances at the doorway again. "I mean, we're usually pretty close to the same anyway, but..."

"What's this about, Sam?" I've never detected any hint of romance between Sam and Maisie, despite their obvious closeness, but maybe I've been wrong. Maybe Sam has a crush on her.

He takes another step in. His words come out in a quiet rush. "There's this dude at school—kind of a bully. He's...interested in Maisie, but she's not interested in him. She told him so but... he showed up at the cabin, at Maisie's cabin, yesterday. Scared her. Grabbed her arm. I don't know what would've happened if I hadn't been there. She didn't want to say anything to you, but I don't want her home alone."

I know I'm frowning because the last of the liquid stitches tugs at my skin. "Her mom know about this?"

"She... I don't think Maisie told her. Her mom...has to travel a lot for work."

"But you're around a lot?"

Sam nods. "Yeah. Almost anytime we're not at work or school."

Well, this is frustrating. "Why didn't Maisie want to tell me or her mom? This guy sounds like trouble. Has she considered talking to the principal or somebody at school? Or calling the police?"

He shakes his head and casts another anguished glance toward the dining room. "She doesn't want anybody to know. She thinks it would cause more trouble. She'll be really mad if she knows I talked to you."

"But you think you can keep her safe if I schedule you two the same? You can be around her that much, and she'd be okay with that?"

"I think so. I...practically live there as it is." He studies his hands as I study him.

"Sam, please forgive me for asking this, but if I arrange your schedule like you asked, I'm not going to be helping you stalk Maisie, am I?"

His round, blue eyes find mine. "No, ma'am! Maisie's like my sister. My best friend. Both, I guess." He glances at the door again, then leans a little closer and says almost inaudibly, "Ms. Tate—July—I'm gay. Maisie's got nothin' to fear from me."

"Oh. Okay. Thanks for trusting me with that, Sam." I frown down at the scheduling sheet I've been using, trying to work in the three new employees I hired this morning. "Lemme play around with the hours and see what I can do. I'm going to have to sound her out on this a little. But I won't let on that you said anything."

He nods. "Okay. She's on break right now. I'm supposed to be out there too, so..."

I wave him away. "Go."

He exits the kitchen via the door to the restroom hallway so he'll be approaching the dining room from that direction. Smart boy.

Before I have time to think better, I pull out my phone and text Joe: You nearby? You hungry? Need your opinion on something here. Subtly. Then I get myself a glass of iced tea, tell Donna I'm on break, grab some fruit and a piece of quiche, and head out to the dining room. My phone buzzes on the way out—Joe saying he'll be over in a minute.

I join the kids in their booth. They're talking about the school year ending next week. "I can give you both full-time hours once school's out, if you're up for it," I'm telling them when Joe slides in beside me. "Hey, Joe."

"Hey." His smile isn't just for me the way it used to be.

I don't know why it feels so awful to have him treat me like just a normal person. It's not like he's not nice to normal people.

It just doesn't seem fair for him to be able to do that when his nearness, his scent, his face, everything about him makes every tiny hair and assorted other bits of my body stand up and say, "Hey."

Maisie and Sam greet him with their usual enthusiasm. Sonya bustles over to give him a hard time and take his order.

"How's it going?" he asks us when Sonya heads back to the kitchen.

"School's almost out!" Maisie sounds excited.

Sam adds, "July's gonna put us on full-time for summer."

Joe looks around, taking in the nearly full dining room and patio. "I can see why. Almost full at three thirty on a weekday. Business is good." He gives me a half smile that makes my stupid insides flutter. Makes me want to forget the past twenty years and scoot closer so he can put an arm around me. Kiss and touch me the way he used to when we were young and he loved me.

Focus, July. There's important grown-up stuff to pay attention to here. "What's the bruise, Maisie?" I nod at her wrist as she raises a forkful of salad to her mouth. "We need to fill out a worker's comp form?"

Her eyes widen and she gestures at her mouth, making a big production of carefully chewing her food. She's stalling for time, I know it. Sam looks at Maisie until she finally swallows and says, "No. Just some dumb boy."

Joe stiffens beside me. We're not touching, and it's nearly imperceptible, but I can tell his attention has sharpened on her. "What dumb boy?"

Maisie looks to Sam, who gazes back at her without saying anything. She sighs. "Just a dumb boy from school."

"What'd he do?" Joe's voice is casual. He doesn't look at her as he asks. Instead he points to a slice of strawberry on my plate, then to his own mouth, and makes a pitiful begging face.

I roll my eyes, spear the strawberry, and hand him the fork.

"He showed up uninvited." Maisie shudders.

Joe stops chewing and swallows. "He showed up at your house?"

She nods, looking equally miserable about the situation and about having to talk about it.

To give Joe time to process this, I ask, "Maisie, does your mom know?"

She shakes her head, eyes on her plate. "She...was out of town for work." She darts a glance at me and adds, "But Sam was there, so nothing happened, really. I'm fine."

"What'd he do, Maisie?" Joe has dropped the casual tone.

"Nothing, really." But at a nudge from Sam, she admits, "He was trying to get me in his car."

I look at Sam for the first time since this conversation started. "But you stopped him?"

Sam nods. "Yeah. I don't think he expected to see me. He let go of her and drove away."

Joe's expression is murderous. "He put a hand on you, Maisie?"

Maisie squirms, lowers her eyes, poking at her salad. "Just my wrist."

"Okay." I'm all business now that it's out. "Maisie, you tell your mom, okay? I think she should take you to the police station to talk to somebody, see what they recommend. And maybe talk to somebody at school about it too. Let me know if you want me to give you some names, or if y'all want me to go with you, okay?"

Maisie nods, but her misery is palpable.

"How often are you home alone?" Joe has calmed himself, gotten the deadly note out of his voice.

"Only when Sam and I are on different work schedules." Maisie adds quickly, "He stays with me most of the time when Mom's not there."

Damn, girl, perfect opening. "So if I give y'all matching schedules for a while, until this jerk learns to leave you alone, would that help?"

Maisie and Sam look at each other and nod.

Joe thinks ahead. "What about overnight? Is your mom ever gone overnight?"

"Sam stays with me when she's gone overnight."

Joe's still frowning. "You got phones?"

"Sam doesn't, but I do." Maisie pats her purse.

Joe leans back so Sonya can place his meal in front of him. He thanks her, and then pulls his own phone out of his pocket and slides it across the table to Maisie. "Dial your number from my phone, and then save my number. That creep comes back, you call 9-1-1, and then you call me, okay? I'll come right away, anytime. Tell me how to get to your place."

Maisie gives him directions, and Joe looks at me. "That's on the lake right near the place we used to go." He turns to Maisie and Sam. "I run up that way a lot."

Sam straightens in his seat. He and Joe exchange a look I don't understand, but I don't want to change the subject by asking.

I turn to Maisie again. "You and your mom go get some official advice as soon as you can, okay? Let me know if you need help."

Maisie looks at me with her big, solemn eyes and hands Joe his phone back.

He saves her contact information and slips the phone into his pocket.

Under the table, I find his hand and give it a quick thank-you squeeze. He squeezes back for just a second before letting go.

No matter how sad I am about things between Joe and me—and no matter how hard it is to hide that—I made the right call to pull him in on this situation with the kids. He's freaking great with them.

CHAPTER 16

Dear July,

I've started looking for change in the fucking streets, hoping to find enough for an international call...

Joe

"THANKS AGAIN FOR COMING TO help me with the thing with Maisie." July finishes her stretches, bounces a couple of times on the balls of her feet, and sets off at a faster clip than last night.

The sway of her ponytail above her solid curves mesmerizes me, and it takes me a minute to catch up.

"How did you know she was going to tell us about that?" I've been wondering. And thinking about how odd it felt for July to ask for my input as a...friend? Rather than as her boyfriend. Her other half. In a flash I'm back in her family's kitchen, dazzled all over again by her mischief, by the tiny freckles sprinkled across her nose, by her dimples and her laughing eyes as she holds out a spoonful of something for me to taste.

"Sam came to me privately just before. Asked me to schedule

them together. I pressed him on it, to make sure he wasn't being stalkerish."

"Hard to imagine Sam stalking anybody. And they seem really tight."

"Yeah." She glances over at me. "How worried do you think I need to be about the bully? About her?"

"Definitely worth keeping an eye on." I can't be objective on the subject of men bullying women. "I'll help. I'll try to run up that way more often when they're not working. Especially once school's out."

"That'd be great. Thanks." There's relief in her voice.

"Think she'll tell her mom?"

"I think so? I'm surprised she hasn't already." Her ponytail swishes as she shakes her head.

"Do you know her mom?" July knows everybody else in Galway, that's for sure.

"Just met her once, when they first moved to town. First time I met Maisie."

"They seem close?"

"Yeah. They were really cute together." Her smile reaches her voice. "Her mom must've been young when she had Maisie. It was one of those could-be-her-older-sister things. Why do you suppose Maisie hasn't told her already?"

To me, it seems like a freaking miracle when kids *do* have parents they can confide in. "I can think of a few reasons. Maybe her mom works a lot and Maisie's trying not to worry her. Maybe Maisie's afraid her mom'll blame her. Or...people hide relationship stuff. Bad stuff."

When July finally responds, it's so quiet I can barely hear her over our footfalls on the pavement. "Joe, how did you turn out okay?"

"What?" *Who says I'm okay?* "I don't know. Wait, yes, I do. Some people have good role models, right, to show them how to act. I had a role model show me exactly how *not* to be. So I just...avoid being my dad." As much as I can, anyway. A guy in Germany—a would-be bully who picked on me one too many times right after I gave up writing to July—probably still has scars. And he was lucky his friends pulled me off of him because I'm not sure I would have ever stopped hitting him.

But I can't tell July that.

Another pause, another soft question. "Was your mom good to you at least? Tell me to hush if this is too nosy."

"Mom was...okay as long as I didn't try to talk her into leaving my dad. As long as I didn't bad-mouth him. As long as I didn't say we should tell somebody or get help."

"But he hurt you too, didn't he?" First time I've heard steel in her voice.

"She'd try to step between him and me. I tried to do the same thing for her. Didn't work—he'd just hit both of us."

"Didn't anybody ever notice? Like teachers or neighbors?" Steel with an edge now. The concept of not helping must be completely foreign to her.

I shrug as I run. "I'm sure people suspected things sometimes. Maybe that's why he moved us around so much. Keep us off-balance. Keep us from making friends who could help us get away."

"Joe, I'm so sorry I didn't know. I'm so sorry I didn't ask."

That's just silly. "Why would you? Why would you even think of it? You have a really nice family. You'd probably never seen anything like mine, had you?"

"Not in real life, no. But I saw that big bruise on your back that one time."

"I'm sure I gave you an excuse for it." Like Mom always did. "I should've kept asking, Joe."

"No. You know what I've just realized lately? Watching how Maisie and Sam are—how young they are—has made me see that we were just kids too when we knew each other. How were you going to see and understand what was going on with my family? And how the hell could you have fought it?" I glance her way.

Her jaw juts out. "I would have tried, Joe. I wouldn't have let you go home to that."

"I know. But I didn't want you to know. I didn't want to, like, dirty you with it. Didn't want you to see me as part of it either."

Her next words are practically a whisper. "I didn't think we had any secrets."

I don't have an answer for that.

It's four blocks before she speaks again.

"You're so good with Sam and Maisie. But you've stayed single, right? How did you learn to be so good with kids?"

I think about my answer for a few strides. "I just...like people. Unless I see somebody like my dad staring out their eyes. The young people who worked for me were really interesting. How they thought, what they hoped for. How they'd screw up and what they'd try to do to fix things. How often they were stuck in a bad situation they didn't make. Sometimes it helped them just to have somebody listen."

She turns her head. Meets my eyes. "That why you decided to go into social work?"

"Yeah."

"You're going to be really good at it, Joe." Her smile is tiny and private. One I don't remember from our past.

Her words feel like a physical touch. A soft, warm gift of a touch.

———————

July

I didn't even think Rose and Andi knew each other well, but here they are, on a Sunday of all days, leaning in and talking up a storm when I bring Rose's meal out on my break.

"What y'all talking about?" I slide her salad and my sandwich onto the table, sit down beside her, and take a long drink of my iced tea.

"You." Rose spears a sliver of chicken and pops it into her mouth.

"You and Joe." Andi meets my eye matter-of-factly.

What the—? "There is no me and Joe."

Rose swallows her bite. "Exactly. Why the hell not?"

Across the table, Andi opens the take-out box she'd come in for and pulls out half of her sandwich. She doesn't say anything but she's smirking.

I sigh. "Rose, I told y'all already. I killed any chance we might've had before it even got started."

"But you all are running together now." Rose drizzles vinaigrette on her salad.

Andi nods, not looking up from her food. "And playing ball."

What did I do to deserve this today? It was a perfectly nice morning. I was in such a good mood. "Yep. Nothing remotely romantic about that. We don't even have to talk if we don't want to."

There's a pause as we all chew in silence. I'm just starting to breathe normally when Rose speaks up again.

"Do you?"

Oh, for the love of god. "Do we what?"

"Talk?"

This would be a good time for me to look into her sweet, caring face and tell her to mind her own business. I sigh. "Yeah."

"About the weather?"

"No." I will her to pick up her fork and jam a big bite into her mouth.

"About your luuuuv?" There's a tiny dimple in Rose's cheek when she's being a pain in the ass. I never noticed that before.

Andi snorts, chokes on her sandwich, and starts coughing.

I reach across the table and whack her on the back. "What is *with* you today, Rose? We're not in freakin' middle school."

Her face falls. "Are you honestly saying there's nothing between you two anymore?"

"I'm honestly saying that whatever is between us now is much different than before. It's platonic. It...doesn't feel magic like it used to." Except when we're asleep. "We're grown-ups now. We don't...click anymore. We've changed."

Rose puts one elbow on the table and turns in the booth to look me full on. "Are you sure it's platonic? Joe shot back to the kitchen to help the minute I told him you were hurt."

Andi regains control of her lungs and joins in, damn her. "He watches you, you know. When we play ball." She holds up a hand as if she thinks I'm going to protest. "And not in a creepy way. You know my tendency to see red flags everywhere. This isn't that. He just...watches you like you're the most interesting thing he's ever seen."

My head hurts and, maybe for the first time ever, I'm wishing I was eating alone in my office. "I'm sure it's platonic, okay? And the reason I'm sure is that Joe told me so. He doesn't want so much as a kiss from me. Things don't feel the same to him now. He said so. So even if I wanted to pursue somebody who doesn't want me—which I don't—it wouldn't do me any good with Joe. It would just embarrass us both."

Kinda like this conversation. I lift the top of my sandwich and peer at the precisely centered tomato slice. Smells good. Ripe. Too bad I've lost my appetite. The idea of chasing an unwilling Joe is, as Rose would say, depressing as fuck. "The guy's been through enough. If he can find some peace here, he deserves it. I'm not going to mess that up by pressuring him to be with me."

Rose picks up her fork again and looks down at her salad, then glances toward the kitchen and opens her mouth to say something else.

I cut her off. "Rose, I think he just missed cooking. Missed working as part of a team. Everybody said he fit right in. Slipped in easy and did a great job and seemed to have fun with it."

She closes her mouth and jabs a piece of arugula, then a chunk of tomato, then a sliver of boiled egg.

"And you"—I point at Andi—"stop looking at me like that. Of course he watches me when we play ball. It's left fielder's job to back up third base. He has to know what I'm doing all the time."

Andi shakes her head and raises her hands in the I-give-up gesture.

"Don't you want him anymore?" Rose's voice is soft beside me.

Yes. "No. Doesn't matter anyway. It's gotta be a two-way thing, and it's not. Besides, y'all saw me that first couple of weeks after he came back. I was a wreck. That's no way to live. I don't want that."

Andi reaches back into her carryout box for the other half of her sandwich. "So you're saying if one of the women on the team develops an interest in him, you'd be okay with that? You'd be just fine watching him go out with somebody else?"

No. The idea makes me want to puke. And cry. And puke while I cry. "If that's what would make him happy, yes."

That shuts them up. I feel them staring at me as I pick up my sandwich. "Can we change the subject, please? Rose, what you got going on at the foundation?"

Rose sighs, but then perks up as she tells us about a project someone proposed this week: tiny homes built around a community garden where the old supermarket used to be, on the east side of town. Angus is excited about that too, she says. He works two jobs, and one involves counseling veterans. And vets—especially homeless vets like my friend Devon—will have first shot at the tiny houses.

This news makes me feel a lot better.

Andi's excited about work too. She has a mysterious new idea for how to present material on sexual assault and domestic violence to the football team at Galway High. She won't tell us exactly what she's planning, but I know one of the volunteers is an excellent videographer, so it should be interesting to see what develops.

We talk away the rest of our meal, and I relax once I see that they're really going to let the subject of Joe and me drop. Thank god. It's depressing enough to think about it without having to explain out loud to other people that yes, I'm completely sure I've broken what we had. The thing that I'd hoped—and yeah, feared—could be amazing again, with the only person who ever felt that right to me.

But I meant what I said. If he can find some peace here, let him. Let him be. I'll do what I can to help, quietly, and do my best to be a friend to him. And then I'll just let the man be.

I'm working on convincing myself that I'd be just fine with that when my phone buzzes in my pocket. I fish it out.

Speak of the devil. A text from Joe: Need help with kids. Not quite emergency but can you come? Maisie's cabin.

I'm on my feet on my way to the kitchen, belatedly waving goodbye to Andi and Rose, before I even know I'm moving.

CHAPTER 17

Dear July,

Please don't be mad at me. Please. I would never have left you if I had any choice.

Joe

WHEN I WAS SIXTEEN, EVERYTHING about the lake seemed magical to me because of its association with July. The glittering water that grew colder when we dived deeper. The rich, layered greens of the trees over us where we lay on my old blanket, the undergrowth privacy-screening our clearing. That scent of sweet Carolina air I've never found anywhere else in the world.

Then I came back and had my hastily resurrected dreams sexorcised right out of me, and the lake became my solitary refuge. A place older than me and my mistakes. A place where maybe, if I'm patient and look hard enough and don't get distracted by the memory and feel of July, some wisdom and peace might seep into me.

But today I've just gotten to our—my—rock when I hear shouting and a girl scream, and any remaining magic shatters.

All that's left is the sound of my heart and breath ragged in my ears, my feet pounding over the roots and ruts of the trail down to the cabins, and when I burst into the clearing and see two guys, one with his hand on Maisie, and Sam doubled over holding his gut...*I'm gonna kill that motherfucker.* Rage distorts my vision as I dive straight at the guy, catching him in the solar plexus with my shoulder, taking him down and landing on top of him hard...

"She's on her way." I slide my phone back into my pocket.

Everybody nods.

Birdsong has started back up farther into the woods, but here, where I wait with the kids and a mirrored-glasses sheriff's deputy, it's quiet. None of the other cabins show any sign of life. A half-full laundry basket sits in the grass near us, a few T-shirts pinned to Maisie's clothesline above it. She's pale and shaking, her eyes huge, her thin arms wrapped around Sam. He's holding on to her too, looking a little less green than a few minutes ago, just rocking her and staring beyond me to where another deputy has the kid who grabbed Maisie handcuffed in the back of a cruiser.

At first it wasn't clear who they were going to cuff.

"Where'd Willard go?" Sam's voice is hoarse. There's murder in it.

The deputy near us perks up. "Who's Willard?"

"The other asshole. Curt's friend. He was here too, till Joe tackled Curt. I didn't see where he went after that." Sam rubs circles on Maisie's back.

Our deputy waves over a third officer, a woman, and speaks too low for me to hear. She nods, goes over to the cruiser, and says something quietly to that deputy.

July's little car wheels into the circle of cabins with a spray of gravel. She must've broken a land-speed record to get here this fast. Everyone, including the deputies, turns to look. I don't think it's my imagination that we all take in a deep, relieved breath. Swear to god, some of the birds start singing again in the trees around us.

My desire to laugh is entirely inappropriate.

She's out of the car, still wearing her apron, reaching for Maisie and Sam before anyone can even greet her. "Y'all okay?"

They nod and she turns to the deputy without taking her arms from around them. "Hey, Cade. What's going on? Can I help in some way?"

"July. Mr., uh"—he consults his notes, jerking his head at me—"Anderson here suggested we have you come up. We need to talk to these three"—he nods at Sam, Maisie and me—"separately, and he thought you should be here for the kids, since their folks aren't here."

July's eyebrows raise and her eyes find mine for the first time. "Okay, sure."

She stays with Maisie. The woman deputy comes over to talk with them. Cade seats Sam on the steps of the cabin next door, and they wait, silently, for July to finish with Maisie. The third deputy waves me over to the cabin nearest the cruiser.

He leads with, "Kid says you beat him up pretty bad."

"What? No. Not true. I tackled him and told Maisie to call 9-1-1. I held him down while we waited for you all to get here. Never hit him." I'm telling the truth—the miraculous goddamn truth because my fingers still itch to pound him, to close around his throat and squeeze—but sweat prickles at my back anyway. I hated my dad, but his message about police not being our friends must've stuck. I'm a newcomer—still mostly a stranger—in a small town, an adult who tackled a minor. At least I assume he's still a minor, despite him having a couple of inches and at least thirty pounds on me.

"Okay, why don't you tell me from the beginning? What were you doing up here anyway?"

I tell him about going for a run up to the picnic spot, hearing yelling, and coming down to see what was going on.

"Why'd you care enough to come see?"

I tell him about what Maisie had told us at the restaurant the other day. "I didn't know if it was them I heard yelling, but I had to make sure they were okay."

"And when you saw them, you hit the Curt kid, knocked him down, and pinned him?"

"No." I keep my breathing slow, my tone quiet. "I didn't hit him. I was still running. I tackled him to the ground and held him there."

He nods, takes down my contact information, finds a few more ways to try to get me to admit to hitting Curt, and when I correct him each time, he finally seems satisfied. "All right. Stick around till we're done with these kids, okay, in case we have more questions."

I lower myself to the porch steps and watch as he approaches July and Maisie and their deputy. July seems to be just listening, close by Maisie's side but letting her stand on her own. Maisie's hugging herself, her hands holding her elbows. Her face is pale and serious. I can see her mouth moving, but she's speaking too softly for me to hear anything.

I glance over to the next cabin at Sam. He's looking at me. I give him a nod I hope is reassuring and he nods back. I think he'll be okay.

The kid I tackled is still in the back of the squad car, his head tilted back against the seat, not moving. *Yeah, you just sit there and pray, asshole, and rethink your life.*

My eyes are drawn back to July. She's steady as a rock beside Maisie, posture alert and easy, arms by her sides, sunlight dappling her hair and shirt, her pretty face calm as she listens. She's taken off the apron and tossed it across her shoulder. Her blue T-shirt is snug across her chest.

In a flash I'm back in her apartment on her sofa, moving in her, her bare breasts full and soft and pale in the early morning light, her eyes on mine, heavy-lidded, satisfied, and I'm...twenty years too late.

I have to blink away to remind myself where I am.

July doesn't speak, doesn't try to do anything, but Maisie and Sam look less scared just having her here.

I feel better too. I don't know whether we're friends exactly, but she's a hell of an ally.

When the deputies finish with Maisie, July catches my eye, raises her brows, and I know just what she's asking. I nod and make my way over to sit with Maisie on her steps while July goes with the deputies to talk with Sam.

"How you holding up?"

"Okay." Maisie glances at the cruiser where the Curt kid still waits. A tiny shudder ripples through her.

He's too far away to see it, but I'm not. I stretch and get to my feet, "accidentally" moving between her and the car so Curt won't be able to see her.

Her eyes shift to me. "What do you think they're asking Sam?"

I shrug, shaking out my hands and arms. "Probably the same stuff they asked you. What happened, who did what."

"Are we going to be in trouble?" Her voice is tiny.

"What? No! Why would you be in trouble?"

Her turn to shrug. "It just feels...weird. I've never had to talk to the police before. It feels...bad. Like if I wasn't doing anything wrong, I shouldn't have had to."

I nod. "Yeah. I kinda felt that way too."

"You did?" There's surprise in her eyes. Maybe even a hint of a smile.

"Yeah."

"That was great, what you did." Her eyes are solemn again. Huge in her face.

I don't know what to say to that.

"Come on. Show me how to hang laundry," I tell her finally.

She laughs, but she climbs to her feet and leads me over to her abandoned clothes basket.

July

Sam's story is nearly identical to Maisie's. I listen with one ear as I watch Joe with Maisie. He's helping her hang the wet laundry for heaven's sake. I can tell he's purposely picking socks and towels, and looking away as she hastily scoops up the underwear and hangs it behind a sheet. What a funny, kind, sensitive guy.

Sam says, just as Maisie did, that Curt had punched him, "and then Joe came flying down off the trail and tackled him." To hear them tell it, you wouldn't think Joe's feet even touched the ground. "And he bent Curt's arms up behind his back and told Maisie to dial 9-1-1. And he just...held Curt down and asked me if I was okay."

The deputies have a few more questions for Sam. Nothing I haven't already heard until they ask for his contact information. "This is the best place to find me. I'm…pretty much always here when I'm not at school or working at July's." His voice has gone quieter.

No mention of when Maisie's mom is gone. Just "always here."

The deputies ask about the kids' jobs with me. I say they'll be full-time starting next week. They nod, tell us how to request a copy of the police report, and then as they head toward the squad car, Joe intercepts Ginny, the deputy who questioned Maisie. I hear him say quietly, "Can you get somebody to tow Curt's car so Maisie and Sam don't have to look at it, and so he and his buddies don't have any excuse to come back up here?"

I hadn't noticed the old Toyota on the other side of the squad car, but Joe had and thought ahead to solve a problem before it even arose.

Ginny looks Joe over and nods. "Yeah, we can do that."

The kids and Joe and I stand and watch as the deputies leave with the Curt boy.

"Y'all okay?" I ask the three of them, just as Joe says to the kids, "You two doing okay?"

Our laughter doesn't quite break the tension.

"Come on." I nod at the empty laundry basket under Maisie's arm. "Put that inside and lock up. Everybody in the car. We're going for a drive." I glance at Joe. "That means you too."

"Yes, ma'am."

"You there, Mr. Hero," I say when we're on the road, Joe beside me, his seat pulled forward to give the kids more room, his tanned knee right near my gear shift. "You find some good music. And, y'all..." I meet Sam and Maisie's eyes in the rearview mirror. "It's your job to groan and gripe about whatever the old man picks."

They play along like I've been bossing them around their whole lives, Joe trying station after station, song after song, the kids booing each one. Finally he finds "I Won't Give Up" and nobody hisses. In fact, from the back seat comes quiet singing.

"Oh, *come* on." Joe twists around to glare at them. "*Really?*"

"It's a good song!" Maisie says it. Sam nods.

"How do you all even know Jason Mraz?" Joe's cranky that they didn't like his Red Hot Chili Peppers, I can tell.

"There's a K-pop group that sings it too."

Before they can argue anymore, I turn the volume up, and then we're barreling down country roads into Spartanburg County, belting out the lyrics at the top of our not-always-on-key voices. It's cathartic.

Just north of Spartanburg, I turn east to take us to a farm-store diner Andi and I discovered a few years ago. They serve the biggest, greasiest plates of food you can imagine, and they finish you off with homemade pie and ice cream.

We order burgers and fries and a big plate of onion rings to share.

"Your stomach okay?" Some of the worry has crept back onto Maisie's face as she turns to Sam.

He pats his belly. "Yeah. I'll probably have a bruise, but my guts are fine."

Maisie frees her silverware from her napkin and then looks from Joe to me. "What do you think's going to happen with Curt and the police?"

Joe raises his brows at me in a silent *You take it.*

"I don't know the exact steps. I think they'll take him to the police station and charge him. Decide whether to let him out on bail. His family or somebody will have to take care of that to get him out, I think."

Sam leans forward, elbows on the table, twisting a straw wrapper in his hands. "What do you think they'll charge him with?"

I shrug. "Probably assault for hitting you? Maybe something like attempted kidnapping for trying to make Maisie go with him? I don't know much about this stuff."

Joe says quietly, "They're probably going to look for the Willard kid. Question him. He might be charged with something too, depending on what all he knew about Curt's plans."

Maisie and Sam share a look and go silent.

"A judge will probably order them both to stay away from y'all." I know this much from the women at work. What I don't know is whether those boys will have the sense to listen.

Maisie nods.

"Your mom going to be home soon? How late does she work?" Joe is, once again, thinking ahead.

Maisie exchanges another glance with Sam. "I don't think she'll get home until tomorrow."

"You should call her right away. Ginny—the deputy, remember?—is expecting your mom to call her as soon as possible." I don't understand why Maisie doesn't seem to get how important this is.

She sinks down in her chair a little. "I'll call her when we get back to the cabin. It's...sometimes it's hard to reach her. She's in meetings a lot."

"Let me know if you want me to be there when you call, okay?

However you want to do it is fine. You just have to do it soon." I stop there. Any more will push her away, I'm pretty sure.

Maisie nods.

I'm glad Joe speaks next because I don't know what else to say. That rarely happens.

"Anybody ever teach you all self-defense?" Joe looks from Maisie to Sam.

He tells them about some good online videos and sources of information. It's a great subject change, really, to get them thinking about what they *can* do rather than all the things they've got no control over.

I lean back and listen. He asks them questions, some serious, some silly, and tells them good tips mixed with funny stories. They listen and smile and, eventually, laugh.

The server brings our food. It's hot and fresh and delicious, the fries thin and crispy just the way I like, but I can barely swallow past the lump in my throat.

How many of these things does Joe know because he had to learn how to defend himself and his mom from his dad?

This Joe looks tougher—harder and lean rather than skinny— than young Joe. There are faint lines at the corners of his eyes. From laughter, I hope. His thoughtfulness and sweetness are still there, his gentleness in full evidence as he talks to these two traumatized kids.

I think about excusing myself to go to the restroom. Maybe lock myself in a stall and have a good long cry about all three of them. About the resilience of youth, and the strength of kindness and hope. And selfishly, about all I lost when I hurt this amazing man.

But I don't want to leave them for a second. So I sit and listen and smile at appropriate moments. I sip my tea and force down tiny bits of my food and watch them.

And after they've finished their burgers, and Joe and Sam are arguing about which kind of pie sounds best, I see Maisie gazing from one of them to the other. First at Sam's face, then his stomach. Then at Joe. And when she turns those big, scared eyes on me, I know she's wondering what would have happened to her today if Sam and Joe hadn't been there. Hadn't been such good guys. Hadn't put themselves in harm's way sticking up for her.

"I think," I cut in, interrupting their good-natured squabbling, "you both deserve as much pie as you want." I meet the bemused server's eyes. "Bring us two of everything, please. And a whole lot of forks."

And Maisie's wobbly smile across the table about breaks my heart.

CHAPTER 18

Dear July,

I miss you so much I can't stand it. Please write when you get this. Let me know how you're doing. Tell me a story from home.

Joe

WE DIDN'T RUN LAST NIGHT. July didn't want to, and for once I didn't either. I stayed in, alone but somehow not lonely, in the space Angus and Rose have made into a home for me. Parked my ass on my new purple couch Rose had described as "just trust me, this is The One." I watched the TV Angus centered on the floating shelves he built along one brick wall. Fixed dinner in my efficient little kitchen and ate it sitting at my new dining table beside the bright congratulations-on-your-new-space! plant the restaurant—not July herself—had delivered. Started on the paperback thriller Dirk from softball loaned me.

Tonight's quite a bit warmer, and as we set out running, I have to keep my eyes firmly forward, off July's strong, curvy legs and arms. Also the bare nape of her neck, where those baby-fine blond hairs grow that used to tickle my lips and nose. Basically, I keep my eyes off all her exposed skin.

This is ridiculous. My brain and gut and body are all mixed up with wanting her, reminding myself she's a stranger, and arguing back that she's really not anymore.

July glances my way. "You're quiet tonight. You okay?"

"Yeah. Thinking about my nice new apartment." Not a total lie.

She gives me July smile number twelve: the I'm-so-tickled-that-you-too-appreciate-these-people-I-love smile. "They did a good job for you, huh? They're an amazing team."

"They really did. Why doesn't Rose work with Angus full-time? Seems more fun than an office job."

July shakes her head, her ponytail sliding over the smooth skin of her shoulders. "That office job is her passion. She loves figuring out ways to help people."

Like someone else I know. "Speaking of. How were Maisie and Sam today?" They hadn't taken us up on our offers for a place to stay last night. Just looked at each other, squared their shoulders, and said, "We'll be okay."

July doesn't immediately answer. When I glance over, she's frowning. "There's something..." She shakes her head again. "I keep feeling like something's going on there." She meets my gaze, her gray eyes darker than usual. "Ginny—the deputy?—came to talk to Maisie again. To check the number Maisie had given for her mom. Ginny said she hasn't heard from Maisie's mom and doesn't get any answer, just a voicemail-is-full message when she calls. She asked Maisie for her mom's work number, and Maisie said she didn't know. Said she always uses the cell. So Ginny asked for the employer's name, and Maisie said she couldn't remember.

Said it's a temp place out of Asheville, and they send her mom out on different jobs."

Now I'm frowning. What kind of temp work sends people out of town regularly to a job that involves lots of meetings? "Weird. What do you think is going on?"

"I have no idea."

Our strides match perfectly. The sound of our footsteps landing together, time after time, is…a comfort. A lulling, misleading comfort I should not get used to.

"Joe, what if the kids are lying?" July's voice pulls me back.

"Lying about what?"

She shakes her head again. "I don't know. About her mom, I guess. Maybe she's got a substance abuse problem of some kind? I mean, she goes off and leaves Maisie by herself for days."

"Possible." She sure wouldn't be the first. "What's up with Sam's family? Why are they okay with him staying with Maisie so much?"

"You know, I don't think I've ever heard them mention his family at all. I can tell from his accent he's from around here. There's a family or two with his name living out past the lake." She frowns for another quarter mile. "What the hell is going on with them?"

She doesn't need to be taking on any more responsibility. Any more worries. Half the town is enough.

This calls for silliness. "I'm thinking they're cannibals. They seem nice and innocent until midnight during the full moon. Then they come out of the corn like zombies. Really hairy zombies. Waving knives and chainsaws. Chanting, 'Redrum. Redrum.'"

She laughs. "How many movie plots did you mangle for that theory?"

"I don't know." I'm just happy to see her smile. "I'll look out for them, okay?"

"Thank god you were there yesterday, Joe." She's frowning again. "You know, I've seen that Curt kid before. He's bigger than you are."

"I had the element of surprise. And once you pin somebody, it's hard for them to get out of it unless they've had training." I preferred the horror movie discussion.

"Did you have to learn that because of your dad?" She's looking straight ahead.

"Some." Shit, I hate this. "July, I don't want to have a poor-abused-Joey conversation, okay? I'm grown now. I'm fine. My dad's been dead for six years. I'm done with that part of my life." And after yesterday when I managed to keep my rage in check, I'm no longer so afraid part of him still lives in me.

Now she looks over at me. Searches my face. Nods finally when I raise my eyebrows, and we run another half mile in silence.

"I'm sorry. I guess I do keep bringing it up, don't I? I won't do that anymore." Her voice is soft but firm. She means it. I can trust that.

I focus on the road ahead of us. "Yeah, let's talk about you for once. Tell me why you always change the subject when I ask you what it was like for you when I left."

Silence, for at least a block and a half.

I try again. "Okay, then, tell me why you're still single."

Another silent block.

Then she sighs. "The two things are related, I guess."

I wait while she works out in her head how to say whatever she wants to say.

"Okay, I'm going to tell you, and it may be more truth than you wanted, but you asked, so suck it up."

I smile at her bluster. I know this girl and her fake-tough love. I ache for her, for the fear I hear behind her words. "Hit me."

"After you left I fell apart, okay? Completely. For a whole year. Dropped into a depression—I didn't even know I was capable of depression. But it was bad. I was suicidal some of the time. Didn't take care of myself. Stopped ea—everything. Got real sick. Almost had to be hospitalized." Her voice is stunningly matter-of-fact. She might as well be talking about a book she read.

I can't speak. The night sounds around us swell to fill my brain: bugs and faraway traffic and creatures in the dark. And our footfalls, carrying us together through the center of it.

This is so not what I expected. I can't even picture my golden July like that. Makes my stomach turn to try.

I have a million questions and no idea which ones might be okay to ask. I want to stop right in the middle of the road and hold her. Anchor her. Save her from the past. Our past. My parents. The idea of my goddamn family making my laughing, grounded, bighearted girl want to die…shreds me.

She shoots me a glance. "There are exactly six reasons I'm still here. Jen, Brendan, my mom, my dad, Angus Drummond, and Angus's grandma."

My words come out as a croak. "How…? What…?"

One side of her mouth quirks up, but it's not exactly a smile. "I get that you don't understand. Some people come out stronger when they're tested. I think you're one of them." She shrugs, but it's not carefree. It's more like she's shifting an uncomfortable load. "But some of us break." Her last word cracks.

Ten strides before she speaks again. "I had the perfect life up to that point, you know? No disappointments, no losses, no real challenges. Thought I was strong. Capable. Thought the rest of my life would just…fall in line too. When I met you, I assumed you'd be part of the rest of my charmed life. Of course you would, right? I believed in soul mates."

So did I.

I don't want to hear the rest of this. It's like we're peeling back the top few layers of our skin, exposing everything underneath to the sting of the night air. But I have to listen. Have to know.

Twelve strides. "When you disappeared, suddenly I could see all those assumptions like a spotlight was shining on them. And then I could see them crumbling to dust, one by one. All the things I'd taken for granted about the world and love and how life works. About my own judgment. I mean, clearly *that* couldn't be trusted. Because I had been *so sure* about you, Joe. About us. And then it turned out I was wrong—or I thought so for twenty years, anyway—and I felt like I had zero control over anything in my world. Even my own brain." Her voice drops lower as if she's talking to herself. "It would have been easier if I'd ever had any doubts."

I should reach out. Take her hand. Pull us to a stop. Hold her. Show her she wasn't wrong.

But she keeps running, and her words keep flowing, stinging like acid although her tone is calm. "At first I thought you must be sick. I went over and saw your truck there, but nobody answered the door. No signs of life. Finally a neighbor saw me hanging around, told me he'd spoken to y'all that night and your dad had said something about Germany." She looks at me now, her eyes wide and dark. "I didn't know what had happened, Joe. I had a bad feeling. Didn't even know if you were still alive."

Oh, shit. It never occurred to me that she'd have been worried about me. But of course she would have been.

"I was so sure you wouldn't just leave me without saying anything. I waited and waited for you. I was so sure. I got my folks to talk to the police, to get them to do a wellness check. They found mail piling up in your mailbox. Checked with the landlord and found out y'all had moved." She raises her hands, swipes at the corners of her eyes. "And that's when I quit being sure of anything."

I have to stop, have to hold her, but she speeds up.

I push to catch up. "But your family..."

"My family was wonderful. For a whole year, I didn't want to do anything but lie on my bed or try to literally outrun my thoughts. Jen and Brendan would make popcorn, snuggle up close, and just sit with me. Like they knew I needed their body heat to stay alive."

Thank god she'd had the family she has. Thank god. "And Angus?" Did she and Angus have a thing? Is that why he seemed so protective that first day I was back?

"At the end of junior year, Angus caught me in the hallway at school. Most people had given up trying to talk to me by then. But Angus pushed a piece of paper into my hand. Said, 'Call my grandma. She needs help this summer.'" July glances over at me, a faint smile on her face. "His grandma was a saint. His grandpa too, I guess, but she was the driving force. She spent all her free time helping people, trying to make sure people had what they needed. Your house burn down? Mrs. Drummond would line you up a place to stay and help you replace what you'd lost. Lose your job? Your family hungry? She was the person who'd get you fixed up and fed. She was the Mother Teresa of Galway."

"And now you are." There's a smile blooming somewhere in my chest, even if it hasn't made it to my face yet.

She shoots me a startled look and a frown. "What? No. But

she put me to work helping her that summer, and it straightened me out. Gave me some perspective on what real need and loss are." She nods to herself. "Gave me a purpose. Saved my life."

We're at the halfway point of our run, and she swings into a wide turn. Shakes her hands and arms like she's shaking off something cold. "Anyway, that's one reason why I'm single. Not strong enough to go through that again."

We head back toward the square.

"And not to make an excuse, because there is no excuse for what I tried to do to you, Joe, but that's why I was so freaked out when you first came back, and I felt my head and my feelings getting all jumbled and overwhelming again, and I couldn't sleep. I was afraid of a relapse."

I watch our feet keep perfect pace with each other, so close and so far away.

She sighs. Says quietly, "So you were right that we're pretty much strangers now. Because the girl you knew shattered into a million pieces when things got tough. I'm just the pieces that were left, glued back together kinda sloppy. Everything doesn't quite match up right anymore."

July

I'm in the kitchen cranking out a big order and trying to ignore the fact that Joe's brought Rose and Angus in for a thank-you dinner. And that when I went out to say hi and deliver their drinks, he looked wonderful, a slim, button-down shirt tucked into his faded jeans, his hair messy as usual, his scent clean and woodsy and delicious as always.

I've never felt this urge to run my hands all over anybody else. Just Joe.

We didn't run the past two nights—I had back-to-back board meetings for the shelter and the free clinic Tuesday and we had softball last night—so I haven't had much chance to gauge his reaction to my confession the other night. He was really quiet afterward. Realllly quiet.

I was hoping we might eventually have a friendship. I hope I haven't wrecked that by oversharing.

But dammit, he asked. And asked. And asked. So now he knows.

He *used* to be a safe person to share with.

It's probably better for him to know I cared too much than to think I hadn't cared enough.

Better for him, anyway.

Sonya pops her head in from the dining room as I put the finishing touches on the big order. "July, somebody's here for you."

It's Ginny Lewis and another deputy. I dry my hands on my apron as I greet them. "Hey, y'all. What can I do for you?"

Ginny's grim expression tells me they're not here to eat. "July, I need to talk to the kids. They here?"

Shit. This doesn't sound good. "They're in the kitchen, but we can go upstairs to my apartment where it's more private." I glance over to where Joe and Rose and Angus have finished their meal.

Joe's watching, his brows raised. I gesture him over. He hands his credit card to Sonya, says a few words to Angus and Rose, and joins us.

"Let me get the kids. Joe, would you like to sit in too, so they both have an adult with them?" I touch his forearm below his rolled-up sleeve and feel the tension there.

He doesn't show it. Doesn't hesitate. His voice is easy. "Sure."

I round up Maisie and Sam, and turn over supper service to the evening team. Donna says she'll stay late to make up for me stealing part of the crew. Her eyes are worried. She knows the story and has enough life experience to take it really seriously. I know she's wondering, like I am, what fresh hell that Curt asshole and his little asshole sidekick have cooked up.

We troop upstairs in silence. Maisie's got big waif eyes again. The kids sit together on the sofa. Joe pulls over a chair from the dining area and settles beside Sam. I squeeze in next to Maisie on the couch, leaving the deputies the armchairs.

"All right." Ginny flips open a notepad, all business. "This case has taken an unexpected turn, and I need y'all to tell me what's going on." She eyes the kids, who huddle together looking scared and much younger than usual. "Maisie, I think you know I haven't been able to reach your mom, and she hasn't tried to reach me. The cell number you gave me still says voicemail full."

She flips to the next page of notes. "This afternoon I got phone records for that number, and I learned something interesting: no outgoing calls or texts have been made from that number for months. Not a single one. And the only incoming calls have been very short and were all from the number you gave me for you. So. That's one mystery."

She turns her attention to Sam. "Meanwhile, Sam, I've contacted your parents, and they tell me they have not seen or heard from you since New Year's, and that they know nothing about your activities but would not be surprised to hear if you are in trouble. They asked me not to contact them again."

Sam's face is impassive, but Maisie shoots him an outraged look and then picks up his hand and holds it tight between both of hers.

Joe shakes his head, his mouth twisted with disgust.

Ginny turns back to Maisie. "We've done an online search for your mom. Her social media activity stopped around the time of her last outgoing phone call. Her bank account shows some modest transactions: the deposit of your paychecks, online bill payment for insurance and utilities. No record of other economic activity or employment in her name for months." She closes her notebook and draws a deep breath. "Our assault investigation seems to have opened up a whole new can of worms. So we have two big questions for you two today. Where's your mom, Maisie, and why have you two been lying to us?"

Nothing about Curt or his friend. This is bigger and even scarier. Joe looks as shocked as I feel.

No one speaks for what seems like an eternity. Maisie's barely holding back a sob, and Sam disentangles her hands from his— gently, so gently—and puts his arm around her.

Ginny tries again. "You know, this looks really bad. You seem like good kids, but this looks like y'all might have done something to your mom, Maisie. Tell us what really happened."

Now Maisie's horrified. "I didn't! We didn't! I wouldn't! I love my mom!" She looks at Sam. He nods at her, his eyes sad, his arm tight around her. She turns back to Ginny Lewis. "And Sam didn't even know her. He never met her. He's never done anything wrong. It's his family that sucks." She's fierce. Angry.

Ginny nods encouragingly. The other officer quietly begins to take notes. "Where is she, Maisie?"

"I don't know," Maisie wails, misery and truth evident in her voice. I open my hand on the cushion between us, and Maisie seizes it. "But…I'm afra—I might have an idea." Tears stream down her face.

Joe gets up and grabs some paper napkins from the dining table. Hands them to Maisie and sits back down just as she says, almost inaudibly, "I think she was the person in that bus crash in Asheville."

Oh god. "That one a few months ago?" I probably shouldn't have spoken, but I can't help it.

Maisie nods, swiping at her face with the napkins. "Four months and four days."

Ginny Lewis leans forward, her voice gentle. "Why do you think it was her, Maisie?"

Maisie's face crumples, and she has to force the words out. "Because she went to Asheville that day and she never came home. I was supposed to go pick her up from the bus station when she called, but she never called. And she didn't answer my texts. I fell asleep in the chair waiting, but she never called."

My god, this poor, poor child.

"Why would she have been on a bus in Asheville?" Ginny's doing all the talking, but the other deputy is scribbling notes like his pen is on fire. "She has a car."

Maisie makes a heroic effort to calm herself, sniffling and wiping her nose. "She went in to check out the temp agencies. We had just moved here from Illinois, and she was looking for work. She wanted me to use the car to stock us up on groceries and cleaning stuff—she gave me a big list—so she had me take her to catch the Galway bus into Asheville, and then she was going to use Asheville city buses to get around town there. Then she was going to take the Galway bus back here and call me to come get her from the station. She never... I haven't heard from her since that morning."

I'm dredging my memory for facts about the bus crash. There

was a lot of speculation about it in the restaurant. The weather was still cold. An Asheville metro bus was broadsided by a drunk driver in an SUV. Both vehicles caught fire, and both drivers and almost all the bus passengers sustained severe injuries. One passenger had been trapped on the bus and died, the body burned beyond recognition. The authorities were fairly sure that the person who died had been a woman in her early to mid-thirties, probably white, but beyond that, without a clue of where to search for dental records or a DNA match, identification was impossible. To add to the mystery, no one reported a person of that description missing.

I remember multiple news reports asking for anyone with information to come forward.

Ginny Lewis must be thinking the same thing. "If you thought that might have been your mom, Maisie, why didn't you contact the police?"

Maisie huddles closer to Sam and looks down at the soggy napkins clenched in her fist. "Because I didn't want to have to go to foster care. I'm almost seventeen. Grandpa left the cabin to me. I can take care of myself."

Brave, stubborn, gutsy girl.

"How can you be sure your mom didn't just take off?" Harsh question, but again Ginny's echoing my own thoughts.

Maisie frowns, ferocious. "My mom would never do that! She would never leave me. If she could come back to me, she would."

Ginny draws a deep breath and blows it out. I suspect she and Joe are as unsettled by these revelations as I am.

After a minute she turns to Sam. "Sam, where do you fit in this picture?"

"I live with Maisie. We take care of each other."

"Are you boyfriend and girlfriend?"

Both Sam and Maisie shake their heads.

Ginny tries again. "What's the deal with your family, Sam? Why don't you live with them, and why would they think you might be in trouble?"

Maisie rolls her eyes and makes a rude noise.

Sam just looks resigned. Maybe a little nauseous. He raises his blue eyes to meet Ginny's gaze. "Because they think I'm demon spawn," he says finally. "They threatened to throw me out because I stopped going to church with them. Then somebody told them I'm gay, and they did throw me out. I've never gotten in any trouble. They just think I'm a sinner, and they don't want me around my little brothers and sisters." He mutters almost to himself, "As if I'd ever hurt them."

I glance at Joe. His expression shifts from bleak to angry to blank.

"How long ago was this?" Ginny's gentle again.

"Winter break."

Jesus Christ. These so-called parents threw their child out in the dead of winter? I want to kill. And cry. And burn things down. I shift so my arm is around Maisie and my hand on Sam's shoulder. On Sam's other side, Joe leans into him too.

Ginny's brows raise. "So you two have been living together all that time?"

Sam shakes his head. "No. I didn't meet Maisie until a little later."

"Where did you live, then, before you moved in with her?"

Sam looks down at his knee, picking at an imaginary spot on his jeans. "Mostly under one of the cabins near Maisie's."

"*Under* the cabin? You were homeless?"

He nods.

I check Joe's expression and find zero surprise there.

"How did the two of you end up living together?"

"Maisie—" Sam breaks off and looks at her. She gazes back, her eyes sad and full of love. "Maisie started going to my school. She was the only person who'd sit with me at lunch. After a while she figured out I was homeless."

Maisie speaks up then, to give him a break, I think. "I was really lonely. And sad and scared. I was trying not to do anything that would make anybody notice me, so I didn't talk to anybody. Sam noticed me but he never gave me any trouble. One day...we had a long talk and found out we knew each other's secrets. He knew I was all alone in the cabin."

Sam takes up the story. "She was afraid I'd freeze to death or starve. She asked me if I wanted to stay in the cabin with her."

Maisie tosses him a tiny smile. "I had to really talk him into it."

"I was filthy... I stank. And Maisie asked me to live with her anyway, and that first night while I was in the bathtub trying to scrub clean, she wrote a little note and put it in the room that's mine now. She wrote, *Welcome home, Sam.* So that's my home now, and Maisie's my family." Sam says it fiercely, looking around at us one by one, daring us to try to separate him from his chosen sister. "We go to school. We go to work. We pay our bills. We don't bother anybody. We take care of each other. We're doing fine."

"Except for Curt," Ginny says dryly.

The two kids fall silent then. The rest of us are quiet too, contemplating the situation. Finally Ginny rises. "I need to make a couple of calls. If y'all don't mind, please wait here."

She heads downstairs. The other officer stays with us in the living room, finishing up his notes and then sitting quietly.

I shift to face the kids. "Listen, I don't know what's going to happen, but y'all will not go through this alone, okay?"

"We'll help." Joe's determined face makes me feel better, so I know it must help the kids some too.

Sam nods, looking stoic, and Maisie gives us a tiny watery smile. Then we sit in silence until Ginny Lewis rejoins us.

She drops into the armchair with a weary sigh. "Okay, here's the deal." She looks from Maisie to Sam. "I can't let y'all stay in the cabin by yourselves. We have to find you some kind of temporary custody. You'll be assigned a caseworker. Maybe two, one for each of you. You probably will have to enter the foster care system, at least temporarily. And a detective from Asheville will be coming to collect a DNA sample from you, Maisie, to see whether it was your mom on that bus. The dates on the phone activity and the bus crash do match up."

"Temporary custody." I've not heard that phrase except maybe in relation to jail. "What does that mean?"

"Somebody who cares about them and can keep them until they enter the system. It's usually a family member or family friend."

Everyone looks at Maisie and Sam, who shake their heads. "I don't have any more family," Maisie says. "My mom ran away when she was fifteen because her family…abused her bad, and she never wanted them to know about me. I don't even know their names. And Grandpa was the last person on my dad's side."

Sam grimaces. "All my family's friends go to their same church. They call gay people an abomination. They wouldn't want me. And even if they said they did, I wouldn't feel safe going with them."

The kids exchange glances and then say at the same time, "We want to stay together."

I can't stand the idea of them being separated after all they've already lost. "Ginny, I know them, and I care about them. If they'd feel safe being with me, can I provide the temporary custody?"

Maisie and Sam look at Ginny. I think that's hope in their eyes.

Ginny stands. "That might work. Let me check."

CHAPTER 19

Dear July,

Remember that day we were joking around about artichokes? Goofy. But I'd trade the rest of my life for one day to be with you somewhere talking about artichokes.

Joe

"I'M NOT SURE HOW I feel about the idea of them filing for legal emancipation." July's stride is as smooth and steady as ever, but there's a tiny furrow between her eyes as she glances over at me.

We're running later than usual on account of having to go with the kids to the cabin where they silently loaded their must-have stuff and perishable food into my truck for the trip back to July's. Then while I collected my air mattress and its bedding for them from my apartment and the kids went back to work, July performed one of her social miracles, summoning people to an emergency meeting. She brought together Angus and Rose, another couple—Meg and David—and two other friends who were a social worker and a family lawyer. Meg and David brought their own three foster kids.

July pushed together a few tables in the dining room and sat us all down with Sam and Maisie to discuss their legal options and to give them a chance to ask questions about foster care. Both Maisie and Sam perked up when the lawyer mentioned the possibility of them petitioning for legal emancipation. "Sam, you're sixteen and you've lived in Galway County your whole life. You could apply for emancipation tomorrow. Maisie, you meet the age requirement, but you'd have to wait until you've been here six full months."

"That's a few more weeks." Maisie cast a glance at July.

July reached out and touched her arm. "That's okay with me."

But the social worker shook her head. "The county probably won't let you stay with July that long, with July not being an approved foster parent and only having one bedroom. You'll probably be in foster care for part of that time."

It's true; July's apartment was feeling pretty crowded when we left a few minutes ago. Sam will be in her bedroom, July will be sleeping on the couch, and Maisie will be on my air mattress in the corner near July's dining table, a folding screen giving her a little privacy.

Now I study July's clean profile as we navigate deserted streets. It was hot and humid all day, and she's in flimsy running shorts and a tank, her golden skin mesmerizing me as we move in and out of the streetlights' glow. "What's bothering you about it?"

Her frown is back. "It's just...I want to support what they want, right? And it's obvious that's what they want. But it seems like...a final declaration that they'll have to fend for themselves. No turning back." She shakes her head, the end of her ponytail whipping in the heavy air. "I was just hoping they'd see how great Meg and David are. How happy their kids are. I want them to have somebody like that to help take care of them and love them."

She's not wrong. David and Meg are young and energetic and obviously adore their three children, who just as obviously return the feeling. But… "Maisie and Sam have been doing a great job taking care of themselves. They seem really proud and happy about that. I think it's important to them."

She sighs. "That and their freedom, I guess."

"Mm-hmm." But I know she's still not convinced.

She turns her head to look at me again. "But what about an emergency? Who will take care of them in an emergency?"

"They'll manage what they can. And we'll be there to help with the rest. We're not abandoning them, July, whatever the courts say. We were already helping some, and now that we know what's going on, we can be more useful."

"Well, that's…true." She sighs again. "I just hate this for them."

"Yeah. It would be better if everybody had a good family." I don't add "like yours" but I know she's thinking about that as we run a block in silence.

We're not quite to our turnaround point yet, but the air feels like we're breathing through a wet towel, and suddenly the street goes white in a brilliant flash of light followed immediately by an earth-shaking boom of thunder. The skies open up, and we're drenched before we can even speak.

I'm grabbing for her arm even as she reaches for me, and we dart into the dubious shelter of a used bookshop doorway. We press back under the shallow overhang, dripping all over ourselves and each other. A foot in front of us, rain comes down in sheets, pounding awnings and vehicles, hissing as it hits the hot street and sidewalk.

"That seemed scary close." But July is laughing, eyes shining, her smile wide and her voice breathless, sharing her joyful relief with me as she reaches up to slick water off her hair.

And just like that, something inside me rises up and rolls over, belly up, begging for her attention, basking in her glow even in dim street light on a stormy night. I slip willingly under her spell like we're in that high school cafeteria all over again. I thought I was done with her.

I'm not.

She's part girl who stole my heart, part miracle-working, sexy as fuck lifesaver of a grown woman, and she's taken full possession of me. And I'm not sure how I feel about that.

"Yeah, we should stay put till the lightning stops at least." I glance away, trying not to think about how close she is. How I can feel the warmth of her bare skin next to me. How I'd like to smooth the rain droplets on her face one by one with my fingertips. Kiss them off of her neck. Suck them off her lips. Lick them…

Shit.

She clears her throat. "What were we talking about?"

If her voice was shaky, mine's a croak. "Emancipation."

"Yeah. So…if they decide to petition for that, do you think we should support them?" She's holding herself a little away from me, watching water rushing and gurgling in the gutters.

"Yeah."

She looks so sad I reach out and touch her bare shoulder. "It's not like we're cutting them off from anybody they've got now. And we're here if they need help."

She nods. The storm seems to have dropped the temperature by twenty degrees. Goose bumps have formed on her exposed skin. The tiny blond hairs of her nape and her arms are standing on end.

I can't pretend not to see. "Cold?"

"Not too bad." But her teeth chatter.

I turn and pull her to me, wrapping my arms around her, rubbing my hands up and down her back, the way I've wanted to all night.

"Oh god." She sighs. Drops her head to my shoulder. "How can you be so warm? You're not wearing much more than I am, and you don't have as much padding."

I don't answer. I love her padding, and I'm not sure I can speak, with her breath tickling my ear and our bodies pressing together and my renewed feelings filling me up to my eyes.

She sighs again. "I just want...the world to be better. So kids like Sam and Maisie don't have to think about supporting themselves before they're even done being kids."

I rub her arms, my hands sliding over the silk of her skin, the sensation comforting *me*. "I'm surprised you don't have a bunch of kids of your own, the way you like taking care of everybody."

She shrugs. "Never really thought about it. There's a lot of other things I want to do."

"Like?"

"Stuff for Galway. Make it a place where we take better care of each other." She raises her hands, rests them at my waist. It feels tentative, like a butterfly that might take off if I move.

"Stuff you want to do for other people, then." I keep my movements slow and easy, but in a minute, I'm going to have to ease away from her or shift position so she can't feel that I'm getting hard while she's trying to talk to me about important things.

"Yeah, I guess." Her voice is soft. Dreamy.

I lift my face from her hair and look in her eyes. "I get that. But what do you want for yourself?"

Her gaze flickers from my eyes to my mouth and back.

Christ. If I'm going to have a hope of loosening my hold, of moving away instead of pressing closer, it's got to be now.

July

"But what do you want for yourself?"

The man I've dreamed about all my life, the guy who is a hero to kids and everything I've ever wanted in a lover and companion, and who has his warm hands on me *right this minute*, has a hell of a lot of nerve asking me that when I've been doing such a goddamn fantastic job of respecting what he said about not wanting me anymore. Of not asking or hoping for more. Of admiring him chastely from afar.

Well, from at least a foot or two away.

But at this moment, our bodies might as well be one, and his body says he's not any more unaffected by it than I am.

The world seems hushed as I gaze at him, first into his mountain stream eyes and then at that mouth I know can be both gentle and hungry. His hands slow on me and mine pull him closer.

"What do you want for yourself?" I want you, Joe. I've always wanted you. Even when fear and exhaustion make me do stupid things. I've always wanted you.

His lips are two inches, one inch from mine, I'm raising up on the balls of my feet, and he should really pull back if he isn't interested in me anymore because I am fixing to kiss the hell and the foolish, dangerous questions right out of him...

And then a bright light that is not lightning illuminates us both.

"Everything okay here, Ms. Tate?"

I pivot away from Joe, squinting and holding up one hand to block the light so I can see who's talking.

Jimmy Moran. A young guy I used to babysit for, grinning cheekily at us from his police cruiser. The rain has stopped, and I don't have a clue when that happened.

Jimmy turns off the bright light, still looking mighty pleased with himself.

Brat. "Everything's fine, Jimmy. Since when do you call me Ms. Tate?"

"Since I became a public servant, ma'am, dedicated to public safety and stuff."

I feel my eyebrows shoot up. "Oh, now you're *ma'am*-ing me. What'd I do to piss you off, Jimmy?"

"You broke my heart, Ms. Tate. You promised you'd wait and marry me, and now I find you kissing some strange guy in a doorway."

I feel the blush creep over my face as I spare a glance at Joe, who still has his hands on me and is looking from Jimmy to me with interest. And a smirk. "I'm not kissing him. And he's not *that* strange."

Joe snorts and lets go of me.

I don't like it, but it brings me back to my senses. I focus on the smart-ass in the patrol car. "And besides, you were only eight when I said that, Jimmy. And I was only fourteen."

Officer Jimmy shakes his head sadly. "A promise is a promise, Ms. Tate."

"You're almost thirty now, Jimmy. I waited as long as I could, but you never came around to make good on your proposal. I suggest it was *my* heart that was broken, and that if I *were* kissing Joe here, which I was *not*, it would not be an act of unfaithfulness."

Jimmy rubs his chin, looking thoughtful. "I don't know, July;

that didn't look like a not-kiss to me. Lotta leaning going on there. Looked like you were about to really lay one on each other."

I shake my head. "Jimmy, we were sheltering from the storm. That's all." I feel a little queasy at the realization of how close I had come to making Joe have to reject me again.

"I don't think it's legal to fib to an officer of the law, Ms. Tate." Jimmy lifts one hand, palm up, and shakes his head sadly when no rain falls in it.

"You're cutting into my evening here, Jimmy. Just tell me straight out. How long before this story is all over town?"

"I get off in five minutes, Ms. Tate."

"So...say, six, six and a half minutes?"

"Sounds about right, ma'am."

"I'm gonna tell your mom you were hassling me, Jimmy."

"No need, ma'am, she's gonna be my first call."

I drop my chin and give him my fiercest babysitter glare. "You've grown up to be a real pain in my ass, Jimmy."

"Yes, ma'am." He grins and puts the car in gear. "Y'all have a nice night." He drives away and I can't tell who's smirking harder, Officer Jimmy or Joe.

I shove Joe's arm. "You're both a pain in my ass."

He laughs. "It's pretty cool how you know everybody. But I can definitely see how it could grow to be a pain in the ass."

He steps out from under the overhang and tilts his head in the direction of home. I square my shoulders and follow him out. Our wet shoes make squishing noises as we run.

"Why'd you invite Rose and Angus to the meeting tonight?" His voice is light. Easy.

I'm glad he's restarting the conversation because I wouldn't have been able to, not with the feel of him holding me so fresh in my mind. "Rose because I thought she might know about something relevant going on in Galway." She used to ask *me* for town and county information, but she's worked hard, and now she's the expert everyone goes to. "Angus just because…well, one, he's a therapist, and two, if anything needs to be done to the cabin to make it safer or to help it weather the time until the kids can move back in, he'd be my first choice of someone to do it."

Joe glances over at me. "You planning on paying him, or would he do it for free?"

"Probably a little bit of both. The kids almost certainly couldn't afford him. But he almost certainly wouldn't charge them his usual rate."

"And what if they need a lawyer? You going to pay for that too?" This time he keeps his eyes on the street in front of us.

"Yeah."

"I'll help." His voice is firm.

"You don't have to do that, Joe. I'm the one who called a lawyer in tonight. I'm the one responsible for them right now."

He laughs. "And we were *just* talking about how we'd both be there for them if they need us. Even if they get emancipated. I'll split it with you."

Guess I better get used to the idea of supporting the kids' quest for emancipation. And of having someone to help me with that.

We run the last few blocks in silence.

He doesn't repeat his question about what I want for myself. If he knows I was about to kiss him, he doesn't let on. If he's sorry I didn't, I sure can't see any sign of it. Thank god for Officer Jimmy, interrupting a mistake that would have resulted in my heart breaking all over again.

I'm such a freaking snowflake.

CHAPTER 20

July

DAVID AND MEG MUST HAVE contacted Galway County
Foster Services right after our emergency meeting at the restaurant. Maisie and Sam are only with me for a couple of days before
we load their stuff back into Joe's truck for the drive up to Meg
and David's rambling new house high in the hills on the far side
of the lake, where there's plenty of room for even more kids, in
case Meg has quintuplets or she and David decide to foster half
the kids in the county.

Two days after the move, the DNA results come back, confirming that the unidentified woman who died in the bus crash
was Maisie's mom. Maisie is at work when Ginny Lewis brings
the news.

We all crowd around, Donna hugging her especially tightly,
Tina handing Maisie tissues and helping Sam hold her as she cries,
Sonya's and my eyes welling up as we join the swaying, clutching
huddle.

"I hate knowing she's really gone," Maisie forces out on a sob, before gathering herself and standing straighter. "But I knew she wouldn't have left me."

Not a dry eye in that kitchen for the rest of the shift.

————————

It's a perfect day at the lake, the sky deep blue overhead, the greens of the forest and hills layered around the gentle ripples of the water. Somewhere nearby something is flowering, its sweet scent mingling with the smell of rich earth. A light breeze tugs at my skirt and musses Joe's hair. I grip my hands together tighter to keep from smoothing it back down with my fingers.

It's a Sunday, and I closed the restaurant a couple of hours early so we could all spend the afternoon up here at the cabin. This memorial was Meg and David's idea, and although there have been tears, there have also been laughter and good memories and hope. We're telling stories about Maisie's mom. Well, Maisie is, because none of the rest of us knew her mom, although I do contribute the tale of the day I met them and they tried to make me say whose driver's license photo was worse. That seems like a lifetime ago.

Maisie is still having to wipe an occasional teardrop from her cheek, but some of them are catching in the corners of her smile. Every time she finishes a story and falls silent, Sam or one of Meg and David's kids prods her with, "Tell them what you told me about when your mom…"

Sam, of course, is right there beside her, like a good brother should be.

God, I'm crying myself. I dip my head and shove a hand into my pocket for a tissue. I feel Joe's hand hovering at my back, not quite touching me, just a trace of warmth.

He must see me as weak now that he knows about my break-down. Poor July, liable to snap at any moment. My stomach drops at the thought. He doesn't even know the whole story.

Movement nearby brings me out of my thoughts. David is murmuring something to Ruby, the second-youngest of the foster kids. Joe whispers something to Rose. A couple of the restaurant night crew members head inside the cabin, probably to start laying out food. Birds chirp and rustle overhead as the rest of us shift, at Meg's direction, over to a spot under an enormous loblolly pine where someone has placed a small concrete statue of a serious-looking child with angel wings. Meg, one hand deep in a canvas bag, turns to her newest foster daughter. "Maisie, we wanted to do something to help you remember your mom. The kids and I picked out this statue, and Joe and Rose have brought some flowers to plant around it."

The group parts with a murmur to allow Rose and Joe to step through with a flat of rich, velvety pansies and a bag of potting soil. David and Ruby are right behind them with a guitar. Meg pulls hand trowels and garden kneeling pads from the bag and passes them to Sam, Maisie, Joe, and Rose. Meg's voice is softer when she continues. "Ruby told David you've been singing her a good-night song your mom used to sing you. She wanted David to help her sing it to you today."

I've heard David sing before—he's a songwriter and a member of Galway's favorite hometown band, the Blue Shoes—but I've never heard him do anything like this. As the four flower plant-ers kneel around the statue and Rose shows them how to gently loosen the pansies from their plastic containers, how to gently separate and spread the roots so the little plants will be able to absorb nutrition from the soil, how to dig just deep enough to have them level with the surrounding earth, David begins to pick out a slow, simple tune on his guitar. Three rising notes, repeated and lazy.

It takes me a minute to recognize the song. Years ago, Andi and I went through a Dixie Chicks phase, where we learned every word to every one of their songs. They're the Chicks now, and David's low voice is a lot different from Natalie Maines's sweet tones, but the song is "Lullaby," and it's beautiful. My heart and my throat clench as little Ruby joins David, her voice as pure and sweet as only a child's can be.

It's not clear whether the song is for a baby or a lover, but whoever it's addressing, the singer is full of wonder at this amazing, cherished person they're singing to, asking them how long they want to be loved. And whether forever would be long enough.

Ruby takes over the melody, and David drops back to an almost-whispered harmony and echo. Melly, Meg and David's youngest, edges forward to stand beside Maisie as she works. Julian, the older brother of the two little girls, places himself between Sam and Maisie, standing straight and vigilant, awkwardly, vulnerably protective of his new older siblings.

How did these wonderful people come up with such perfect, heart-stretching ideas for this day? When did they plan this? I hear a soft sigh from Tina beside me, see her hand tighten on Donna's, as Ruby and David sing the last verse, which seems like a parent stepping back, assuming a guardian angel role, watching her beloved child venture into the world alone to discover new things. Reminding that child that she's always loved. Always.

The music rises around us as the gardeners finish their work. Maisie is crying softly, tears dripping into the soil she gently presses down around the little flowers.

The Chicks' lyrics become a different question in my mind.
Instead of *How long...?* I'm hearing *What do you want for yourself?* and I'm back under that overhang with Joe in the rain, lust
and honesty rising in me, almost forcing me into a mistake that
would have only broken my heart. Because you can break things
that seemed like forever if you hurt someone enough. If you selfishly destroy their trust.

But god help me, as I watch Maisie sit back on her heels and
reach for Ruby and Melly to wrap them in a hug so tight I think
we all feel it, I see Joe, quiet in the background, a few salty droplets of his own on the dirty hands he's wiping on his jeans, and
I think if only I could undo what I've done to hurt him, forever
might just be enough.

Maybe.

Joe

I don't know where the hell they got that song, but goddamn, it's
still ringing through me long after we've finished the planting.
Long after we've carefully watered the new little flowers and gone
inside to wash up and fill plates from the potluck feast that covers
the kitchen counters.

Ruby's high, sweet little voice and David's soft harmony singing those words had me right back in the high school cafeteria
the first day I saw July. Right back in the steakhouse my very
first day of work, watching July ring up a little old lady whose
lipstick mouth was drawn way outside her real lips and who visibly brightened when July lifted her tray and carried it for her,
talking and laughing the whole way, to a prime little table by the

salad bar. I was right back in the middle of our first date here at the lake, when July didn't laugh at my ratty old truck or turn her nose up at warm pop and a can of mostly broken chips.

She was a miracle to me. A rare, impossibly good, magical creature willing to beam that warm smile on anybody who needed it, just because. And I had never in my life seen anyone or had anything like that, and goddamn, I needed it. I soaked it up, every drop, as if my whole life up to that point was a desert and July was my first rain shower.

Forever was—is—exactly what I want from her.

The whole restaurant crew is here, night shift and day shift, along with Rose and Angus, David and Meg, and a buttload of kids. Several people brought folding tables and chairs, and we've settled at them outside so the kids can run around and play after they eat.

Ruby and Melly and Julian, though, stick close by their new foster sister and brother, asking them questions we adults could never get away with. We duck our heads, focus on our plates, and listen for all we're worth as the little ones ferret out more of Sam and Maisie's story.

"Did you really live here all by yourself?" Melly cranes her neck to look around the clearing.

When Maisie and Sam nod, Ruby says, "But you didn't have the same mommy?"

"Nope," the older kids answer together.

The serious-eyed boy, Julian, speaks up. "How did you start living together?"

"Well, first we had kind of a fight…" Maisie laughs a little, looking at Sam.

He explains. "We were kind of friends before, but not really.

We just sat together at lunch. Sometimes we rode the school bus together."

"What'd you fight about?" Melly again.

"We figured out each other's secrets"—Maisie gestures with a carrot stick—"but we were both afraid the other one would tell on us."

Ruby frowns. "Were you doing something bad?"

Maisie shakes her head. "No, but we didn't want grown-ups to know we were living by ourselves because we were afraid they'd make us go live with a bad family."

The younger kids eat quietly for a few minutes, then Julian asks, "But why did you fight?"

Sam fields this one. "Maisie figured out I didn't have any place to live. But when she asked me about it, I was afraid she was going to tell somebody, so I said, 'Oh, yeah? Well, I know you're living all alone in that cabin without any grown-ups.' I wanted her to think that if she told anybody my secret, I'd tell hers. I thought that would make her not want to tell on me."

Maisie must see Melly's confused expression. "Sam wasn't really mad at me. But he was scared so it sounded like he was."

Sam nods. "But then we started talking and told each other our stories, and then Maisie asked me if I'd come live with her."

Maisie laughs. "At first he didn't want to. He made up all these reasons why he couldn't."

"Why?" Julian's brow is furrowed.

Maisie looks at Sam, who answers quietly. He's so patient; he must have been a great brother to his biological siblings. "I'd been living outside. Everything I had was in two plastic garbage bags and it was all dirty. I didn't have any way to do laundry." He toys with the crust from his turkey sandwich. "I was embarrassed to bring my dirty stuff into Maisie's cabin. I was afraid I'd make everything smell bad and she'd be sorry she asked me in. I could take a shower in the gym on school days, but then I'd have to put my dirty clothes back on. I didn't want to mess up Maisie's place. And I didn't want to be a charity case."

"What's that?" Melly, of course.

"It's when somebody gives you something, but you don't have anything to give them back." He glances sideways at Maisie.

She nods. "Sam's very nice and very stubborn. I had to really talk him into moving in. I had to tell him how lonely I'd been, living alone with nobody to talk to. And how scared I got sometimes, especially at night. I had to convince him that he *did* have something to give me. He'd be making me feel safer and less lonely. He'd be somebody I could talk to without worrying about giving away my secret."

Julian's still frowning. Boy's a thinker. "How did you figure out each other's secrets?"

Beside me, July's knuckles are white, she's clenching her fist so tightly. I know just how she feels. When I nudge her hand with one finger, she glances at it and then holds on.

Maisie and Sam exchange glances. Maisie speaks first. "Sam had been sleeping up here under a different cabin. He didn't want to get caught, so he paid real close attention to who was nearby. These are mostly summer vacation cabins, and it was winter, so I was the only person around besides him. There weren't any grown-ups. He didn't know why I was alone, but he could tell I was."

Sam takes over. "Maisie didn't know where I was sleeping, but she noticed I was always dirty. She knew I didn't eat lunch... I'd just sit and draw. And then one day, she came back into the cafeteria after lunch to get something she'd forgotten and"—Sam draws in a big breath—"she caught me eating pizza from a trash can."

It's a miracle none of us adults gasp.

Leave it to the littlest one to speak with honesty. "Ew, why were you doing that?"

Sam looks at her, his blue eyes serious. "It was the only way I could get food."

July squeezes my hand so tight I can tell we're going to have to draw straws for the honor of killing Sam's worthless-ass parents.

"I didn't have any money. There are places that will give meals to homeless people"—Sam flicks a warm glance at July—"but I was afraid to go. They might think I was too young to be on my own and try to make me go…live with a bad family. So every day I'd wait till the other kids left the cafeteria, and then I'd go to one of the fuller trash cans and take out as much food as I could, real fast. I'd eat some of it right there and put some in my backpack for later. I could only take stuff that wouldn't spoil right away. On Fridays I'd try to take more, but I usually couldn't get enough to last through a weekend, and unless it was really cold out, it went bad or got all full of bugs before Monday anyway. So on Mondays I was always really hungry."

Sam sets the crust back on his plate. "I tried to get a job so I could buy food. I put in applications everywhere I could think of, but nobody was hiring. And then after a week or two, all my clothes were dirty and were starting to smell bad, and people didn't even want me in their stores. Nobody would even talk to me about hiring me by then. So…I ate out of trash cans."

There's absolute silence at the tables. And there it is. Sam's just given me my life's mission. All the damn times I've heard people say, "Get a job!" as if that's an easy answer to homelessness. As if homeless people should have to eat garbage if they can't find work. I'm a goddamn chef on his way into social work, with a building just waiting to be put to good use. I'm going to open some type of shelter for kids in trouble. Feed 'em. Have a shower and a washer and dryer they can use. A safe place to rest and keep up on schoolwork.

July flinches and I realize I'm gripping her hand too tightly.

I let loose and lean forward to whisper, "Want to go see our old rock?" I need to be alone, or alone with her.

Adults have taken up the conversation, and David and Meg's kids join the others in a game of tag. I know Rose and Angus and Donna and Tina and Sonya see July and me slip away to the trail, but nobody says a word.

No sooner are we out of sight of the clearing than July doubles over, arms hugging her midsection, a gasping sob wrenching out of her. I pull her into my arms, feeling the outrage and sadness vibrating through her. "My god, Joe," she says into my shoulder, her fingers clenching my T-shirt as I rub her back.

Sometimes it seems like the whole world sucks, like everything is a battle, but this one instant of this one afternoon, with this woman in my arms, turning to *me* for comfort…this is how it's supposed to be. July and I together against all the hard, cold things of the world.

The circles I'm rubbing turn into hearts, and I wonder if she notices. I murmur nonsense in her ear. Her harsh breathing calms bit by bit.

"Thanks, Joe." She laughs a little, shakily, and eases her grip on my shirt.

There are tears on her cheeks, and I raise both hands to wipe them away. Lean in to press her forehead with my own. Open my mouth to offer my undying love and seal it with a kiss... No, to kiss her first and *then* declare my undying love...

But before I can do either, she's out of my arms and striding up the path, calling back, "I haven't been up here since a week after you left. I wonder if it's changed..."

She's read my intentions and is rejecting them firmly, kindly, · before I can embarrass myself.

CHAPTER 21

Dear July,

*When I got home today, my dad was beating my mom. Again.
I grabbed him and threw him across the kitchen. He hit the
cabinet, maybe broke his nose? His damn turn to bleed. I've
never been able to do that before. Might've scared him. He
yelled some shit but didn't come at us again. Just stomped
out. Then I got to hear my mom try to justify the things
he does. Try to make me "understand." I fucking understand
everything just fine. I fucking hate this life.*

Joe

THE QUESTION I'M WRESTLING WITH, as I drive to our last
ball game, is whether friendship is the most I can hope for with
July. I thought at least she still wanted me for sex, and hell, it isn't
what I want but…friendship with benefits with July would be
way more—and way better—than anything I've ever had with
anybody else. And I thought the other night in the rain she was
wanting to kiss me. But no, apparently body heat and the momen-
tary comfort of hugs and hand squeezes is as far as it goes.

Nothing special here, Joe. Move along.

I mean, I figured she'd never feel the way she used to. But somewhere deep inside me, some little spark of hope kept burning until she ducked away on the path at the lake.

But I'm not leaving Galway again. Maybe...maybe July's just not there yet.

Besides, I want to open that youth shelter *here*. I like Galway, and my building is really growing on me. My research has given me some great ideas for fitting out the downstairs with a computer/homework area, a table for eating and gathering, a kitchenette with a Crock-Pot, sandwiches, and fresh fruit and vegetables right there so hungry kids can help themselves. A stacking washer and dryer beside the restroom, where I'll add a shower. Maybe I'll put in an area for some kind of dance game in the front room. Bookshelves with fiction and school resources... Maybe I can work with the school district and Rose's organization to make sure I've got current textbooks.

It's almost exciting enough to distract me from the thought of living and working so close to the woman I love, who already has five times more friends than she knows what to do with and who counts me as just another one.

But I've got friends here now too. And I can make more.

Maybe some of the team would want to have a regular hangout night. Get together every week or two for a beer or something. Maybe I'll see if Rose and Angus want to go to dinner in Asheville with me one week, eat at that Spanish place I've heard so much about. As long as I'm good to July, Rose won't plot my death, and as long as I don't flirt too hard with Rose, Angus won't take me apart with his bare hands.

Tonight's the last time I have to stand behind July with a

front-row view of her body moving with power and grace while I remind myself to keep my drool inside my head. That'll be tough, since I've held her recently enough to be able to close my eyes and map her contours with my hands, recreate my memories of where she's the warmest, where she's the softest, and just where her breath teases my throat when she's in my arms.

Jesus, it's going to be a rough night.

I park alongside Dirk's pickup and shoulder my bag. Dirk's already warming up with Hiromi, but Tom needs a partner. To my surprise, he holds up a ball and raises his eyebrows at me. At my nod, he tosses it easy at first, and then harder each time, soon with more zing than is strictly necessary for warm-up.

But maybe that's just a shortstop thing. He's been okay lately. Guess he can tell he's got nothing to fear from me where July is concerned.

She's almost late. Comes jogging up at the last minute, breathless, and joins Andi and the catcher where they're throwing, over by the parking lot. I try to keep my focus off her, but my damn brain and eyes and assorted other parts are having none of it. Gets worse when we take the field and I'm behind her, forced to look in her direction so I know what's going on in the game. I practically feel every one of her movements, her sprints toward the ball, her dips to scoop it up, her smooth, powerful throws. It's like she's pressed against me so that my body gives whenever and wherever she needs space. She steals my breath from fifty feet away.

I grit my teeth and do my job. It's a low-scoring game, but we take a one-run lead and hold it. Then, in the bottom of the last inning, with two outs and a speedy runner on second, the other team's cleanup batter steps up to the plate.

"Let's go now!" Tom yells. "One more out to keep our streak."

In the dugout during our last at bat, I heard him say something to Hiromi about this being the team's third undefeated season in a row...if we win this one. We need to get this batter out before the runner on second can score. I yank my focus off July and concentrate on the batter. No way am I going to be the cause of us breaking the streak.

The guy pops a mile-high foul outside the third base line almost exactly halfway between July and me.

"Mine!" She charges after it—a foul fly ball is as good as a fair one for an out—and I'm moving to back her up when I see the barrel.

What jackass would position a giant metal trash can so close to the field, in playable foul territory?

July's headed towards it at top speed, but since she's running backwards, it's in her blind spot. She's going to catch that ball—no doubt in my mind about that—and then she's going to hit the rim of that monster can at her rib level and hurt herself bad.

It's too late for me to call her off of the ball. I move between her and the barrel, putting the warm metal against my back, and when July's glove closes over that fly ball and she hits me like a truck, I wrap my arms around her and hold on. The can tips and we flip over it, through a shower of used water bottles, crushed candy wrappers, and soggy napkins.

My liver—or maybe that's a spleen—is not going to be happy with me later, but July holds her glove high to show the umps she's still got the ball, and when she turns to me, her expression incredulous, and says, "Joe, you colossal doofus, are you okay?" all I can do is laugh.

Just wipe a piece of mustard-smeared hot dog bun off my forehead and laugh.

And when the umpire calls the game for us and July hauls me up with her free hand and the team gathers around to make sure we're really both okay, I feel as good as I can feel under the circumstances. Because I helped her win the game for us and because she's okay and because I've got another memory of the two of us together to add to my pathetic collection.

July

The man is a complete and total whack job.

Or maybe I am.

I *cannot* make sense of him. Why did he risk getting hurt like that? Can he just not resist being a hero? Putting his body between me and that stupid trash can... I outweigh him by probably fifty pounds, and I hit him like a freight train. Flipped him end over end. How freaking embarrassing.

And he lay there laughing.

I park in my spot in the alley and head for Lindon's for our team celebration. I'm halfway there before I realize I'm still wearing my cleats. Joe's messed up my mind. Again.

And what the hell was that on the trail the other day? It almost seemed as if he was going to kiss me. But I know *that* can't be right...unless... Oh god. What if it was going to be a pity kiss because I'd been crying?

My long-ago dinner rolls in my belly. The thought of him donating a charity kiss to poor, fragile, upset July makes me want to vomit all over the sidewalk. That would have been the worst. It would leave me with no pride. Surely he knows that wouldn't have been a good thing, right?

I'm shaking my head, one hand on my stomach, when I get to Lindon's. Andi's a few steps ahead of me and holds the door.

"Interesting play you and Joe made there at the end," she says in my ear.

"Shut up."

She laughs. "You okay, really? No injuries from your crash?"

"I'm fine. But he's clearly got something wrong with him."

"Yeah? What's that?" Her tone is a lazy drawl. "Because I'm having trouble seeing it. Makes a woman rethink her commitment to singlehood. If you don't make a move on him soon, July…"

I swivel my head so fast I get a crick in my neck. Another reason to glare at her.

Andi throws up her hands, laughing. "Kidding! Seriously though, what in the hell is stopping you now? You've gotta see he's warmed up. Way, way up."

I wish. I shake my head. "Nah. It's just…we're friends now. We bonded over a couple of kids in trouble."

She nods as we head to the bar. Several of our teammates are shoving tables together in one corner, so we'll grab beer. "Rose mentioned something about that."

"Since when did you two get so cozy?" They're both my friends, and two of my favorite people in the world, and both of them could use another good friend. I just don't like the idea of them talking about Joe and me.

Not that there's a Joe and me.

Andi shrugs. "She's helping with something for the shelter. Roof sprang a leak a little earlier than my budget allowed."

"Oh no! Anything I can do to help?"

"Nope. Thanks. We've got it covered." Andi gives our order to the bartender.

By the time we join our group with two pitchers and two fistfuls of empty mugs, most of the team is there. They've saved us seats between Joe and Tom. I take the one next to Tom, ignoring Andi's raised eyebrows. After a second, she settles beside Joe.

I busy my hands pouring and passing.

Hiromi holds her mug up for a toast. "To July...and Joe...who kept us from a shit show that last inning!"

Everybody laughs and pretends to pick trash off our hair and clothing. Joe says something smart-ass—I can't make out the words, but I'm sure he was self-deprecating—and then everybody's reliving the season, bringing up all their favorite plays and hits and umpire calls.

This has always been a great group. Nice people, good sports, lots of laughter. This season is better, though, because Joe's joined us. I don't think it's just me who thinks so.

I sip my beer and watch Dirk and Andi giving him a hard time about a game where he got a triple because he just didn't stop running. The other team kept throwing the ball a minute too late, and he'd be halfway to the next base.

"Wonder if I'd be that fast if I were that scrawny?" Tom says, beside me.

"He's not scrawny." The words are out of my mouth before I think about it. "He's just really...lean."

Compact and cut is what Joe is. Not a bit of extra. I haven't seen him without a shirt on since he's been back, but I've been pressed up against him enough times to feel the ridges of his body, his hard pecs and biceps. God knows I've seen those tennis star legs of his enough lately.

Something flips low in my belly, and a little growl comes out of my mouth. I have to cover it by clearing my throat and taking a quick swallow of beer.

Conversations swirl around me. On my right, Tom's talking to the catcher and the right fielder about looking for a new car. Across the table our two pitchers are squabbling about which of the umpires is the fairest behind the plate. And to my left I hear Joe say, "So do you all get together through the year, or just during softball season?"

Hiromi eases her ponytail band down her silky hair, setting the shining mass free. She eyes Joe as Dirk and everyone else looks at her gorgeous hair. "You know, we should do that. We could get together here every week or two."

"Yeah," Dirk breathes. "Let's do that." Poor guy has been head-over-heels in love with Hiromi for at least two years. I'm not sure she's noticed.

Beside me, Andi shrugs. "I'm in."

Joe smiles at her before his eyes slide to me.

"I'm in," says Tom, not to be left out of anything involving his own team. "When I can, of course." It wouldn't do for us to think he's not a busy, busy man.

One by one, everybody agrees. Joe is still looking at me, and Andi turns to look too.

"Sounds fun." What else can I say? It probably won't be any more torture than running with him every night.

Hiromi tosses her hair back, gives Joe her best smile—a damn pretty one—and clinks her mug with his. "It's a date, then. Wednesday nights at Lindon's."

He smiles down at her, his eyes crinkling in that way I've always loved.

Okay then, I take it back. Seeing him with other women will be much, much worse than running with him.

But I wanted him to find a home here. Friends. People he could turn into family, so that he wouldn't be so alone. And I've succeeded.

Yay me.

I take part in exactly three more conversations, and then I mumble something about needing to go shower the garbage off of me.

Joe turns those bright eyes on me as I stand, but then he blinks back down to hear what Hiromi is saying.

And I slip out the door. I may not enjoy the idea of Joe getting close to other women, but I guess it's preferable to having him aim pity kisses at me.

CHAPTER 22

Dear July,

I didn't mean to write about that. I meant to do my usual thing where I tell you that I miss you so much it feels like my heart is being ripped out. Then I meant to ask you again how you're doing, and then I meant to beg you again to write me back. I'm sorry. I'm feeling really, really bad tonight. I really need you to write, July. Please.

Joe

"HEY, JOE. WHATCHA DOIN'?"

A big family-sized van slows beside me, and a grinning Maisie waves out a back window. Sam and Meg and David and the three younger kids look at me with interest too.

"Want a ride?" David must've hit some button inside because the side door slides open.

Maisie unbuckles her safety belt and scoots around the seat to join Julian and Ruby in the wayback, making room for me.

"Thanks." I hop in, stow the plastic bags I'm carrying, and fasten the belt so as not to be a bad example.

We've only got three blocks to go, but I'm glad for the ride. It's a scorcher out. Probably wasn't smart of me to try carrying fifteen pounds of raw meat in this heat, even if it was only a seven-block walk.

The younger kids are so excited at the prospect of swimming that Meg has to raise her voice, laughing, to make sure they all put sunscreen on before they got in the van.

It's Sunday and a perfect day for a pool party. Rose had pounded on my door Friday at lunchtime, and when I answered she handed me four grocery bags full of raw sirloins and ground beef. "The Sam and Maisie support group meeting has been moved to our house Sunday. Three o'clock. This is your contribution." When I peeked into the bags at the meat, she added, "July says you were great on the grill at the steakhouse and that you're a genius at seasonings now." She waved her hand at the bags. "Do something with that, will you? Marinate it or dry rub it or whatever. Angus says you'll be helping him grill it Sunday."

She was gone before I even got a word out.

So I did my thing with the meat, and then yesterday I went to the farmer's market in Asheville and came home with a beautiful selection of peppers and onions and mushrooms which are now ready for grilling along with the meat. And a few minutes ago, I loaded it all back into bags and set out for Angus and Rose's.

July had pointed their house out to me on one of our runs. It's an immaculately kept little Victorian just a few blocks off the square. Apparently Rose and Angus fell in love when she hired him to do renovations. "They have me to thank for that." July flashed me that grin that melts my knees. "I recommended him to her. So yay me!"

We haven't run since the last softball game. At first she claimed soreness from our collision with the trash can, but by last night I was pretty sure she was coming up with reasons to avoid me.

I won't pretend that doesn't hurt.

Maybe today I can show her it's okay, I get it, we're just friends. If I act normal enough—polite without being too friendly, disinterested without being rude—maybe I can at least have my running buddy back.

Or maybe for the next twenty years, we'll avoid each other except for the occasional can't-skip gathering like this one.

She's in Rose's kitchen when we get there, the two of them laughing over some joke we just missed. Rose is stirring a bowl of corn and black bean and tomato salsa. July is moving what looks like cheesy potato puffs from Tupperware containers onto baking sheets.

"We can just pop these into the oven a few minutes before we're ready—" She breaks off when she sees me, but Meg and David's family streams in with Sam and Maisie, everybody carrying some kind of food, before an awkward silence can form.

"Joe, Angus is outside." Rose waves me to the back door.

I step out into an area that could be straight out of a magazine. "Wow." A lattice-shaded flagstone patio stretches across the back of the house, leading to a big in-ground pool surrounded by flagstones surrounded by beautiful plantings surrounded by privacy fencing. It's like a private tropical resort.

"Like it? Rosie designed it and we did it all ourselves, except for the pool." Angus steps out from behind the grill and surveys the yard.

"Nice!" I guess I'd look satisfied if I built paradise with the love of my life too. But I'm not going to think about that today. I hold up the bags. "Meat."

He takes one and peers inside, sniffing. "What'd you do to it?"

"Magic."

He snorts and leads me over to the grill. "You'll be in charge, but I'm going to stand here with you and look busy."

His reason becomes clear as the back door bursts open and the kids race out, Sam and Maisie behind them warning, "Don't run near the pool!"

Another minute and David comes out too. He keeps one eye on the kids, who have shed their T-shirts. Julian and Melly are navigating the stairs at the shallow end, but Ruby's having none of that. She does a cannonball that splashes everybody within range.

David closes his eyes, tips his head back, and laughs. "Want me to put up the net?"

Angus shakes his head. "Give 'em a few minutes to get some of that energy out. Then I'll help you." He points at a big cooler in the shade. "Help yourselves. Plenty of soda and beer in there. Cans. We don't bring glass out here."

The women come out then. They root through the cooler for drinks, then settle on lounge chairs on the far side of the pool, pulling off their swimsuit cover-ups and passing around a jumbo tube of sunscreen.

July's suit makes me want to smile and cry at the same time. It's not revealing and it's very practical—a snug tank with skinny straps and drawstring shorts with dolphins on them—but her silky skin begs for my mouth and hands. Maybe a little bit of teeth. I have to force my eyes away from her as she smooths on the lotion.

"You look like you need a cold one," Angus mutters as he and David step around me to set up the net for water volleyball.

Christ. He's not wrong. I fish out a Fat Tire from the cooler and try to look busy at the grill. "How long before you want us to eat, Rose?"

"Give the kids a few minutes before you start grilling. Don't wanna have to pull them out of the pool right away." She raises her Coke to me in an air-toast.

Angus comes back over when everyone else gets in the pool for a quick volleyball game. After a few minutes, I put the meat on the grill and try not to be too obvious about where my attention really is.

"Jesus, dude, just ask her out." Angus's low rumble lets me know I failed.

"Nah, man, she..." I shake my head. "Just nah."

"Why the hell not? Why waste time?" He sounds genuinely curious.

"She's not interested. I thought maybe she was...but I was wrong." Don't know why I'm telling him this.

He frowns a little, his eyes on the way I've arranged the meat on the grill. "Did you actually ask her?"

"No, but I..." *Huh.* No, I did not. "Sorta."

He cocks one brow at me. "You've had something with her in the past. There's still *some*thing between you."

"Something. Yeah."

"And you want something more." He cocks his other brow.

I just stare back at him.

"We're not kids anymore. Just ask her." He glances toward the pool. "She's it, right? Your person?"

I don't give permission but my head's nodding anyway. Reluctantly.

"Don't waste a minute of that, man." His eyes are on Rose.

She seems to feel it. Looks over, gives him a little wave and a brilliant smile. And the giant, scary dude beside me melts. His whole face softens and he smiles back at her.

What the fuck am I doing?

————————

July

When Joe and I got together the first time, everything seemed so easy. He asked me out not long after he started working at the steakhouse. We spent time together every day—usually at the lake, talking for hours—for two full weeks before he even kissed me. I hadn't really had a boyfriend before that, so I didn't have any expectations. Didn't even recognize all my feelings. But after that first kiss, it seemed more natural to be touching each other than not. We never stopped talking; we just did it with our arms around each other.

But Joe's disappearance not only broke me; it made me question everything. And now everything between us feels mixed up and confusing. Are we friends? Are we not? Can we even *be* friends? Is there any hope for anything more between us?

I do a pretty good job, in a totally middle school kind of way, of not staring at him when he's over at the grill. But then, when all the food's ready and Rose calls everyone over to start fixing their plates, Joe wipes sweat from his forehead, glances at the pool, and then quietly moves toward the water as he pulls off his shirt.

His board shorts hang low on his lean hips, and I see that my instincts were right. He's filled out some across his chest and shoulders. Not a lot, just...enough.

And now when I look at him, I know exactly what lust feels like, exactly what I'd like to do with him—slowly and thoroughly with my mouth, my hands—and exactly how I'd hope he'd respond.

But now I have trouble remembering how it was so easy to touch and talk and laugh and feel confident and comfortable all at once. I'm not sure I can do that anymore.

So when, after swimming silently halfway across the pool underwater, he comes up for air, slicks his hair back, and finds me with his burning eyes, I blink away, moving to the kitchen door as if I actually have some thought of food at this moment.

I don't think I've been hungry since he's been back. I have no idea how many meals I've skipped without realizing it until my head starts to hurt. It's not on purpose this time, but it scares the hell out of me. I can only seem to focus on one thing at a time. Any more makes me drop the self-care ball. Or the work ball. Or both.

I'm still pretending not to notice him—that's how mature I am—an hour later as we're eating Italian ice and popsicles in the shade. He's still shirtless, sprawled in a chair with a grape pop-sicle, admiring a sketch Sam made of the kids jumping into the pool. But I am so not noticing.

"Maisie, Sam." Meg starts off the conversation, our reason for being here today. "You're still wanting to apply for emancipation next week, right, after you hit your six-month milestone here, Maisie?"

Maisie nods. "Yes. Sam too, at the same time. We've been reading all about it."

Meg looks at me.

My cue. I lean forward. "Joe and I want to help you guys with that. Remember the lawyer you met at that meeting at the restaurant? We want to hire her to help you make the best possible case."

Maisie and Sam look from me to Joe, who nods.

Rose goes next. "Angus would like to look the cabin over to see how we can make it sturdier or more weatherproof for you. He'd check the roof and the wiring, make sure there's nothing weak structurally. And I'd like to fix up a good study area for you. I understand you've been working and eating at an old folding table…?"

The kids nod.

David says, "The point is for everyone to respect you as adults. So it's up to you, how much we help."

Sam and Maisie look around the circle at each person's face. The younger kids are silent, seeming to understand the seriousness of the moment.

Maisie leans over and says something softly in Sam's ear. He nods, then replies too quietly for me to hear. Maisie squeezes his hand and looks at us all again. "We'd really appreciate your help. But we want to be able to give back." She looks at Meg and David. "To you two too."

Sam says, "We can babysit or paint or clean, or do yardwork or laundry. I can do a mural or sketch anything you'd like. So everybody think of something we can do for you."

My vision blurs and I have to clear my throat. We've known these two are resourceful and mature, but this… Raised brows and tiny nods from around the circle. The others are as impressed as I am.

"Okay, then." Joe reaches out with his bare foot and shoves Sam's knee gently. "Well done."

"I know what I'd like." Rose's eyes are bright. "Ever weed a vegetable garden?"

Soon she's got Maisie and Sam over near the tomatoes, pointing at the ground and answering Maisie's questions about growing produce.

"You think we could put in something like this up at the lake?"

Rose shrugs. "Probably, if you've got a sunny spot and good soil."

Sam and Maisie exchange a glance and a nod. Another challenge they'll meet together.

I'm so proud of them.

I swipe at my eyes, hoping no one's noticed my sentimentality. How is it that some people—Maisie, Sam, Joe—can rise above massive obstacles at a really young age while others of us...can't?

I admire that strength. That grit.

Wish I had that in me.

We clean up the dinner mess and get back in the pool for cutthroat volleyball. Well, as cutthroat as you can be when there's a seven- and a nine-year-old playing. We make a rule that six-foot-four Angus has to stand flat-footed in his position. And another rule that only Ruby and Melly can spike the ball, which doesn't stop the adults from lifting the little girls up high to spike. Eventually David puts one girl on his shoulders, and Joe puts the other one on his, which makes Julian laugh so hard that we're all cracking up.

Rose and Meg argue that they too are short enough they ought to be able to sit on someone's shoulders. Angus volunteers to loan them his trench coat. Says together they'd almost make one normal person. At which everyone hoots. "Honey," Rose says, patting his arm, "nobody believes you'd have a trench coat."

Through it all, I manage to keep my hands to myself, even when Joe's smooth back is only a foot away. Even when his eyes crinkle and shine. Even when he's making sweet kids laugh and clutch his hair and shriek in triumph at their first successful volleyball spike. And miraculously, even when he turns to me and includes me in that big crooked grin of his. Lord have mercy.

Then it's getting dark and the bugs come out to feast on us and we've all worn each other out. I go inside to put my empty— I'd baked forty-eight cheesy potato puffs, and not a single one is left—Tupperware containers in a bag for the walk home. Meg and David offer me and Joe a ride, and heaven knows their van could transport a small army, but I thank them and tell them I'm up for a stroll.

Joe looks at them and then at me and says he'd like a stroll too.

And the next thing I know, I'm calling out, "Thanks!" and "Good night!" and letting myself out Rose and Angus's front gate with the man who is temptation on two legs right behind me.

CHAPTER 23

Dear July,

I don't understand why you won't answer. Please, can you write just once to explain it to me? Did I imagine the way you looked at me and the way you held me? Because that really felt like love to me. I don't have a lot of experience with it, but that's how I always thought it must feel.

Joe

IT'S A SILENT WALK FOR the first two blocks. Just the slap of our sandals on the still-warm sidewalk and the occasional whine of a mosquito in my ear. But I hear Angus's low rumble from before: *Just ask her.*

And it comes out of my mouth. "Did I do something that upset you?" I focus on my empty hands as I ask. I'd offered to carry her bags, but July wasn't having that.

She matches my stride for a few paces in silence. Then, softly, "No, you're fine, Joe."

Which is obvious bullshit. If it were possible to get mad at

July, I'd think that's a spark of anger I'm feeling now. "Then why have you been avoiding me?"

"I—" She breaks off and shakes her head. Her hair, left down to dry, shines under the streetlamps. "I'm sorry. I just didn't want..." She lifts her free hand in a vague gesture.

"Didn't want what?" Didn't want me to kiss her. I know that's it, and I know it will hurt like hell to hear her say it. Let's just rip off the Band-Aid. Get it over with.

She raises her gray eyes, that nighttime gleam I've always found fascinating in them. "I thought you were feeling sorry for me. I didn't want you to feel sorry for me."

I stop and stare. "Why the hell would I feel sorry for you?"

She gestures me into the alley that runs behind the restaurant. Guess she wants to go in the back way. I follow, still waiting for her answer.

"I don't know." But there's something in her voice...something she's not saying. "I thought maybe because I was crying over the kids."

That doesn't make any sense. "You thought I was feeling sorry for you because you were upset...about the kids...and that made you avoid me?" My voice is rising. I rein it in. "Why in the world would that make you avoid me?"

She reaches her car and sets her bag on the hood, rooting in the pocket of her cover-up for something. Just as she pulls out her keys, the bag slides off the car, and we both step forward to catch it, ending up a breath apart, my hand covering hers.

Back here there's no sound but our breathing and the moths fluttering around the light bulb over the door.

Nothing to look at but her face, her eyes shining up into mine with...memory? Wariness? Want?

Her hand is warm, the skin velvety smooth and soft under mine, her knuckles little ridges that feel way more fragile than I know July to be. I trace them with my thumb. My words rumble out in an unfamiliar Angus-like register. "Why would you avoid me, July?"

Her eyes close for an instant. Her tiny sigh is lemon ice–scented.

"You make it sound stupid, Joe." Her voice is quiet. Defeated.

"It doesn't feel stupid."

What? There's nothing remotely stupid about this woman. I would never want to make her feel that way. "I'm sorry. I know it's not stupid. Tell me. Please." I dip my head to look into her eyes again. Rest my forehead against hers.

Her laugh is a short sound with no humor in it. "On the trail, when you did this forehead thing? I thought you were about to give me a pity kiss. I don't want pity kisses from you, Joe."

I don't know when my hands moved but they're cradling her face now. I sweep her cheekbones with my thumbs, try to clear a pathway from my eyes to my heart so she can see inside me, see how unnecessary that worry is.

And she looks. And looks. I don't know what she's seeing or what I can say to ease her fears, or even why she would think I pity her. Lust for her? Yes. Admire and respect her? Yes.

Love her?

Yes.

But pity? And kisses based in pity? Never.

I open my mouth and what comes out is a whisper. "How about other kinds of kisses?"

She doesn't speak. Her gaze moves from my eyes down to my lips. Her free hand rises to my waist and rests there.

I tilt closer, inch by fraction of inch, watching her for any sign of...anything...but she's still and silent as a statue. I pause, a paper-width slice of air between us. I can't take something I'm not sure she wants to give. And I can't read her like I used to.

"Joe..." she breathes into my mouth, and our lips brush, catch, brush.

It feels like our first kiss again. Nothing is the same except my partner—it's night instead of day, an alley instead of lake's edge, a history behind us instead of a whole future ahead—but the *feeling* is the same. Heart-swelling, momentous, forget-to-breathe, this-is-The-One same.

I tunnel my hands into the silk of her hair and angle my head to kiss her better. Her lips feel just as soft, taste just as sweet as they did when she was sixteen. I pull back long enough to locate her sprinkle of freckles in the flickering light of the moth bulb, and then I kiss every one of them, one by one, hoping she's listening hard enough with her heart to realize that each kiss is a promise, a reassurance, a statement of love and faith. A "thank you for showing me love exists." No pity anywhere in there.

Her lips find my chin. The bag clatters to the ground as she brings her other hand up to the back of my neck. My breathing is harsh in my own ears as I wrap both arms around her and crush her to me. Mine. Finally, she's mine again.

A tear squeezes from between my closed lids as I hold her tight, marveling at this miracle, and then I find her mouth with mine and open to her, devouring her. I lay her back on the hood of her car and she tugs me down on top of her. She's so soft and strong and warm under me...so alive she makes *me* more alive. She murmurs my name between kisses, rakes one hand through my hair the way she used to, and I'm dizzy. Dizzy with longing, dizzy with memories, dizzy with lust. Dizzy with getting to share this with my girl again. My woman.

I open my mouth on her jaw, breathing in her scents—sunscreen and chlorine and July—nipping her there before finding her pulse with my lips. Her neck, her beautiful throat…I kiss every part of it, drinking in her soft sigh and gasp, and she arches into me, one of her knees coming up to lock around me, pressing even closer.

This is all I want. A life of being with her, holding her like this, knowing we will have years together to talk and laugh and make love and take care of each other. A life like this, starting tonight. And this time nobody can separate us.

I'm touching every part of her I can reach, caressing, stroking, squeezing, claiming her. Her swimsuit cover-up is in my way. I tug down the front zipper, spreading it open to see the shape of her. The rise of her breasts, the long, tantalizing slope of her torso down to those flirty little shorts…all before me like a feast.

With shaking fingers I push aside the straps of her tank, peeling it down to see the full pale curves of her breasts. I remember how she used to like to be touched: firm pressure, my fingers catching and squeezing her nipples between them. It still makes her groan and arch with pleasure, and that still makes me smile and throb and ache to be inside her. I lower my head and tease her nipple with my tongue, and when she whimpers, I suck it into my mouth.

I will gladly pleasure this woman any way she wants, as long as she wants, for the rest of our lives.

July

When he stared at me in disbelief at the idea that he might feel sorry for me, I realized I'd been wrong—he wasn't trying to give me a pity kiss at the lake.

When he takes my face in his hands and leans in to a hair's breadth away, I know this isn't going to be a pity kiss either. And god help me, I want it. Don't know what kind of kiss it *will* be, but it's from Joe and I crave it. So I take it. I cover that last sliver of space between us and touch my mouth to his...

And I'm back at the lake for our very first kiss again. Back in that suspended moment of hope and joy and disbelief that this amazing person might actually want me the way I want him. We'd spent two weeks circling each other back then, talking and laughing and learning each other's stories and thoughts and dreams. Two weeks of growing close and closer without touching except for the occasional brush of a hand or arm when we were in the water or perched on our big rock together. Two weeks of shared, private I-like-you-I'm-looking-forward-to-time-with-you-later smiles at work, of me watching him notice the people nobody else saw. The new boy with the terrible complexion who got lucky enough to have Joe be the one to train him on the grill. The shy girl who worked the salad bar and whose name nobody else remembered. Joe could make them both talk and laugh. Make them open like flowers in the spring.

And after two weeks of precious time alone with him at the lake, he was inside my soul, filling my thoughts and my heart, making me want to open like a flower in spring too, making me burn and ache to touch him. He'd stand, laughing, to do a shallow dive off our rock, mesmerizing me with the taut shape and flex of him. We'd race out to a shallow-water warning buoy, and I'd fall back a little so I could watch the lean, hard arrow of his body slicing through the water. He'd turn and call out with his crooked, joyful grin, and my eyes would trickle over him like the water sluicing off his sun-browned skin. Sometimes, if I turned my head quickly when we were sitting together, I'd catch him gazing at me with a burning look in his eyes, but then he'd smile and tease me or distract me with a question, and by the end of our second week together, I was afraid he was never going to touch me. Never going to kiss me. I was afraid we were just buddies in his mind, just good swimming buddies.

And so when, on our fifteenth day together, he fell quiet, gazing out over the water to the dark line of trees on the far shore, I thought our time was coming to an end. Thought he was just trying to figure out how to say it. I gathered my courage, asked what he was thinking. Gave him the opening I thought he was looking for.

And instead of diving through it, he turned to me, his eyes moving over my face...my eyes, my cheeks, my lips. "I'm wondering how you taste," he said, and you could have pushed me off that rock with a single gentle fingertip.

And I recognized that look from all the times I'd turned it on him when I thought he wasn't watching. And my smart mouth took over from my stunned-blank mind, even though the words came out a hoarse whisper. "If only there were some way you could find out."

His eyes flared. One corner of his mouth twitched in an almost-grin.

And joy began to fill me as he angled himself to face me and looked at me some more, and then reached out one shaking hand to touch my hair. He laid his palm so gently against my cheek. He raised his eyebrows in an *okay?* and when I nodded, he leaned in just like he does tonight, slowly, slowly, stopping just a hair away until I meet his lips with mine.

Just like then, the contact seems to galvanize him, to set loose something inside him, and he takes my face in his hands and presses kisses all over it. Wraps his arms around me and hauls me tightly to his hard body.

And tonight something inside me loosens too, with a sigh and a *yes* and a *finally*. I pull him close, where he's supposed to be, and run my fingers up into his hair. It's as soft as I remember, and his kisses just as sweet. Just as hungry. And I'm hungry too—no, starving. My mouth, my hands, my eyes, my heart, all starving.

I relearn his body with mine, fitting him to me, all the lines and angles and hard slopes of muscle; his scent of sunshine and chlorine and coconut; his taste of pure, sweet, sharp Joe. And though we've both changed some, the fit is still perfect, the relief of coming together still overwhelming.

He lays me back against the hood of the car, baring me, kissing and touching and making my world spin in circles and loops. I'm dizzy and giddy and drunk with him.

This is what's been missing from my life. What's been missing with every other man I've tried to be with. This amazing coming together of all the parts of me with all the parts of another person. A person I think is wonderful, with a brain and a giant heart and a sense of humor he only ever uses for good. And a way of holding me close that is, truly, holding me. Close.

My hands are on him, sweeping down the worn-soft fabric of his T-shirt, heading for the loose waistband of his board shorts when it hits me. This is what Joe was talking about—what he knew was missing from the sexorcism night and the morning we woke up entwined on my couch. He knew I wasn't all in then because he knew what it felt like for us both to be all in together.

He knew because we'd had it before. He knew, and he wanted us to have that again.

And god help us both, he thinks we've found it. Somehow, he thinks he's found it again with me.

And his hands are in my swim shorts, cupping my bottom, squeezing, and he's murmuring words—I don't catch them all, but I think one might have been *love*—in my ear. Part of my heart cracks open and spills out tears and love, and part of me freezes in horror as I put my hands on his chest and push him up off of me.

"Joe, no, stop!"

And because he's Joe, he does, right away. He lets go and steps back, his eyes wide with concern. "I'm sorry! Did I...? Was I...?"

He thinks he did something wrong. He thinks he's the problem. With all that's wrong in the world, all that's gone wrong in his life, all that's good and gentle and perfect inside him, somehow he thinks *he's* the problem.

A huge knot of tears rises to block my throat. I am so sick of tears. I force the words out around them. "I'm not strong enough for this, Joe. I'm not strong enough for *you*. I'm so sorry."

And he watches me, eyes tragic, arms at his side, as I scoop up the bag and my keys, and fumble to open the back door locks. He's still standing there as I tug the heavy metal door closed behind me.

The tears burst out of me then, in giant, harsh sobs as I make my way upstairs into my apartment, cursing myself for being a careless, hurtful, selfish monster of a woman hurting Joe again because I can't stop my own wanting.

It doesn't seem to have registered with him when I told him how I broke when he left. How I'm not the same brave, ready-for-love girl he knew back then. I don't think I can ever be her again. I didn't tell him the whole story, so he doesn't know.

But *I* know that every time I focus on too many things at once or on something just for me, everything goes wrong. All the little cracks in me begin to vibrate and split apart, and I fly to pieces and can't hold up my end of anything for anyone. I can't take care of myself or think or work...can't do anything but try to ride out all the wild, clashing feelings. It's like living in a blender.

I can't handle a love like ours.

And I have to make him understand before I hurt him any more. Have to make him back off to a safe distance. Have to make him understand just how serious the breaks in me are.

I go into my bedroom, into my closet, and dig out a box of things I kept from high school. Photos. Yearbooks. My varsity softball letter from senior year. A citizenship award they gave me at graduation.

The only journal I've ever kept. The year after Joe left. It's at the bottom of the box because it scares me to read it. My ramblings are terrifying.

Joe bared his soul to me when he gave me those letters to help me see that he hadn't forgotten me, hadn't give up without a fight. Maybe this journal will help him understand my fight too. And why I can't go through that again.

I tuck in the worst photo, scribble a note on the page after the last entry, stuff it in a plastic bag, grab my keys, and am outside his building pounding on his door before I know it.

When he appears in the hallway across the front room, shirtless, T-shirt in hand and a hopeful, wrecked look on his face, I steel myself. Hold up the bag for him to see. Hang it on his doorknob and take off back to my place like the coward I am.

CHAPTER 24

Dear July,

When you said you loved me, I really believed you. I didn't doubt you for a minute. I thought you were the realest, warmest person I ever met.

Joe

WHEN I HEAR THE POUNDING, my heart leaps from somewhere down around my heel up into my brain, making me dizzy enough to grab the rail as I tear down the stairs. *Please, let it be July. Please let her have changed her mind...* Not that I have a clue what she's thinking. What that was all about in the alley.

It is July, but I barely have time to make that out before she waves another one of her damn bags at me and disappears.

My mouth still has the sweet taste of her on it. I'll be damned if I'm erasing that with food tonight.

But I shuffle over to retrieve the bag, relock the door, and head upstairs with it because her will is mine.

It's not food though. It's a notebook, an old spiral one. I

turn on a reading light and drop into a chair, running my fingers over the battered, stained cover, not sure whether I want to open it.

Of course I have to open it. It's from my July, written in her familiar, loopy, sixteen-year-old penmanship, the entries twenty years old.

She's given me this for a reason. There must be some kind of answer for me in here. I flip to the first page and start reading.

July 7

I believe in soul mates because I've met mine. When Joe holds me and looks in my eyes, I feel precious. Not too big or okay or good—precious. Like he treasures me. Like what we have is treasure.

We're not virgins anymore. I don't think I should have been thinking of him as a boy I like. It's not that I believe any of that stupid you've-had-sex-you're-a-man-now stuff. It's just that I'm not sure Joe has ever been a boy. He is sweeter, more generous, more loving, and more seriously grown-up than most of the adults I know. Yeah, he laughs and teases and jokes, but his core is true, strong, solid, grown man.

Tonight wasn't sex; it was a promise. Joe's it for me. I am gonna be with this man forever.

I have to stop reading for a second. Press my hand flat to the page. She's laid her heart there, and I need to touch it again. Because I know what happened next.

July 8

I don't know what's going on. Something is wrong.

    I [illegible, water spots, smeared ink] so scared.

July 9

I was sure I'd wake up and find out this was a nightmare. I don't know for sure what's happened to Joe. He wouldn't have left me. I know it. I am praying and praying that he is okay.

    I am so scared for him. This is so not like him. I sat up most of the night, hoping he'd call. I'm still waiting.

July 10

Joe, where are you? You have to call and let me know you're okay. Please! I talked to Mom and Dad. They've been worried about me and about why you haven't been around. Tonight when I couldn't eat supper, I told them everything I know about y'all leaving so suddenly. I asked them how I can find out if you're okay.

    Dad says he's got a friend at the police department, and he'll ask him what he can do to check on you.

    If y'all flew to Germany, you'd be there by now unless you stopped somewhere else on the way. PLEASE call and let me know you're alright. I miss you. I love you. I'm scared for you.

July 12

Dad got some officers to do a "wellness check." They said your landlord said y'all moved out. Mom and Dad said that if you are in Germany, it might take a while for mail to get here. Joe, I just don't get why you wouldn't have told me you were leaving. I miss you so much.

July 29

It's been three weeks. Mom finally admitted she thinks I would have gotten a letter by now if you had written when you got there. And that if you were going to call, you would have already.

Last week there was a "For Rent" sign in the yard of your house. This week the sign is gone, and a new family with a little kid is living there.

Joe, I [unintelligible streaked ink, water blotches]

July 30

Should I have seen signs that you were ready to be done with me?

I can't stand going to work anymore. Putting a big plastic smile on my face. People asking about you, or worse—just staring or whispering. Salad Bar Girl asked me if you were okay. Her eyes were as worried as I feel. I couldn't answer. Everybody thinks I should know, but I know nothing. I asked Mom and Dad if they would think I was a loser if I quit. They just hugged me and said that I'm sixteen and I don't have to work unless I want. So I gave a week's notice tonight. That's four more shifts. I hope I can make it.

Joe, I don't get it. Why'd you leave like that? Why

didn't you tell me? Why don't you call or write? I [unintelligible]

July 31

I wish I just knew for sure that you're alright. Some horrible part of me sometimes thinks that if you're not alright, at least it would explain why you haven't called or written. But that's a terrible, selfish thought. I don't want you to be hurt. I want you to be okay. I just want to be with you wherever you are. Well, and I want you to want me there. I don't know whether to be mad or heartbroken or scared out of my mind for you. Everything feels horrible all the time. Even food is disgusting. Nothing is okay.

Brendan and Jen are being so sweet. I don't go out anymore. I just stay home with the people who love me. We miss really liked you, Joe. How could you leave us like this? We...I miss you so much.

Aug. 2

I feel like a colossal bitch for being so upset with you when I don't know for sure if you're even okay. Yeah, I know the signs point to it. Maybe I'm in denial. I just—I KNOW you wouldn't have wanted to leave me. I KNOW that you weren't faking how you felt. Nobody could fake like that. But I think if you weren't okay, if you weren't still in the world, I'd feel it. I'd know it. I think you're still alive. ~~So why~~

Joe, come back or call me. Or write. Please. I can't stand this.

Aug. 5
School started today. I don't care. I don't care about anything. Becca Friedrich asked how much weight I've lost. I just stared at her. How much does a heart weigh?

Aug. 8
I must be the stupidest, most gullible person on the face of the planet. Are you somewhere laughing at me for thinking that you meant all those things you said? It's not like any other boy ever showed that kind of interest.

I guess now I know why you chose that night to bring a condom. But really, that was kind of dumb on your part if you just wanted sex before you left because I would have given it to you anytime. You had me completely. I'm so stupid.

I look at the future, and all the plans I had seem stupid now. What was I thinking? Somebody with judgment like mine can't run a business.

At school people talk to me, and I have to stand there and replay everything in my head to try to remember what they just said. Every day is so long. I come home and crawl in bed and try to remember how it felt to have your arms around me, and then I hate myself, and I try to forget how it felt to have your arms around me. Then I cry. Then I hate myself for crying.

Oh my fucking god. My girl…my poor girl. I'm doubled over, reading her pain.

Sept. 10
Mom and Dad are making me go to a counselor. I know they're scared for me, and I'm sorry about that, but really, what's the point? Just let me sleep. Just leave me alone. Just let me fucking die. I'm too stupid to live anyway.

Nov. 15
Stupid fucking pills make me feel like a zombie. I didn't need pills for that. Mom said my clothes are too big—she wants to take me shopping. Who the fuck cares about clothes.

Dec. 24
Joe, I [unintelligible] you.

April 23
Jen needed me today, and I couldn't help her. I heard her scream from the bathroom—she'd burnt herself on the curling iron—and I jumped up from the bed to go to her, but there were all these black spots, and I think I passed out for a minute. Then I couldn't push myself up from the floor. I hollered to her to get the aloe gel under the sink and then to get some ice in a towel… I had to just yell because I couldn't get up.

I've let you destroy me, Joe. All my strength is gone. I couldn't even help my baby sister when she needed me.

I was crying when Mom came home later. I had to tell her I need help.

Oh holy Christ.

My guts are a giant knotted fist. If my dad were still alive, I'd hunt him down and kill him just for what he did to my sweet girl.

There's a photo jammed between the next two pages. I pry it out and stare at it, not sure what I'm seeing. It's a girl with death in her eyes. A frail girl with thin, lank blond hair and delicate bones and death in her eyes. She looks a little like Jen, but there's Jen right next to her and Brendan on the other side.

My lungs seize up. Jesus fucking Christ.

It's July. But about half the size she should be, with only a flicker of life and spirit left.

Jesus fucking Christ.

The whole world almost lost my girl.

I will myself not to throw up, but I can't stop moaning. Have to wrap my arms around my gut the way I would around July if she were here. Rock and moan, just rock and moan.

But there are more entries, so I wipe my eyes and read on.

May 2

I ran into Big Angus today. Literally ran into him. Almost fell on my butt. He caught me and asked if I was okay, and when I said yeah, he looked at me like he didn't believe me and said, "Really?" I tried to leave, but he kept walking beside me with those long-ass legs and asked if I would help his grandma collect stuff for the homeless shelter. I must've looked at him like he was crazy because he started telling me about how they need lots of stuff, and his grandma wanted him to get high school kids to help. I asked why he was asking me, and he said because he hates to talk. I said Angus, "It's May and I've spoken like fifteen words this entire school year." He said, "Yeah, but you need to talk. And you're good at it. And people need you."

Dammit. Sometimes I hate that overgrown mind-gamey son of a bitch.

I told him I'd call his grandma.

July 7

Joe, it's been a year since I last saw you. I don't know where you are or how you're doing. The biggest, kindest part of me hopes that you are okay. Dammit, I wish I didn't cry every time I think about that.

A mean, little part of me hopes that, if you are alive and healthy and just didn't write or call, you're every bit as miserable as I have been. It scares me how close I came to not making it. Mom and Dad and Jen and Brendan would've been wrecked if I died, and I was so, so close. I hope I never ever have to go through that again, and that nobody else has to either. I can't—well, I just can't.

The last entry is in a more adult scrawl, dated today.

Joe, when you came back, I started to dream dreams for me again. Started to have hopes for us again. And I immediately began to fall apart. Started forgetting to eat. That's how my eating disorder started last time, when I was depressed and felt so out of control. Then I realized I had control over what I ate or what I didn't eat.

I'm terrified, Joe. It took me months to build back my physical strength, and I still have to be careful. I look at myself in the mirror and do daily affirmations, just to talk myself through tough times. Because emotionally I'm not strong, and I don't know that I ever will be.

None of this is your fault in any way. You are a wonderful man, and you deserve the best. I'm...not it. I need to just keep my focus on other people so I can hold it/me together. I'm sorry.

Love always,
     July

The damn notebook is damp in my hands by the time I finish.

When I was in Germany thinking she didn't care enough to answer my letters, it truly did almost break me. I let anger carry me through the grief and pain and sense of betrayal. Meanwhile, July was here, with those same feelings, plus a fear that something terrible might have happened to me. No wonder she broke.

But she's wrong if she thinks she's still broken. The July that built that wacky restaurant family, the July that gives and gives to anybody and everybody who needs anything, the July who came to the rescue and loaded me and two traumatized kids in her car and calmed us all down and got us to sing, for Christ's sake, is so not broken.

And I'm not either.

I fish my phone out of my pocket, find the song I want, and text it to her. Then I go to bed. Nothing else I can do.

———

July

"I think we ought to take corn chowder off. Maybe come up with some kind of street corn dish." Donna looks at me over the top of the menu we're considering updating.

"Smokin' Joe's Pepper Pasta's been a big hit. Maybe we should ask Joe if he's got any street corn recipes. Where's he been, anyway?" Tina's tone is a little too innocent. She came in to make dough, but she's been lingering out here where Donna and I are on break.

Where's he been? In my dreams every night. In my imagination and my memory every freaking waking moment of every day.

It's been almost three weeks since I've seen him. The first week was the easiest. Jen went into labor and had her baby and our folks came up from Florida and I spent as much time as I could with them and Brendan and Jen and my precious new nephew.

They asked about Joe too. I accidentally started it by asking who the gorgeous pink and coral roses were from. I knew they couldn't be from Jen's asshole husband.

Sure enough, Jen beamed up at me, her eyes tired but bright. "Joe sent those. Aren't they beautiful?"

"How'd he know you had the baby?" My voice sounded fairly normal. Fairly casual. Gotta take pride in what I can when I can.

"Oh." She waved her free hand dismissively. "He was supposed to come for dinner the day I went into labor. I had to call and ask him for a rain check."

My mom leaned forward to adjust little Patrick's sock. Precious baby can't keep socks on for anything. "How *is* Joe doing? I was so glad to hear he's back in town. That was terrible, what his parents did, but I'm glad to know there was a reason you didn't hear from him, July. He seemed like such a nice boy."

"Seemed like he was doing okay when I saw him at Lindon's the other night." Brendan glanced over at me. "He was with Hiromi and that friend of hers… What's his name?"

"Dirk." I picked up Jen's empty glass and went to the kitchen to get her a refill. And to keep from hearing one more word about Joe.

It's bad enough that I can't go to sleep at night without playing that damn Jason Mraz song we sang in the car, the one about not giving up on us. Every night I pull up Joe's text on my phone, see his message, You are so much stronger than you think, and hit play on the link. Then I lie there wondering what he's doing, what he's thinking, what it would be like to have him lying there with me, holding me tight and steady, his bright eyes crinkling at me.

Since my folks left, I've been working nonstop, trying to banish my flesh-and-blood ghost. I leave work only long enough to take treats to Jen and pace around the yard with Patrick so my sister can nap. During the day I set a timer for every five hours so that I won't forget to eat.

Now I study Tina, wondering whether everybody's in a conspiracy to push me into Joe's already-way-too-appealing arms. Before I can tell her that I don't know where he's been, my phone buzzes.

It's Andi. No-nonsense, as usual. Lindon's tonight. You, me, Rose, Happy Hour 5:30.

Donna's quiet voice breaks into my thoughts. "If that's a social invitation, you should take it. We're getting too soft around here, both shifts fully staffed now and you still working day and night." She taps the table with one long, slim finger. "Don't want you getting sick again."

Ain't that the truth, even though she's talking about the bronchitis and ear infection, while I'm thinking about something bigger and older.

"Is it Joe?" Tina chirps. "If it's Joe, you should definitely go!"

Donna groans and I roll my eyes at Tina. "Lord, woman, you are the nosiest person on the face of the planet." I try to stare her down but she just winks at me.

"Fair enough. But is it Joe?"

I push up out of the booth and pick up my mostly empty salad bowl. "All right, y'all can tell the evening crew I'm taking the rest of the day off. I'm out of here. Call me if you need me."

Upstairs I change clothes and take a long, slow run. It's hard not to listen for Joe's footfalls keeping pace beside me. Harder not to miss it. He should give up on us. On me. Why won't he?

Might be a mistake, going tonight. Normally I love doing stuff with Andi or with Rose. It's still a little weird to think of them as a pair, but they really seem to have hit it off, which could be a problem if they decide to matchmake me and Joe again.

I'm home with just enough time to shower and get to Lindon's by 5:30. My friends are already there, huddled together over Rose's phone at a table in the back.

"What's up?" I slide into a chair across from them and pour myself a beer from the sweating pitcher on the table.

"I outdid myself!" Rose gives me one of her sweet, dimply smiles. "Look at this." She passes over the phone.

It's photos of Maisie's cabin, but better than I've ever seen it. One corner of the living room—a corner that seemed gloomy and useless before—is now a bright study area with an L-shaped two-person desk topped with a whiteboard, pale bulletin boards, and bookshelves. The chairs look comfy, and there's task lighting mounted under the shelves for the work surfaces.

"Wow, you really have, Rose!" I pass the phone back to her with the smile she deserves. "It's so cute and so practical! I didn't remember the cabin even having outlets there."

"It didn't. That was Angus. He was insulating everything and decided to rewire the place to make it safer. Added a bunch of outlets while he was at it."

Andi doesn't know Sam and Maisie, but I'm sure she's heard the full story by now. She's nodding in approval. "Have the kids seen it yet?"

Rose nods. "They've been in and out. Meg and David are really good about letting them spend some daytime hours up there. Sometimes the whole family goes up together to the lake. The younger kids love it."

Maisie and Sam have continued working too, just as reliably as the rest of the crew. I shake my head, thinking about them. "Donna told me she and Tina sent the judge letters of support from both crews last week."

Every one of the restaurant staff is amazing. They've been through stuff I've never had to face—abuse, death of loved ones, custody battles, poverty—and they survived and came out on this side better, surer, and still kind enough to go to bat for each other.

They're strong like Joe.

I clear my throat, raise my mug for a drink, and swipe at my watering eye.

Andi's watching me. "Where were you the other night? The

rest of the team was here, all cleaned up. Weren't even sweaty or smelly. Nice change."

"I was...probably working? Or maybe at Jen's. I got a perfect little nephew now, you know." And major avoidance issues.

They fall for my subject change, saying, "Oh, yeah!" together and making the appropriate oohing and ahhing sounds when I pass around my own phone with my own pictures.

"Joe said he was a cutie. He was right."

There it is. The Joe mention I knew was coming. Andi hands my phone back, and I stick it back into my pocket, muttering, "I guess he's already been over to see him too."

"Yeahhh..." They're both staring at me oddly.

"Did you two have a fight or something?" Rose asks, just as Andi says, "There something we should know about him?"

I wave them off. "No. Why would we fight? He's a great guy." Just so tempting it's taking all of my energy to resist.

Andi busies herself with the pitcher, topping off our mugs, while Rose stares at me with a tiny frown. "July," Rose says finally, "if Joe were to tell you he's madly in love with you and wants to try again, would you want to?"

Oh lord. How in the world can I answer that without either lying to my friends or laying the whole mess out on the table? I really don't want to talk about this.

I must hesitate too long because Rose sucks in a breath and exchanges a look with Andi. Don't know when they started reading each other's minds, but it's annoying as hell.

Andi comes right out with it. "He did, didn't he? He said it." She shoots Rose a glance. "I knew it. It's all over his face every time he looks at her."

I rub my jaw. Look over at some guys laughing about

something on the TV behind the bar. Think some more about how to answer. "Not...exactly." I sigh. "But kinda."

"July!" Rose's voice reaches a squeaky pitch I've never heard from her. She reins it in to say more quietly, "Then what's wrong? You've loved him forever, right? Why are you not with him right this very minute?"

I glare at her, then at Andi. "It's not that easy, okay? I don't want...the same things I used to want."

Rose makes a great show of reaching into her purse and pulling out a notebook and pen. She flips it open and reads aloud as she writes. "Reasons...crazy-ass July...would reject...a guy... like...Joe."

"Number one," Andi supplies immediately. "He's too nice. She prefers her dicks in the metaphorical sense."

"I see what you're doing," Rose mutters as she scribbles, "testing whether I can spell *metaphorical*." She barely pauses before continuing. "Number two: Too sexy. Devilish eyes and washboard abs... Bleh, *so* overrated."

"Number three." Andi again. "Too much stamina. Have you seen how that dude can run? Bound to exhaust partner through excessive orgasms."

I roll my eyes and listen to them and wonder why it is that nobody—not Joe, not Tina and Donna, not Rose, not Andi, not a single one of them—can see that I am not up to this. It's like they think I can just choose love and everything will be fine. They of all people should know better. Why can't they see I can't do this?

Andi finally takes pity on me. "Okay, we'll stop. But just in case it matters, you should know that I think Joe's one of the truly good ones. And you know me, I've got plenty of reasons not to trust men, and I've never been serious about one in my life. But if I met somebody like Joe, who looked at me the way Joe looks at you, I might reconsider."

And that, from Andi, is a stunning admission.

CHAPTER 25

Dear July,

When we talked about the future, were you just playing? I can't imagine you laughing at me, exactly, but I can't make sense of this. If you can just help me understand why you don't even want to write to me, maybe I can let go. If you don't want me, help me figure out how to stop loving you.

Joe

EVERYONE ELSE IS ALREADY AT the courthouse when I get there on the day of the kids' emancipation hearing. Sam and Maisie's lawyer goes into the courtroom with the county caseworker to report them present. Everybody else is gathered in the hallway. Meg and David are here with their kids to show support and act as character witnesses if needed. Angus and Rose are here for the same reasons.

I stopped by the restaurant on my way, but July had already left. Donna and Tina both wanted to come, but with the others out, they're needed on the day crew. They told me to give the kids a hug for luck.

Sam seems ill at ease, fidgeting, raising his hands to his hair. David and I took him out yesterday for a shorter haircut and court clothes, so today he's in chinos and a button-down shirt and tie instead of his usual worn jeans and T-shirt. Maisie looks more comfortable. She already had a navy dress Meg and the lawyer declared suitable for court.

July is beautiful, her hair piled up, showing tiny gold knot earrings, a white sweater over her pale yellow dress, her tanned legs bare and smooth. I have to clench my hands and will my feet to stay rooted where I am. She only meets my eye for a second before turning to speak to Angus.

At first we all stand around waiting in a big group, making small talk to fight our nerves, but after an hour, we break into smaller clumps. Meg and David's kids have brought a board game, and Maisie sits on a bench and plays it with them. She leans some on Sam and he leans back, even though he's pulled his sketch pad out and is working intently on something bright. His hands seem steady and sure as he shades in the edges of the frame he's drawing. Art must relieve his stress.

Meg, Rose, Angus, and David are standing together talking near the younger kids.

A woman walking by—a lawyer?—greets July, and they move off down the hall together.

I stand twiddling my thumbs, waiting and trying not to think too hard.

My phone vibrates... *Hallelujah!* A distraction in the form of a call from Colorado. My former employees pass the phone around at their end, catching me up on how the restaurants are doing and all the gossip and goings-on. I'm actually smiling as I wander down the hall toward the water fountain. I tune out the sounds around me and enjoy their long, convoluted story of how a manager at the Fort Collins store just got engaged to a manager at the Loveland store.

By the time we end our call, I'm in a better mood. I stoop to take a drink from the water fountain just in time to hear a woman out of sight around the corner say, "I heard Jimmy Moran mention seeing you with that guy from high school. I didn't realize he was back or that you're with him. Be careful, July. Is he even working anywhere? You sure he's not looking for a free ride? I heard his dad was a real piece of work back in the day. Real asshole."

Well, fuck, that was...a lot. I straighten slowly, wiping a water droplet from my mouth, and debate what to do next. The part about my dad was true, but the rest? Harsh and unprovoked and so, so wrong. I don't get paid for working on my building or reading ahead for my social work program or making notes for a youth shelter, but they still count for something. And I've probably got way more money in the bank than July does, at the rate she gives it away.

It totally sucks that this woman's put July in this awkward situation with her nosy questions.

Should I walk away and pretend I didn't hear? Stroll around the corner and assure this stranger my intentions are honorable and I don't need July's stinkin' money? Or maybe just tell the truth and let her know she's got nothing to worry about because July wants no part of me?

Before I can decide, July says, in a voice colder than any I've heard her use, "Stacy, this isn't any of your business, and Jimmy Moran's a hopeless gossip. I'll tell you like I told him: Joe and I aren't together. But I'm not sure why you'd think he's a user anyway. He's the most decent guy I've ever met, and I know a lot of good guys. He's not after my money—he's got his own. What he wants is...a real connection with somebody. A *real* one. And if I could be the one to give him that, you bet your ass I would, and I would count myself blessed because he is beautiful inside and out. And if you hear *any*body talking bad about him, please shut that shit down. Joe is *not* his dad, and he deserves *so* much better than that."

There's a pause, and then the other woman says, "Oh. Well. Okay then. Sorry."

And I turn and walk back down the hall the way I came, my heart full to bursting from July's defense. She has my back. She may not want me, but she gets me. She trusts me. And she laid it all out there for everybody (well, a courthouse gossip, which is pretty much the same as everybody) to see. *Goddamn.*

If I've had doubts over the last month—late at night, staring at my ceiling alone, my phone silent—July just removed them. Somehow, through some miracle, I've found The Right One twice. And I am just as head over heels this second time as when we were sixteen.

No sooner do I rejoin our group than the doors open and the kids' lawyer beckons us in. I start back down the hall to fetch July, but she's already headed this way. When she sees us moving toward the courtroom, she breaks into a sprint, and I linger, wanting to be the one to hold the door and walk in with her. Pretending she's running toward *me*. Eager to be with me.

July

The judge asks to see Sam and Maisie one by one in chambers. He has them in there for at least fifteen minutes, ratcheting up the tension for those of us in the courtroom.

I don't need more tension. I could strangle Stacy Billings for what she said about Joe. And then I'd report the crime to Jimmy Moran so I could strangle him too. Busybody assholes. I could barely look Joe in the eye as we came into the courtroom, and he held the door and gave me one of those knee-melting smiles of his anyway. I could feel the warmth of his hand hovering at my back as I moved past him.

He deserves *so* much better than to be talked about like he's some kind of human leech.

I'm still grinding my teeth over that when Judge Fox enters the courtroom and settles at his bench. He's a lovely, soft-spoken man whose dark skin is smooth despite his white hair. His eyes are tired but kind behind his glasses, and I'm glad he's our family court judge.

He places his hands on the thick files before him and lets his eyes rove over all of us before turning his gaze to Maisie and Sam. "I have reviewed the facts of your cases and all the materials very carefully, and I'm prepared to rule. Emancipation cases involve one young person at a time, but I want to address you, Maisie, and you, Sam, together today."

The two kids nod and straighten, visibly bracing themselves.

Beside me, Joe shifts and leans forward a fraction, as if willing them his support and strength. I want to gather all three of them up in my arms.

Judge Fox adjusts his glasses and glances at the files before him. "From these materials, it's clear that you are two extraordinarily mature and resourceful young people who did an excellent job of taking care of yourselves under circumstances that would severely challenge many adults. You showed clear reasoning ability, fine decision-making skills, and a truly impressive ability to keep your future in mind as you coped with a difficult present. Your grades dipped only briefly last year and then improved again. You have a safe, sturdy place to live, and you have cared for it well. You have obtained the jobs you needed in order to live up to the adult responsibilities of paying bills and keeping your-selves fed. You are dedicated students and reliable workers, and your futures are bright before you."

Pride wells up in me in the form of tears. I try to be subtle as I swipe at my eyes, but Joe tilts his head to look at me, gives me a small crooked smile, and takes my hand.

Judge Fox clears his throat. "I wanted to speak with you together today to commend you both not only for your ability to care for yourselves, but also for your ability to inspire the love and loyalty necessary to create the support system you have here, as illustrated by the presence of so many people in this courtroom and by the written testaments of so many more who were unable to be here today. You have many fine people showing faith in you and willing to help you in your future as adults."

Lord, the man is going to have me sobbing. They do—they do have a net. We'll catch them if they fall. We'll help them back on their feet again.

Joe squeezes my fingers, his hand a warm, sturdy anchor.

"But the main reason I wanted to rule on your cases together rather than separately, even though your circumstances differ considerably, is the wording you each used when you spoke to me in chambers a little while ago. You did not sound rehearsed. You each told your own story in your own way and your own words. Yet you both ended with a plea that made quite an impression on me. Both of you said some version of, 'My sibling and I take care of ourselves. We take care of each other. Please let us live together in our own home.' You did not speak of each other as friends but as family. Family you have chosen, despite the certainty of difficulties ahead, because your relationship *matters*. The relationship you described to me was one of family members fiercely and loyally looking out for each other. You spoke with great love and great respect for each other...and great faith and trust in each other. You have instilled me with that same faith in you.

"Your path will not always be easy, but you have a strong and loving support system should you need help. Turn to each other in times of trouble, and turn to these wonderful friends." To my amazement, Judge Fox winks at me, tips the files on end, and raps them on the bench. "I am certain that Ms. Tate in particular will be a formidable advocate. I approve both emancipation requests."

I'm aware of happy noise rising around me, of squealing and hugging and clapping and backslapping and more hugging, and I'm sure I take part in some of it myself, but the biggest uproar is occurring in my head.

Family you have chosen, despite the certainty of difficulties ahead, because your relationship matters... Fiercely and loyally looking out for each other... Great love and great respect for each other... Great faith and trust in each other. Your path will not always be easy, but you have a strong and loving support system should you need help. Turn to each other in times of trouble and turn to these wonderful friends... Ms. Tate in particular...a formidable advocate.

Judge Fox's words are like a kick to my head, jarring pieces loose so that they drop clattering into a new pattern.

The ability to love—to handle and survive love and loss—isn't an innate thing I lack. It's a *choice*. A brave *choice*. A choice about what to value and what to honor.

So what am I going to honor: love or fear? What am I going to value: an empty, false "safety" or the people and relationships I've been blessed with?

I'm not a shell-shocked sixteen-year-old kid anymore. I am a grown-ass woman. A *formidable* grown-ass woman, according to Judge Fox. A formidable grown-ass woman with a wonderful support system to fall back on in times of trouble.

Joe doesn't threaten what I value; he's *part* of it.

Turn to each other...

Beside me, Sam and Joe throw their arms around each other, their grins fierce and triumphant as they pound each other's backs and Maisie hugs them both. Then the three of them turn and tug me into their circle of love.

CHAPTER 26

Dear July,

I feel so stupid and slow, like I'll never get it. But I finally give up. I won't bother you anymore. I'm sorry for everything.

Joe

OUR HAPPY GROUP PRACTICALLY FLOATS across the town square to July's for a celebration lunch. The only people who don't seem completely thrilled are David and Meg's little ones. Apparently they really enjoyed having sweet older siblings.

"Okay, but you can come see us." Maisie takes Melly's hand and swings it. "Maybe Meg and David will do a date night, and you guys can come over and watch movies and eat popcorn and play games with us." The little one gives an excited skip at that.

"And y'all can come over for dinner whenever you want, and we can have our holidays and birthdays together." Meg's a little misty, smiling at Maisie and Sam. David slings his arm around her shoulder and presses a kiss to her temple.

July's smiling too, but there's a tiny tremble to her lips. She's looking around wide-eyed at everybody as if it's the first time she's seen us. When she gets to me, I expect her to turn away fast...but this time she doesn't. She blinks down for a second, almost shyly, and then right back up at me, her gray eyes shining.

And I almost crash into the door Angus is holding open for us. He stops me just in time with a big hand on my shoulder. "Easy there." He pats my back as I pass him, laughter in his tone. Sympathy too.

Inside, there's a line of pushed-together tables reserved for us. Tina peeks out of the kitchen, and July gives her a big smile and two thumbs up. Tina ducks back in, and five minutes later when Sonya's finished taking our orders, the rest of the day crew comes marching out singing, "For they are jolly good fellows." In the lead is Tina carrying a beautiful, flower-decked sheet cake that reads, *Congratulations, Maisie and Sam!* I'm betting the lettering isn't dry yet, that the cake would say something different, something comforting, if July had given Tina a thumb down about the judge's decision.

Everybody in the place joins in on the singing. After the cake is cut and pieces passed out, the kids'—I guess I should stop calling them that—lawyer raises her water glass. "To Maisie and Sam, two of the bravest, most resourceful young people I know!"

Their caseworker goes next. "To Sam and Maisie, who really know how to adult!"

"To Maisie and Sam, the best kids we almost had." Meg's toast comes with hugs.

Then it's Maisie's turn. She holds up her soda glass and waves at the whole room. "To friends," she says, her eyes full of tears.

And quiet Sam stands up and hugs her and raises his glass too. "To family."

Nothing could top those, and we all know better than to try. We've got watery eyes too.

I check to see how July's holding up. I'm still surprised she chose a seat next to me when there was another empty one right beside it. Sure enough, she wipes her eye with one finger before leaning forward to tug off her sweater.

And...that pretty yellow dress is a sundress. Which means I am now inches from her silky, bare shoulders and arms and back, and suddenly the room is a lot warmer and I'm wondering whether I should sit on my hands, just to make sure I keep them to myself.

She glances over at me. Is that a blush? "Wasn't court appropriate without the sweater," she murmurs.

I clear my throat. "It's beautiful. You're beautiful." And I am an awkward high school dork.

She smiles, and I swear it's that sweet private smile she used to give me. Quick and dazzling and full of all the warmth of summer. Her lashes lower, and then she raises them to look me in the eye. "Joe, could I talk to you after this? Could you stick around?"

Woman, I am yours. For as long as you want. "Sure."

I can't tell you how much longer lunch lasts or what I eat, who I talk to, or what I say. All I'm conscious of is the scent of July's baby shampoo and soap when I lean to catch her sweater as it falls off the back of her chair. The tendril of hair that has worked its way free from her updo, and that I'm sure would be as soft as chamois if I rubbed it between my fingers. The fondness that crinkles her eyes when she smiles across the table at our big kids, and the little snort-laugh that bursts out of her when Donna pauses beside her a moment to say, "And don't come back—you're fired."

Seconds or hours later, finally everyone is gathering their

things and standing. Sam and Maisie are going to ride up the mountain with David and Meg to pack their things one last time, to move back into the cabin.

Rose leans toward the kids. "What's the first thing you're going to do when you get home?"

Maisie's answer is prompt. "Unpack and make a grocery list."

Sam's is equally sure. "Test that drawing table you put in our new study area."

At that, Rose beams at them, and Angus beams down at her, his big hand rising to squeeze the nape of her neck gently. She leans back against him, and the tie between them is so tangible I swear I can see it, swirls and tendrils of rose gold.

The back of my throat aches with wanting that.

July touches my arm, and the warmth of her fingers yanks my attention back. "I'm just going to carry some of these plates to the kitchen. Meet you in the hall at my stairs?"

"I'll help." I gather glasses and flatware and follow. Not sure what's going to happen here. I'm afraid to hope. But this is my first actual invitation upstairs. Her first actual indication that she wants to really talk. About us. My heart thumps loud in my ears as we drop off the dishes and tease the kitchen crew. Because you always have to tease the kitchen crew.

And then we're in her private stairwell, climbing up into her personal space, and this time I know I'm welcome, for however long as it takes her to say whatever she wants to tell me.

She pauses at the top of the stairs. "Want something to drink?" When I say no, she looks from the dining area to the living room area as if unsure where to seat us. Finally she moves to one end of the couch.

I take the other end and wait, willing my heart rate to slow, mentally turning off the mechanical squirrels jumping around in my head and my gut.

She shifts to face me, her hands clasped around one drawn-up knee, her brow furrowed. She presses her lips together as she seems to be deciding how to begin, and then she meets my eyes. "So I had a kind of revelation in the courtroom today."

This could be good or bad. "Okay..." *Thump, thump, thump* in my chest.

"I've been..." She frowns again. "It's kind of like if every time I saw a sunny day, I hid out in the basement because one sunny day a long time ago ended with a tornado."

Wut. "Um..."

She laughs and I'm lost in pleasure at the sound. "I was trying to find a good analogy, okay? What I'm saying is, I've been hiding out from relationships, including and especially a new one with you, because the last time I let myself fall in love, it ended really, really badly and almost killed me. So when I was listening to Judge Fox today, I realized I've been denying myself all the sunny days, living my life without sunny days, because I was afraid they'd end badly."

If I'm understanding her right, I'm not sure I like where this is going. "So...I'm the tornado?"

She throws up her hands, collapses back into the couch cushions, and rolls her head to face me. Her smile trickles over me like slow, warm honey, and her eyes crinkle. "Nah. Joe, you're the sunshine."

Oh. That's...good? It sounds good. Hard to think over the pounding of my heart.

She reaches to take my hand between both of hers, stroking my knuckles with her thumb. "So I've been wasting all the sunshine out of fear it would always end in a tornado. I was letting my fear of some possible future tornado that might never materialize keep me from ever enjoying the sunshine."

"Oh." That's very sad. July belongs in sunshine. July *is* sunshine.

She squeezes my hand. "But today I realized that's no way to live. That's not how I want to live anymore. I gotta be brave like you and Maisie and Sam and Donna and Tina and...normal people, Joe. I gotta be brave enough to step outside into the sunshine." She lowers my hand to the sofa cushion and pats it gently. "So...I'm not sure exactly what you want with me, but...I'd like to try for something with you." She says it firmly enough, but there's a war in her eyes as she fights to keep from putting back up the barricade she's just taken down. She looks almost scared.

July should never be frightened. July's the person who comes striding into every room with a big glorious smile and a plan to make things better for everybody. If she's scared, I've got to make things better for her.

I move closer. My turn to pick up her hands. "What do you need from me? Whatever you want." Speech is almost beyond me, with the scent of her in my nose and her fingers wrapped in mine and the hopeful sound of *Joe, you're the sunshine* ringing in my brain.

July

I know, when he laces our fingers together, that it's going to be okay, and I'm flooded with a warmth and a well-being I haven't felt since I was sixteen. I could melt into a puddle right now, right here on this couch, just holding his hands.

His eyes are changing color in the afternoon light, green to brown to bronzy gold back to green, and above the open top button of his white dress shirt, I see him swallow. I have always loved Joe's throat, solid, sturdy, and tanned, his soft, unruly hair curling at his collar. I lean forward now and press a kiss there and he goes very still, his pulse thumping fast under my lips. Every part of him seems so unique, so precious. I nibble a little, upward towards his clenching jaw, and a sigh gusts out of him, a tiny groan right behind. I open my mouth on the firm column of his neck, where his delicious Joe scent is strong, and touch him with my tongue...

And the next thing I know, I'm on my back, Joe on top of me, our hands woven together above my head as he kisses me. Ravenously. With open lips and teeth and tongue, and a hunger that matches my own.

This Joe is new to me. Young Joe was always sweet and careful and respectful, looking in my eyes and asking, "Okay?" before any physical step we took.

This Joe devours me, thrilling me, growling my name as his hot mouth moves on mine. He grips both my wrists in one of his hands as the other sweeps over me, squeezing, stroking, exploring. Layers of fabric are nothing against his determination, and every part of me rises up to meet him, my thighs straining against his, my heart thudding against his chest, my soft places seeking his hard ones.

"I've been wanting you forever," he murmurs, nuzzling my breast before sucking my nipple into his mouth.

I gasp and free one of my hands and cup it around his ass, pressing him into me.

He raises his head to look at me. "You and me, really

together…and time…and a bed." He tilts his pelvis, grinding into me, and groans.

I nod helplessly, freeing my other hand to help.

"The bed's important." He's intent, hands sliding under me to cradle my ass. "…because things might get a little wild."

I stop wondering why he's still talking and smile up at him. "Yeah?"

That unholy, irresistible light of young Joe is in his eyes. "Yeah. Figure we should start out in the middle of something soft so I don't hurt you." He sweeps my hair off my face and grinds a little harder.

I wrap my legs around him. "Don't worry about me, Joe. You're not going to break me." I say it in my low voice, the one he calls my honey voice, because I remember it makes him crazy.

His smile is slow and sweet. "I know that." He traces my cheek with one fingertip. "I'm glad you know it now too."

Another long, hungry kiss, then he's up off me, tugging me to my feet and toward the bedroom. "Get a move on, girl. It's going to be a long trip, what with all the kissing and the undressing and me taking liberties with you…" His fingers move at the nape of my neck and the halter top of my sundress loosens and begins to slide down. He catches my expression, waggles his eyebrows and grins.

"A liberty for a liberty." I unbutton his shirt and he swallows as he watches my progress. Watches my fingers make quick work of his button fly and his zipper too.

"You chef-types are very skilled." His voice is rough, his breathing rougher as I slip my hand into his slacks to close around him.

One squeeze and then he's got my wrist, pulling me toward the bedroom. He stops to press me up against the doorframe, kissing me so fiercely I barely notice him tug at my dress until it drops to my feet. I do notice when he cups my breasts—cups them and captures my nipples between his fingers and squeezes.

My turn to growl and wrestle with his clothing, shoving his shirt down over his shoulders, his pants and underwear down his thighs, and then we're toeing off shoes and kicking aside puddled fabric and reaching for each other as we fall onto the bed.

We'd had a stiff, embarrassed "all clear" conversation about test results weeks ago, and for the first time ever, I make a conscious decision to not use a condom. Joe stills on top of me, poised to join our bodies, and glances toward the nightstand. He raises his eyebrows in question and I when I murmur, "No need," his answering kiss is fierce.

"July!" His voice is harsh, his gaze forcing my eyes open to meet his even though I'm a mindless melted puddle. "Do you want this? You want me?"

More than anything in the world. I can't believe I ever thought it was a good idea to hold back from him. But his question isn't just about consent for sex... He's making sure I want his love. *Him.* I hate that he's had cause to doubt.

"I do." I say it with all the conviction in my soul, and above me his eyes darken from hazel to near-black. His hold on me tightens and our next kiss is slow. Deep. Possessive.

He's the perfect weight on me. Perfect weight, perfect warmth, perfect textures, perfect scent. My hands come up to rake through the softness of his hair. Caress his cheek.

He breaks the kiss and props himself on his elbows, sliding his hands into my hair, freeing it, spreading it over my pillow, dipping his head to bury his nose in it.

And as desperate as I was thirty seconds ago, as hard as he

is between my legs, as ready as I am for him to be inside me, suddenly I would be fine with making this last all day. Lying here with him on top of me, stroking my hair and looking into my eyes like he's finally where he wants to be after a lifetime of searching.

"I remember all the ways you used to like to be touched," he whispers, tracing my mouth with a gentle fingertip. "But how do you like to be touched now?"

That's pure Joe. Pure thoughtfulness and insight. He's not mentioning that he knows there have been other men since him. Not shaming me for it, not asking me about it, just acknowledging that twenty years is a long time and that we might have changed in intimate ways. Those aren't things our sixteen-year-old selves would have wanted, but he's making them okay.

"My favorite way to be touched," I say, holding his gaze, "is by you." Cheesy-sounding but gospel truth.

Then he's kissing me again, tender and gentle at first, gaining hunger as his fingers slip between my legs. "I didn't think anything could feel better than my memories of you." His confession, like his touch, is the perfect blend of rough and sweet.

And then he is shifting, settling into the cradle of my thighs, pushing into me slowly, his eyes closing and then opening to find mine.

"Holy f—" He's the one who says it, who describes this joining so perfectly, but I'm thinking it too.

I hold on and we begin to move.

I don't know how long we rock together, first slowly, then faster and then slowing again, Joe gasping little bits of praise and command and thanks in my ear, his breath warm on my neck, his hands sliding from my hips up over my ribs to my breasts and my face, leaving every part of me feeling loved. I don't know that anyone else would be able to find the rhythm in what we do, but we find it. We understand it. It's ours. It's us. And I am where I'm supposed to be, with the person I'm supposed to be with, doing this thing that must have been made just for us, our bodies fitting together so perfectly, sliding and capturing, filling and stroking, pressure building inside us until we can't go slow any longer and we're frantic, our bodies colliding so hard we scoot across the bed with each thrust until finally we come, miraculously at the same time, clutching and clutching at each other, laughing, clawing our hair out of our faces, brushing tears off each other's cheeks.

And I look in his eyes and hold him so tight I wonder if arms could lock like this. And whether I'd even mind if they did, as long as Joe was in mine. And he's looking back at me the same way, holding me just as tight, wrapping his legs around mine for a long, perfect, full-body hug. "Click," he says.

And a memory surfaces. We were sixteen and had just climbed into his truck after a long day of work at the steakhouse. He opened his arms, and I slid across that old bench seat straight into them, feeling like it was where I should have been all day. That was the first time he'd said it.

"Click," I answer now, just as fervently.

We spend the rest of the afternoon in bed, wrapped up in each other, talking in all the different ways lovers communicate, with words and breath, kisses and hands, gazes and taste, giving and receiving. I wait for the magic of it—of us—to start to dim, because surely it will, some, the way it always has almost immediately with anyone else once we've satisfied the original hunger, but Joe is still Joe and magic is still magic and my hunger for him ain't going anywhere.

His either apparently. He's become a powerful, attentive

lover with knowledge my young Joe didn't have, but he still has his whole heart in the act. And because in addition to always being sweet and respectful, Joe is fun, we get inventive. In my little kitchen, with fresh strawberries and whipped cream. On my couch while watching *Ted Lasso*. Recreating the Nurse-Joe-finds-July-bareass-naked-on-her-bed scene, only with a much happier ending.

And in my shower at midnight.

"Jesus." I'm panting, gasping for air. I grip his hair and bite his ear as he rises, holding me up so my shaking legs don't give out. Half marathons don't have this effect on me. I close my eyes, wrap my arms around him, and hug him as tightly as he's holding me. "Jesus, Joe."

He turns his face into my neck, whispering in my ear as water streams over both of us, "I don't want to let go of you."

There he is. There's that sweet young man I loved. "I don't want to let go of you either." Why did I ever bother with any other lover? Nothing—no one—has ever compared to this man. Sixteen-year-old July may have been inexperienced, but she was not wrong.

And like her, I am going to love this man for the rest of my life. "Stay with me." I mean tonight. I mean forever. I don't deserve him, but I mean it anyway.

He pushes the wet hair out of my face and presses his forehead to mine. "Yes. Please."

CHAPTER 27

Dear July,

If you ever change your mind and want to write, I'll answer.
I promise.

Joe

BEFORE I EVEN OPEN MY eyes, I know who I'm with and where I am. *Home.*

No home I've ever actually lived in, but it's been in my dreams all my life.

We smell of shampoo and July's sweet soap and each other. She's warm and soft and perfect against me, one leg over mine, one of her hands at my waist and the other curled at my cheek. If I never wake fully up, never move again, that'll be just fine.

I breathe in and smile and ease my eyes open to find her looking at me. She's quiet, studying me, uncurling one finger to stroke along my cheekbone when she sees I'm awake. I gaze back at her, letting my smile melt into something softer. "I missed this so much."

When we were together before, we used to spend hours at the lake, sometimes in the water, sometimes sitting on our rock, sometimes just lying on our towels together, talking and looking our fill. Well, and kissing. Lots of kissing.

"Me too." Her pupils are large in the dim light, extending nearly to the dark rim surrounding the gray. "I was so awful to you that roadhouse night." This comes out on a sigh.

The attempted sexorcism's not my favorite memory either, but I can't stand the torment in her eyes. I slide my hand up and down her smooth back. "It was just one mistake."

"I feel like it was unforgivable. Like you shouldn't forgive me." Her eyes fill, and she looks away toward the window. "It was so selfish. I was so selfish."

Newsflash for me: I feel pain when she does.

I wrap my arms around her, gather her in. Press a kiss to the top of her head. Stroke my fingers through her hair. "Before that, when was the last time you thought just of yourself?"

She's silent so long I wonder if she's fallen back asleep, but finally she says, so quietly I have to lower my head to hear. "Sixteen, seventeen. That year."

I keep my fingers moving in her hair. "And what did you do then that was so selfish?"

She clears her throat. "Worried everybody. Almost bailed on them."

"Why?"

Another silence. Then, "It was like...everything felt bad all the time. Like my feelings were big worms, writhing around in there, eating me from the inside. And there was no way to get away from them because...they were me. So I starved them."

I hold her a little tighter. "So...you were grieving the loss of us. You were sad and angry and worried about me."

She nods, her hair tickling my face. "Yeah. My hope was gone. My interest in the future. And...I couldn't believe I'd been so wrong about you. I thought that meant I wasn't the person I'd always felt I was either."

Yep, that pretty much sums up that period for me too. "And the thing that finally pulled you out of it was wanting to help other people? So you focused on other people for twenty years before you finally had a selfish moment?"

She tips her head back to look at me, a furrow between her brows.

"July, what would you say to Sam or Maisie or, hell, anybody, if they had a twenty-year run like that before messing up?"

She stares at me for a long minute. Her voice comes out tentative when she finally speaks. "I wouldn't say anything." She grips my shoulders. "They'd be past due for thinking about themselves. I mean, it doesn't justify using someone like I tried to use you... but it's not the thinking about themselves part that's bad."

I gaze back at her, watching her let her own words sink in, seeing color come back to her face and light return to her eyes.

"I love you."

Her mouth forms the same words at the exact same time mine does.

"I love you," we say again, again simultaneously, and then we're laughing and rolling across the sheets, trying to get out solo *I love you*s between kisses. Kisses become caresses and then I'm inside her and we're tangling the sheets, making love physically as well as with words, and this is the perfect morning. The best morning anyone has ever had.

Afterward we're quiet again, lying together, looking in each other's eyes when her alarm chirps.

"You work today?"

"Is it a day that ends with *day*?" She stretches and sits up. Stretching does wonderful things to her breasts. So does nakedness.

But I heroically corral my attention. "May I help?" I roll to my side, take her bare hip gently between my teeth.

Her brows shoot up. "Why?" She trails her fingernails up the center of my back.

I shiver and release her. "I'd just like to be with you today. Don't care what we do. If you want me to chop onions with you for fifteen hours, I'm there."

She studies me, her eyes crinkling in a near smile, and then she touches my face. "All right, then, sweet man, let's go take our shower."

So I spend the day working in the kitchen with her.

Tina is just letting Donna in the back door when July and I come downstairs. I see Tina's quick victory fist pump and catch Donna's tiny smile before I slip out to go change clothes.

Word spreads fast, I guess, because no one even asks why I'm there. They fall straight back into heckling me the way they did when July was sick. This time, though, I get to see July in action, and she is a wonder. The woman can churn out ten perfect, beautifully plated orders while giving Tina a hard time and carrying on completely different conversations with Donna and Sonya and the dairy delivery guy. And *still* have time to feel me up in the walk-in before the next orders are due.

This place feels like home too. Home and a real, happy family.

Maisie shoots us shy looks all afternoon after the kids arrive for their shift. Sam doesn't say much, but when he comes back from break, he shoves a small piece of paper into the front of my apron.

I dry my hands and fish it out. It's a drawing of a heart with a beautiful rendition of July and me smiling at each other. I admit, I'm actually a little misty as I tuck it carefully away in my wallet. I squeeze Sam's shoulder next time I pass him. "Thanks, man."

He gives me a quick, silent smile.

Rose and Angus come in for dinner. We join them for a few minutes after sneaking in some alone time upstairs.

Eagle-eyed Rose looks us over, clearly registering something in our faces and the way we're sitting close in the booth. And maybe the whisker burn on July's neck.

I'm going to have to shave more often so I don't hurt my girl.

Rose turns to look at Angus, who gazes back at her with a twinkle in his eye.

"So," Rose says.

"So," Angus rumbles.

July flaps her hand at them. "Oh, don't pretend like you two weren't just doing the same thing. Your shirt's on backwards, Rose, for god's sake."

Rose's eyes go wide. She tilts her head to look down at her blouse, which of course is on properly, and the rest of us burst out laughing.

"They might not have known for sure before, Rosie, but they do now." Angus tugs her close and kisses the top of her head.

She blushes and grins and changes the subject back to me and July. "I'm glad to see you two finally quit beating around the bush!" She frowns. "Wow, that sounded a lot worse out loud than in my head."

Angus snorts into his water. July drops her head to my shoulder, laughing silently.

Rose tries again. "What I mean is, 'bout time. Everybody could see you belong together."

July's turn to snort. "You're a fine one to talk, Ms. Had-a-Big-Beautiful-Dude-Practically-Living-Under-My-Roof-For-Months-and-Didn't-Figure-Out-He-Was-Interested-until-He-Dragged-Me-Out-Back-and-Kissed-Me."

I raise my eyebrows at Angus, who is blushing furiously. "Mr. Big Beautiful Dude, I presume?"

"Not how I usually introduce myself, no. And I object to the word *dragged*... Unless some other guy kissed you out back too, Rosie? And then I'd have to object to that."

Rose waves this away. "Okay, okay. I'm just happy to see you two together, that's all. And now it's time for us to find somebody for Andi."

July shoots her a look I can't interpret. "I think if Andi ever decides she wants a partner, she'll do just fine finding one herself."

She's not wrong. Andi's great. And for all of her baggy soft-ball gear and scraped-back hairdos, she's gorgeous. If she ever unbanks her fire, god help the single people of this town.

July

Joe goes out to get Devon and his guys what they need while I reconcile the day's receipts in the office. When I come looking for him a little later, he's at the far end of the kitchen, whistling, his back to me as he mops the floor. The sight stops me in my tracks.

He doesn't have to be here. There's no money or excitement or anything in it for him. But here he is, looking relaxed and happy mopping a floor at the end of a fifteen-hour workday. He could be somewhere comfortable watching TV or reading one of his books or drinking a beer while he waits for me. But he just wants to be with me. It makes him happy to help me out.

Love and gratitude wash over me like a warm shower. How could I have gotten so lucky as to find this guy twice?

I am starting to believe in soul mates again.

When he finishes the floor and sets the mop back in the bucket, I'm there, slipping my arms around his waist to hold him, my cheek on his shoulder. His arms come around me, and he rests his cheek on my head. Presses his lips to my hair. "You tired?"

"Mm, only a little. You?"

He shakes his head. "I have something I want us to do, if you think you can stay awake a couple more hours."

I tilt back to look at him. This sounds...structured. "Okay."

"Let's get cleaned up. Jeans and comfortable shoes, okay? I'll be back for you in half an hour." He heads for the back door.

"You gonna tell me what it is?"

His grin flashes. "Nope. Not yet."

After I shower and brush my still-damp hair, I let Joe hand me into his truck.

He heads out of town but then pulls into the gravel lot at Woollybooger's.

I eye him as he parks between a battered Ford and an equally battered Dodge pickup. Anxiety nibbles at my gut. "Joe, what's your idea?"

He turns off the ignition and picks up my hand, stroking my knuckles with his thumb. "A do-over night."

The only time we've been here together was the sexorcism night. I'm not sure how I feel about this. What good can it do?

How could either of us forget the hurt I caused him that night? I'm not sure I *should* ever forget it.

He climbs out, comes around to open my door, and gently tugs me out into his arms. "C'mon," he murmurs into my hair. "This is our chance to do what we wish we'd done differently that night." His mouth lands softly and too briefly on mine. "Replace a bad memory with good ones."

Okay, that has some appeal.

He can see my answer in my eyes. He grins, tugs me inside, and pulls me toward the only empty booth, sliding across the bench seat, still holding my hand so I have to slide in after him, and then he puts both arms around me and whispers in my ear, "I won't ever forget that dress you wore. Wouldn't mind seeing you in that again."

I drop my head. "I almost burned it after that night. I shoved it way down into the bottom of the laundry hamper. Haven't touched it since."

He nods, his expression serious, but an unholy light dances in those eyes. "I understand. Gonna take some serious mojo to exorcise the demons from that dress. Maybe you should put it on later, and we'll work on that."

The server—one of Tina's cousins—comes to the booth, and we order the same things we had that Very Bad Night: ribeyes, medium-rare; steak fries; and a frosty pitcher of beer. But this time when the food comes, we eat it all, with lots of laughter and talking and touching. Like last time, we get up to line dance, but this time we don't let go of each other, and I'm not worried my world and I are about to crack apart over this man. Instead, I hold him close, feeling safer and warmer for being with him.

And when, on the way home, he asks if I'd like to see what

Angus and Rose have done with his place, I say yes, and soon I'm upstairs in his apartment, with him handing me a beer as he did that other night.

But this time he's showing me the great changes our friends have made. Angus has refinished the old hardwood floors to a warm, light natural color and put in great lighting and shelves. Instead of a lumpy love seat, Joe's got a sleek purple sofa paired with a coffee table made from a battered old leather trunk on legs, courtesy of Rose.

He flips on a ceiling fan, dims the lights, and settles next to me on the sofa, close but not touching. "Scared?" He watches me as he tips his bottle for a drink.

"A little. I don't know why." I turn my beer between my fingers.

He moves his knee just enough to brush mine. "I know the first thing I wish I'd done differently. I wish I'd been the one to take our bottles and set them aside." And he does, and then he puts his arm around me and pulls me close so that my back rests against his chest. He picks up my hand and traces my knuckles with his thumb. "I knew something was off that night. I could tell you were half somewhere else. I wish I'd taken your hand and asked what was wrong." He squeezes my hand. "Would you have told me if I'd asked?"

"I don't know. I hope so."

He moves his hand to my nape and begins rubbing the back of my neck.

A groan escapes me and I relax against him. "If you'd done this, I might not have been able to speak. I was so exhausted and so upset, I probably would've either gone unconscious or burst into tears."

He presses his lips to my temple and sets me away from him just enough to massage with both hands.

I let my head fall forward. Let him massage the last of the tension out of me. "I wish I'd told you I was scared."

"Of?" He sweeps the hair away from my cheek, kisses me just beneath that ear, and softens the movements of his hands.

"Everything." I sigh. "I wanted you so bad it scared me. But... the time before left me believing I was weak. Like, lacking any kind of coping ability for tough times. And everything was feeling so intense again..."

He combs a hand through my hair and keeps massaging, listening, so I keep talking.

"I was afraid the restaurant, the one thing everything I do hinges on—was suffering because of my...obsession over you. I was afraid I'd lose the one kind of strength I knew I had and be as wrecked and useless as last time, only this time I'd take a lot more people down with me."

He wraps his arms around me from behind and lays his cheek on my shoulder.

"What are you thinking?" I turn my face to his. It's his turn to confide in me.

His voice is as quiet as mine. "I'm wondering what I would have said or done if you had told me all that. I'm hoping I would've just held you." He lies back on the sofa and pulls me down onto him. He strokes my hair and I nestle closer, tucking my head under his chin. Somehow he must have found time to shave, because his skin is smooth, his woodsy scent soothing and delicious.

We're silent for a bit before he says, "I wish I'd offered to hold you anytime you need reassurance. And feed you anytime you forget to eat. I wish I'd offered to come work with you so my hands could make up for any distraction I caused. I just want... me being in your life to be good for you."

I don't want him to ever doubt that. "I can't think of a single thing that could make me happier." I spread my fingers to frame his face and bring him to me for a slow, soft kiss. "You asked, that night of the thunderstorm, what I wanted for me. I want *you*."

Beneath me his body loosens as if I'd said magic words that eased his mind.

I wrap one leg around his. "What if, on the sexorcism night, I had told you how I was feeling and asked you to make love to me? Would you have said no?"

"July, I don't think there's anything in the world that could keep me from trying to give you something you need."

I reach between us and tug the hem of his T-shirt up, pressing my lips to the bare skin over his heart. "Make love to me now?"

I laugh when he flips me on my side, laugh at him through kisses, but it's a relieved laugh. I help him unfasten our clothing and push it down out of the way, and then he's sliding into me, full and hard and hot and perfect.

I sigh with the joy of it. "Click."

His laughter is brief, and then we're moving together, my leg and his hands on my hips pulling us into our own perfect, irresistible rhythm.

"Oh god." I skate my hand up his chest into his hair and hold on. "If only I'd known to just ask that night." Because he is giving me every single thing I need.

Afterward we linger, kissing and touching. I outline a big heart on his chest with one fingertip. "Joe, what were you thinking and wanting and needing that night? And now?"

He strokes my hair back off my face. His eyes have never looked so dark or so determined. He locks his hands together at the small of my back. "I want...I want us not to lose any more years by being apart. I want to spend the rest of my life with you."

There's that warmth washing over me again. "When you imagine that, what's it like?"

He closes his eyes as if to picture it. "Mm. Waking up every morning to realize I've been lucky enough to hold you all night. Knowing at the end of the day we'll be together sharing stories. Laughing and kissing and holding each other. Celebrating good times with people we care about. Getting through bad times by holding on to each other. Lots and lots of holding on to each other."

Yes, he is my soul mate.

"Click," I say, and our next kisses are promises.

EPILOGUE

Not quite two years later

WE'RE AT THE LAKE, SITTING on our rock. I'm leaning back against his chest, and he's got his arms around me, his tanned forearms resting on his upraised knees.

"You're going to ruin that expensive cap and gown, wearing them up here." I've been teasing him about them since he put them on for his graduation this morning. The rental cost an arm and a leg, but they feel like they might have been made from a disposable tablecloth and one side of a cardboard box.

He's not listening. His nose is in my hair, and he's been teasing me too—about him and the kids being "graduation triplets" at their party, which is due to start in a few minutes—but now his voice gets quiet. "I'm full with you," he says. "All my empty places fill up when I'm with you."

And I don't ask. Because I know just what he means.

Read on for a short look at
how Rose and Angus fell in love in
Curves for Days by Laura Moher

CHAPTER 1

Alice Rose

THE WORLD GREW COLDER WHEN Mr. Brown died. That was obvious to me.

What I hadn't realized, when I was cradling his head on that hard sidewalk and he'd shoved the little bag with his weekly Altoids-and-lottery-ticket purchase at me, was that my world was about to implode.

I'm not saying all this money doesn't rock. Hypothetically, it *could*, I guess. But not at this particular moment, as I'm elbow-deep in my ripe kitchen trash, trying to bury three hundred tiny pieces of a note from Timmy Johnson.

I'd waited till three a.m. to check my mail, to avoid my neighbors. I'd turned the key, eased open the box, and…another flood of letters and cards, from strangers, acquaintances, and people who were my friends in high school before the bullying started and they'd backed off to save their own asses.

I tucked it all into the folded-up hem of my sweatshirt and shuffled back to my apartment.

The eighteenth card I opened was the worst. I literally gagged when I saw Timmy Johnson's signature. "Just wanted to say congratulations," he'd written. "We had some good times in high school, didn't we?" *Uh, no, Timmy, that night might've been fun for you—your sadistic friends certainly enjoyed the story later—but not for me.* "Give me a call if you'd like to get together and catch up."

Reading that shit must've burst some dam of rage and revulsion inside me. Growling and panting, I tore that sucker into tiny pieces and jammed them deep into the trash bag, under the slimy salad remnants now sticking to my elbow.

And isn't this just a perfect metaphor for what my life has become: bits of terrible, mashed in with the regular unpleasant stuff?

No, that's not right. I'm *fortunate*. Winning the lottery was *lucky*. I'm being ungrateful.

I ease my arms out of the stinky mess and wash my hands three times because I'd touched something *he'd* touched.

There's still a sizeable pile of unread mail, but the next card is almost as bad. Another former classmate writing to say he'd heard about my winnings, always thought I was nice, etc., etc., and to look him up if I want to go out some time. Pretty sure he's the one who drew the caricature of me as a cow with a huge swollen udder on the board in homeroom.

I mean, it's not like I don't have a fucking mirror. No guy my age has ever shown interest in me without having plans to do something rotten. I wasn't as big then as I am now, but I was never the pretty, popular type. Eighty million dollars may make *them* forget what really happened, but the money hasn't damaged *my* memory or made *me* stupid.

I can't make myself read any more of this stuff. Can't even make myself drop it into the trash. I'm also out of food, haven't had dinner, and can't stomach the idea of seeing anybody, not even a delivery driver, if there's even anything available at this hour. So after checking all my locks again and pushing a chair up against the door, I crawl between the sheets on my lumpy old couch, starving, drift off to sleep...and promptly have my *Jesus Christ Superstar* nightmare for the sixth night in a row.

In the dream, I'm outside surrounded by people, some familiar, many not, and they're all reaching out, trying to touch me, asking, begging for stuff. Like the crowds around Jesus in the movie, everybody wants something, and they turn loud and grabby and angry and scary when I don't immediately respond. I try to get away but two of them seize my arm and tear it off. A third trips me and they push me down. They rip me to shreds and run off with the pieces, all except my eyes.

As always, I bolt upright, frantic, my heart thudding in the silence.

I can't take another day in this place—or anywhere else in Indy—hiding from all the people who want a piece of me. The media's pretty much given up, but hopeful-looking strangers still drift by out front and neighbors hang out in the hall, ready to pounce if I so much as crack open my door. I'm trapped.

The people at the firm I hired for accounting and legal advice had suggested I look into a bodyguard service. Riiight. Where the hell would I put a bodyguard in my studio apartment?

I guess they didn't expect me to stay here. And it's true, the building is dingy and leaky and smelly, but it's familiar. Every other option I've considered—a hotel, a new apartment, a house, a cruise—involves doing things I have no experience with, dealing with a million new people in strange places, at a time when everybody looks at me with, like, hunger. Or jealousy, or anger. I'm alone. I don't trust anyone now, and *certainly* not anybody who knows about the money.

But this place has become a prison. I've got to break out.

So. Four thirty in the morning and I'm tiptoeing around this old place for the last time, looking for things I care enough about to take with me. Not the cast-off furniture and worn-out kitchenware Mom scrounged before I was born. Not the clothing and shoes I can't get the restaurant smell out of.

I shove my Important Papers folder, the Yeats poetry book Mr. Brown gave me, a toothbrush and comb, and my two photos of Mom into her old sewing bag with a pair of jeans, a sweatshirt, and all my underwear. No way am I leaving my undies behind for people to paw through. Then I creep out the back entrance to walk to the bus station, slipping a check and a "Fuck this dump, sell all my shit, I'm moving to Hawaii, Sincerely, Alice" note under the landlord's door on my way out.

'Course, I'm not going to Hawaii. And I'm not going by Alice anymore. From now on I'll be Rose. Always liked that part of my name better anyway. Roses don't take any shit. Gotta be careful grabbing a Rose. Might get a handful of thorns.

A Rose wouldn't let herself be all alone at age thirty-two because of something mean kids did when she was sixteen.

A Rose wouldn't have spent the last two and a half weeks cowering in her apartment as people tried to get at her.

A Rose would bust herself out and go after whatever she wanted.

So a Rose climbs off a Greyhound bus four hours later, halfway between Indianapolis and St. Louis, after spying a pockmarked

Honda in a used car lot. She dusts off her driver's license, changes direction to fool any would-be followers, and heads vaguely southeast, without a single soul giving her a second look.

I'll call my Hail Damage Special Lillian. Rose and Lillian sound like gutsy characters from a classic buddy movie, and I'm ready for an adventure. And a buddy.

She smells like dust and fake pine but Lillian has a valiant heart. Barely pausing at the interstate entrance ramp yield sign, she bursts into traffic with a squeal of tires and a tiny fishtail and begins to build speed. She's just a little four-cylinder, so it takes a bit to catch up to the car in front of us, but we've done it! The Alice part of me reacquaints herself with oxygen, breathing deeper than I have in weeks, and we settle in to flow with the traffic until I've got some reason to stop.

Goals:

1. *Find a hideout for a while, maybe near the ocean. I've always wanted to see an ocean.*
2. *Find a new home where nobody knows about this goddamn money. Is ungratefulness a sin?*
3. *Decide what to do with all this goddamn money.*
4. *Buy a bigger Cuss Jar.*

Angus

When the burst of pain and the urge to maim and destroy passes, I set aside the hammer, fetch the ice pack from my cooler, and stand in the Wheelers' front yard holding it to my smashed thumb.

That's what I get for breaking Rule Number One of working with tools that can do a body harm: Never, ever think about your other job, especially if it involves helping troubled veterans with all the shit they've been dealt.

I'd been hammering down a replacement porch board, my mind on my newest client. Young army vet, recently discharged, wrestling hypervigilance, insomnia, rage, depression. "Man, I fucking *hate* people who think life is just fine, who don't realize the world's full of shit people doing shit things and you can't let down your guard for a single goddamn minute," he'd said in our second session.

Sounded just like me when I got out.

Made me realize how far I've come. Made me wonder if I might be ready for a life with more than just work in it. Question is, have I *earned* more?

Life would be a lot easier if there was a big scoreboard in the sky to let you know how much good you'd put into the world versus how much you'd sucked out of it. How the hell am I supposed to know how many therapy clients I need to help to make up for killing my marriage, watching the light in a good woman's eyes die out day by day? Or how my pitiful counseling efforts stack up against the worry I've caused—worry that carved years off the lives of the two best people I know?

I must've been feeling too cocky after surviving another set of winter holidays and Valentine's, that three-month stretch of frigid hell designed to really rub in aloneness.

Used to love holidays. Grandma'd fill the house with every lonely, hungry person she could find. My buddy Lenny was always there. Some of the other kids with screwed-up families. Neighbors, single people, anybody down on their luck. No telling who'd show up. Grandma'd load 'em up with good feelings and good food. Anybody shy, she'd hand 'em a paring knife and some potatoes to peel. Talk their ear off, making up crazy stories about me or Grandpa. Have them howling with laughter inside of five minutes. Grandpa and I'd be on our way through the kitchen to get more chairs, and he'd give Grandma a wink so quick you'd think you imagined it.

Been four years since Grandpa died. Two since Grandma followed, and now I pretty much hate holidays.

I miss 'em.

And sometimes I miss being married. Having somebody to belong to. Miss the part of me that was husband material.

Couple of weeks ago on Valentine's night, I cooked up a pot of chili for my clients and friends who had nowhere else they wanted to go. We played cards and ping-pong. Talked trash, watched sports. Normal and happy as we could manage. Afterward, I bagged up our garbage and took it to the bear-proof bin in the cold backyard. Night leached the colors out of everything. Reminded me no one was waiting for me inside. The weeds rattling against the fence looked as desolate as I felt. But I'd made it through another wasteland of holidays, dammit, and dragged some other guys with me. That seemed important.

The next weekend, I let Lenny talk me into going out to hear his band play. I sat with James's and Rashad's wives, watching the Blue Shoes work their magic on the crowd at Lindon's. Tisha and Shay started in with their matchmaking bullshit. I shut them down quick, like always, but I guess they got me wishing.

So a minute ago, I was hammering that porch board, batshit-hopeful thoughts flapping around in my head, feeling like I might be close to ready for...something.

Then a car backfired out on the highway and I brought that hammer straight down on my thumb. That's what I get for hoping.

I flex my injured hand. Big blood blister, some swelling, but nothing's broken.

That blister's the universe's big loud *no* to my unspoken question about whether I've built enough karma or grace or whatever to start looking for something for myself. Message received, universe.

It's coming down awful hard for March. Been sleeting and snowing all morning, especially the past couple hours. Thick white flakes. I eye the Wheelers' house. Next job is to climb up and replace rotted trim around the dormers.

Nope. Not in this weather.

I toss the ice pack back in the cooler. Gather up my tools, dry 'em off, load up the van. I'll get carryout and take the afternoon off for once. Watch *Die Hard* again. Maybe even take a nap. I scrape my windshield and head for home.

At the stoplight just inside the *Welcome to Galway, NC* sign, a little Honda is sideways in a plowed heap of icy snow. Tires spin, slinging dirty slush as the driver tries to get unstuck. Nothing happens. The engine whines and the wheels spin faster. Still no traction.

I pull over, put on my flashers, and climb out. The driver lowers her window as I come near. I'm surprised she can see over the steering wheel, she's so short. Thought at first she was a kid, but close up she looks maybe thirty. Messy brown hair, big brown eyes, zero makeup. Kinda cute.

"Need some help?" I add a few more points to the karma board.

She leans out her window to look me up and down. Waves

her hand at the driving lane. "Yeah, could you just, like, pick the car up and set it down over there, please?"

Alright, so *not* cute. Thinks she's funny. Thinks I haven't already heard every giant, lumberjack, yeti, Hulk joke in the world. I point to her trunk. "Lemme get in position. When I nod, give it gas real gentle." Can't help but notice the pockmarked roof and trunk lid as I walk around the car. "Geez, poor li'l thing." I don't expect her to hear me.

She does. Snaps, "Hey! Lillian's sensitive about her complexion."

O-kaaay. I brace my hands well above her temporary plate. God forbid I goose poor Lillian. I give the signal and push.

She eases the car out of the snow and into the lane. Squeals, "Oh, man, thank you so much!" Totally different tone than before.

I head back to the van. "No problem." Wave without turning around.

I'm dripping ice, looking forward to cranking up the heat. Almost to my driver's door when something small and hard smashes into the back of my skull. "What the—" I spin around, slip on the ice, and almost go down.

The Honda driver's eyes are huge, her hands up over her mouth. "Oh shit! I'm so sorry! Thank-you Snickers."

What'd she call me?

She points at my feet. "Thank-you Snickers."

There's a candy bar in the slush. Brown Eyes beaned me with it. *Just help the lady,* my scoreboard had whispered. *Have a few laughs. It'll be fun.* No, that last bit might've been Bruce Willis. *Yippee-ki-yay.*

I rub my head and fish the candy out of the mess. Couple of cars maneuver slowly around us as I open my door and drop the Snickers into my trash bag.

"Sorry! Thank you! Really!" She's waving both hands now, silly grin on her face.

I shake my head. Climb in. Raise my hand, willing her to move on.

Instead she hollers, "Hey, is there a motel around here? I think I should get off the road."

Got *that* right. "B and B, two blocks up." Sabina'll take pity on her being out in this mess if she's not full up. I slam my door. Enough conversation.

Hell of an arm, but the woman's a menace.

Glad she's just passing through.

ACKNOWLEDGMENTS

July and Joe's story has changed many times in many ways from its first draft, and it's much stronger because of the generous help I've received from so many people.

As always, giant thanks to my tireless agent, Sara Megibow, and everyone at KT Literary; to my lovely editor, Deb Werksman, and all the folks at Sourcebooks (especially Susie Benton, Alyssa Garcia, and Jocelyn Travis, but also all the people working behind the scenes to bring our books into the world, including Aimee Alker, Laura Boren, Stephanie Gafron, Rosie Gaynor, India Hunter, Stephanie Rocha, and Gretchen Stelter); and to Andressa Meissner and all the talented people responsible for the gorgeous covers and other art for these books.

Perpetual thanks to Mary Morris, the best critique partner in the world, and to my excellent beta readers and everyone who saw drafts and pieces of this story before it was finished, including Paula, Carol, and Amy. Y'all're the best!

Thanks and love to all my friends and family—especially W, my favorite person and biggest cheerleader!—who have offered encouragement and shown interest throughout this process, and who remain supportive even through my weird, introvert, hermit phases. During those times, I especially appreciated the writers of Twitter and the Writing While Fat group on Discord.

Special thanks to Diane Daane, who helped me think through some of the legal issues in this story (over a yummy Greek lunch), and to Suz Brockmann, whose friendship and support continues to surprise and humble me.

And finally, thank you to my reason for being here: you readers who love love and love stories. You make my dream job possible, and your kind words lift me up when I'm discouraged. Thanks, y'all, so much.

RESOURCES

This book deals with serious real-world issues affecting many people, especially young people. All my love and thanks to the dedicated folks who work to support people facing the following issues. (See my website for links to these and other resources.)

HOMOPHOBIA AND TRANSPHOBIA

The National Education Association (NEA) lists three major take-aways from a 2022 study that focused on youth mental health:

1. Forty-two percent of LGBTQ+ youth—and fifty-two percent of trans youth—said they seriously considered suicide in 2021. Attempted suicide rates also are higher for Black and Indigenous students, according to data from the Trevor Project.
2. Students said the proliferation of anti-LGBTQ+ bills, like the "Don't Say Gay" law in Florida, are intensifying their mental health issues. This legislation has been strongly opposed by NEA and its affiliates.

3. There are ways for educators to help: LGBTQ+ students need supportive adults who use affirming words. They need access to safe spaces and events. And they need to see themselves, positively, in curriculum.

According to a 2017 study by Voices of Youth Count, an initiative at Chapin Hall at the University of Chicago, LGBTQ youth had a 120 percent higher risk of being homeless.

According to research cited by True Colors United, LGBTQ youth make up just seven percent of the youth population in the U.S., but they make up forty percent of the youth homeless population.

The Trevor Project can help. They provide information and support for LGBTQ youth. Visit their website at thetrevorproject.org.

DOMESTIC VIOLENCE

According to the National Coalition Against Domestic Violence (NCADV), in the U.S. alone, nearly twenty people per minute are abused by an intimate partner. That's over ten million people per year: one in four women, and one in nine men. There are many forms of domestic violence, and all can cause both short- and long-term harm to adult victims, to their children, and to the economy.

NCADV can help. Their website contains information, resources, educational materials, and statistics, as well as safety plans to help people get free.

If you yourself are not in danger and want to donate or get

more information on how you can help, you can call the administrative line from the NCADV website, ncadv.org.

They also provide info on how to contact help safely if you believe that your web activity might be monitored in a way that places you in danger.

ABOUT THE AUTHOR

Laura Moher is a former associate professor of sociology at the University of South Carolina Upstate in Spartanburg, South Carolina. Her head is full of stories of flawed people who come together to make each other—and their world—a better place. She had deep roots in the South, having grown up in the Louisville, Kentucky, area before moving to the western Carolinas where she taught for eleven years. She has also lived in Colorado and Illinois and is now happily settled near her son in Minnesota.

Website: lauramoher.com
Facebook: authorLauraMoher
Instagram: @lljzmc